OFF THE
EDGE

THE ASSOCIATES: BOOK TWO

Carolyn Crane

Cover art: Amber Shah of Bookbeautiful.com

Publisher's Note: This is a work of fiction. Names, characters, places, and incidents are either the products of the author's imagination or used fictitiously, and any resemblance to actual persons, living or dead, or business establishments, organizations or locales is completely coincidental.

Off the Edge/ Carolyn Crane. -- 1st ed.
ISBN-13: 978-1494719616
ISBN-10: 1494719614

To my readers, all of you crazy, fabulous word lovers!

CHAPTER ONE

Bangkok, Thailand

Laney Lancaster avoided the restaurant host's patient gaze, trying to think of what to say, hyper-aware that he was waiting, one hand on the back of the chair she was to sit in. The Hungry Steer was one of the best places to get authentic steak in all of Bangkok and this kind host had led her to a lovely little window table. An orchid stood sweetly in a vase at the center of it, and the view of bustling Nakhon Chaisi Road was amazing.

To anybody else, it would look like the best table in the place.

To Laney it looked like Russian roulette.

She was quite familiar with the game. It always used to be Russian roulette whenever her ex-husband Rolly beckoned her over to his easy chair, because there'd be no telling whether he meant to hit her or kiss her. It was Russian roulette back when she used to report him to the local cops for battery, because you never knew which ones were in his pocket. It was Russian roulette whenever she'd try to escape him, because it might mean freedom, but it could just as easily mean the horror of being dragged back to him after defying him. It had been Russian roulette when she'd helped that FBI agent gather evidence to put Rolly in prison, because it was either the end of her problems or the beginning of worse ones.

Laney was so done with Russian roulette.

"*Khap khun maak na kha tae wa chan yaak nang nai thee nang khang lang maak kwa,*" she said, thanking him profusely and asking to sit in the back. She pointed to a table in the dark corner near the EXIT sign. The host shot her a questioning glance. She gave him a sunny smile. Always best just to smile.

He led her to the gloomier but safer corner.

"*Khap khun na kha,*" she said with a little nod. An ultra-polite thanks.

When the waiter came by, Laney gave him her order plus money for the bill and tip all at once. This got her another questioning look. She responded with another sunny smile. What could she say? She was the kind of gal who liked to flee a restaurant with a clear conscience.

A full two years she'd been in Bangkok with no sign of Rolly's thugs, but you never relaxed your guard with Rolly and his thugs.

A friend had once suggested that Rolly was the wrong name for him, because it rhymed with jolly. But actually that happy echo was what made the name perfect. Rolly was the ultimate wolf in sheep's clothing—or python in sheep's clothing, as Rolly would likely put it. Rolly charmed you with his smiles and money and manners, and once you realized he was squeezing the life out of you, it was too late.

Rolly was so powerful that even being in an Arkansas prison couldn't stop his muscular and veiny arm from circling the globe in pursuit of her.

Even dining outside the safety of the hotel where she'd lived and worked these past two years was a gamble, but it was her birthday, dammit! And she was careful, wearing her hat and tinted glasses and taking the gloomy back table.

It was just as she was digging into her mushroom ribeye that she saw Harken, Rolly's right-hand thug, enter the restaurant and walk up to the host's stand.

She nearly dropped her fork.

She couldn't be sure it was Harken—she only caught a flash of his face before he turned, but you didn't wait around with a man like Harken.

You ran.

She pulled her hat low over her ears and rose from her seat—*slowly*. Fast movements attracted attention.

She strolled casually toward the back EXIT sign, heading down the dark little hall beyond it, picking up her pace.

She passed a little door set into the wall and continued on, heart racing. It had to be him. Even the way he stood had set off alarm bells, and you had to trust alarm bells. Sometimes alarm bells were your only friends.

She rushed on, dismayed that there was no corresponding EXIT sign at the end of the long, poorly lit hallway. Thais were a whole lot less keen on safety rules than Americans; it was actually unusual even to see an

American-style EXIT sign. Thai restaurants didn't typically have those.

It was when she felt the tickle of a cobweb over her cheeks that it dawned on her that the EXIT sign might have been put up for ambience, just as Americans sometimes hung up signs with Asian writing, not knowing the meaning. A brightly lit EXIT sign. Festive!

When she felt the floor sag with rot, her belly twisted with that old familiar fear. Trapped. Hopeless. She slowed, walking on the non-rot side, heart pounding. She could discern a door at the end, but did people use it? Could it even be opened?

Still she went forward. Sometimes it was all you had left. When she hit the door, she turned the knob and pushed with all her might.

The door gave a titch, then stopped dead. Boarded up on the other side. She rammed it with her shoulder.

No go.

She spun around, overcome with the instinct to freeze in the dark like a rabbit, to be very small.

No. No freezing. Move, move, move.

She pulled her gun from her purse.

Nobody coming.

Maybe it wasn't Harken out there. Or maybe he hadn't seen her.

But if it was Harken, and if he *had* seen her, he'd know she was trapped. He'd be sitting out there relishing her fear like a twisted connoisseur, enjoying its rich, robust undertones and high notes of hysteria. Harken had enjoyed mind fucking her almost as much as Rolly had. And if he caught her, he'd bring her back to the States and straight to Rolly's prison. For the conjugal visit from hell.

The seconds crept on. She couldn't go back through the restaurant. But she couldn't stay. If somebody turned on the hallway lights, they'd see her and raise a fuss.

The little door she'd passed. Was it a closet? She could hide in there and call for help. She could defend herself in there.

She crept back down the hall and tried the knob. Open. She slipped in, eased the door shut, and flattened against it. When she turned on her phone light she saw it was a linen closet. Dry storage. She spied the hanging string for an overhead bulb, but she didn't dare pluck it. Light would show through the crack under the door. Also, she preferred not to see the spider webs. There would be spiders and all manner of other critters in this little space. That was Bangkok, a city with a teeming jungle in the margins.

And now Rolly's man. She'd been located.

Her intuition had been telling her something was wrong these past weeks. And this was a whole lot of wrong.

Two years. She'd almost been feeling like herself again.

She got up her contacts screen, scrolled to Rajini's image, and hit the call button.

"*Haa-lo.*"

"Rajini," Laney whispered, comforted just to hear her voice. Rajini was her best friend and savior.

"Laney! What? Is something wrong?"

Laney stared into the darkness. "I think I saw Harken."

"Are you sure?"

"No. Well, my gut is surer than my eyes. No, I think it's him. I don't know. Crap!"

"Where are you?"

"In the linens closet of the Hungry Steer," Laney said.

"On Nakhon Chaisi Road? What's going on?"

"I wanted some mushroom ribeye and mashed potatoes. Just as a treat..." She didn't say it was her birthday; Rajini would feel awful to have forgotten it. Anyway, it was her old self's birthday. Emmaline's birthday.

Emmaline was dead and buried. Laney wasn't supposed to think of herself as Emmaline anymore, and most of the time she succeeded. "I saw him and I beelined for the exit that wasn't. Now I'm hiding like a freak. If it's him...Rajini..."

"It's not him. It couldn't be," Rajini said. "Breathe."

"What if it is?"

"I'm coming over there. I'll recognize that jackass anywhere."

"Wait—what if he recognizes *you*?" Laney said.

"Am I not the queen of capers?"

"Rajini!" That's something Rajini liked to call herself. "This is serious. He won't be stupid this time."

Rajini snorted. "It's not him anyway. If he's in Bangkok, it means you've been found. He'd already have you."

"Maybe he's waiting for backup."

"It doesn't make sense. I'm getting in a tuk-tuk right now."

Laney gave her layout details, told her about the door, and described Harken's clothes, not that Rajini needed it.

She'd helped her get away from Harken two years ago. She'd remember the man plain as day.

"Just take a look in the front window and tell me if it's him," Laney said. "Do not put yourself in danger, okay? I got away once, I'll get away again." A lie. Harken would never let her get away a second time.

"If it's him, my brothers will kick his ass. Bangkok is our town. You don't mess with the Shinsurins in Bangkok."

"If it's him, you walk away."

"No, I'll send my brothers after him and pry the boards off that back door myself, in which case you owe me a manicure."

"With jeweled decals," Laney said. "What is wrong with me? Letting myself get trapped. Walking around without cash or a valid passport. I let myself get a false sense of safety."

"What's false about it? There's nowhere safer than the hotel."

"A gal likes options," Laney said.

Rajini snorted, but Laney was serious. Her fake passport had expired months ago. Rajini's brothers had promised over and over to get her a new one, but they never did. What if she had to bolt?

They clicked off. Laney grabbed a stack of linen napkins and put them over her gun. The napkins would act as a silencer if Harken busted in.

She'd only known Rajini three weeks in the States, but Rajini had taken up her cause like a warrior when she realized what danger Laney was in. It had been like a suspense movie, the two women outwitting Harken, and then Rajini had talked her into really disappearing—in Thailand. Rajini had finished her degree by then, she was on her way back home anyway, but still, it was a big thing that Rajini had done, getting her away from Harken and out of the country. Laney and Rajini had traveled to Bangkok together and Rajini had cajoled her gangster brothers into giving Laney a singing job at their Bangkok hotel. Together the women had come up with an old-fashioned nightclub singer getup that involved a hat with netting, which concealed Laney's face and added a note of torch singer mystique. Rajini was like a sister to Laney. More than a sister. Laney owed Rajini everything.

She slid to the floor with her knees to her chest, feeling the top of her sheer stockings. Her birthday present to herself—she'd passed a street stall selling them and couldn't resist.

Rolly would've hated the stockings. He'd always make her dress up like magazine pictures he'd show her. She'd gotten good at being a fashion chameleon, which came in pretty handy on the run. She knew how to blend in.

The sheer stockings had appealed to the girl she'd been before Rolly had come along. They'd appealed to the songstress poet full of funky style.

Her birthday present to herself. And like hell she'd take them off.

Footsteps. Heavy. A man.

She wrapped her fingers around the Ruger .22, feeling the little dots on the grip and fixing the napkins over it.

Quiet as a mouse, she slid up to a standing position against the wall behind the door.

Her pulse pounded so loudly in her ears she barely heard the handle turn.

The door swung open. She backed tight to the wall, hand out, using her fingertips to ease it to a gentle stop so it wouldn't bang into her. The light went on.

Rustling fabric. Paper.

And just like that, the light went off and the door slammed shut.

Her shoulders sunk in relief. Just a staffer grabbing napkins or towels.

You're okay.

Except she wasn't. Everything was wrong these days— eerie in a way she couldn't quite put her finger on.

When the footsteps faded out, she sat back down and risked the flash of light to check her email on her smartphone for the twentieth time. Still nothing from her brother. That was something eerie that she *could* put her finger on.

Charlie had forgotten her birthday.

She and her brother were close as peas in a pod, and he'd *forgotten her birthday*. Charlie was a major birthday celebrator.

Charlie had sounded odd in his emails all month, but this was a new level of odd. Again that belly-twist of fear.

She pressed her phone against her chest. What if Charlie was sick? In trouble? Had Rolly gotten to him? No, Charlie would've given her the signal. Her mind chased in frantic circles.

You're between a rock and a pointy place, Rolly always said to her, eyes lit with glee. He loved to change around sayings like that, and whenever he'd deliver one of his changed-around sayings, he'd stare at you afterward, expecting you to react. He fancied himself a poet of sorts, but he was no poet. Poetry was about connecting with people, not hurting them or isolating them. The dusty old poets Laney so loved—Keats, Byron—they helped her feel less alone, as though she was linking with another soul across time. *That* was poetry.

No matter how bad things got, she'd always had poetry. And now she had her gun, too, and she damn well knew how to use it. The Bangkok Imperiale Hotel Des Roses where she lived these days had a shooting range in the basement under the basement—one of the upsides to the Shinsurin brothers being a little shady. You didn't find a shooting range at the Hilton. What the hell; Laney was shady these days, too, what with her fake name and fake life story. Even her hair color was fake. Burdock brown instead of flaming red.

Not twenty minutes later, there was a soft knock at the closet door, followed by a quick triple knock. Laney let her eyes drift shut with relief. Their old signal. Rajini always remembered things like that. Laney stood and creaked open the door.

Rajini Shinsurin stood there smiling in a purple jewel-toned skirt suit that set off her jet black hair. "Coast is clear."

"Did you see him?"

"Yeah, and it's not Harken."

"Thank you! Uh!" Laney shoved her gun in her purse and threw her arms around her friend. "You're sure? You got a good look? I was so sure it was him. He even *felt* like him."

"It wasn't."

"You saw the one I meant, though, right?" Laney asked, tidying up the napkins. "He was wearing a bright green and white-striped polo shirt."

"I know. And jeans. I passed right by the guy. I looked in his eyes. He probably thought I was hitting on him. I see why you thought it's him, but it's not."

"Is he still out there?"

Rajini shrugged. "He looked like he was leaving. He only had a bev."

Bev.

Rajini talked in restaurant and hotel lingo. She'd been in the States to get her hospitality degree. Destined to manage the Shinsurin family hotels.

"You're sure," Laney said. "I was sure it was him."

"For the millionth time. And, think about it—it was always Rolly's investigators who found you first, and Harken would come after. If an investigator had found you, you'd know about it. And Harken wouldn't be sitting on his ass in an overpriced tourist restaurant."

Laney closed the closet door, smiling at Rajini's little dig. "Though I was looking so forward to that mushroom steak."

Rajini pouted. "You don't like our authentic Western steak entrée?"

Laney snorted. A steak with hoisin sauce was anything but authentic, and they both knew it. But then, the Bangkok Imperiale Hotel Des Roses didn't cater to Americans. It was mostly Chinese businessmen, and this week, a lot of the Shinsurin brothers' scary business partners. Like a convention for sketchy characters.

"I hope I didn't pull you out of anything," Laney said as they headed out of the dark hall.

"A boring vendor pitch. I should be thanking you."

Laney pulled her hat down low as they hit the dining room. The man who looked like Harken was nowhere to be seen. Neither was Laney's steak. Her table had been set with new linens. Well, what did she expect?

The host looked at them funny as they walked through the half-full dining room.

They pushed out the doors into the furnace blast of air that was midday Bangkok. Cars and bikes careened by madly.

"Send a boy for takeout next time. You shouldn't leave the hotel. You're safe at the hotel." Rajini looked over at her. "Has your brother emailed you yet?"

"No. And I'm worried."

"He probably has a girlfriend."

"Something's wrong. He sounds...wrong. What if Rolly's guys got to him?"

"Has he used your code?"

Begonia. He was supposed to use the word *begonia* in an email at the first sign of Rolly danger. *Begonia. Be gone.* "No."

"Well, then?" Rajini waved at a tuk-tuk, one of the colorful motorized rickshaws that buzzed up and down the streets.

"But what if he's sick? Or if Mama's sick? All he emails about is TV and current events. It's like he wants to email me, but not really email me."

Rajini stabbed a finger at her. "This is why you thought you saw Harken. You're spooked about your brother. You watch. You'll have an email from him to-morrow, I bet." She looked down at Laney's stockings, which, okay, looked a little odd with her black sheath dress. "What do you have on?"

"It's a new fashion."

"Are you wearing them for your show?"

"Hell, yeah," Laney said. "I think they're fun." Nobody ever paid attention to her, anyway. She was background music. Music to have conversations by. Laney used to despair about being ignored because her songs were the only deep-down truth in her whole fake life.

Stupid.

When on the run from a murderous and rageful ex-husband, you wanted to be ignored. That was the whole point.

"I need to get a non-expired passport," she said. "I know your brothers are working on it, but this was a sign—be ready for anything. I think I've gotten too secure at the hotel. You don't know what it was like sitting in that closet. I kept thinking, *What if I have to rabbit right now?* Hardly any money. An expired fake passport."

"You worry too much," Rajini said.

"Still," Laney said. "I want to start carrying big money and a valid passport at all times. I'm thinking about going down to Khaosan Road—"

Rajini began to protest. "Laney—"

"I don't want to keep bugging your brothers," Laney went on. "I know they're just busy, but I need a non-expired passport. This was my wake-up call." Everyone knew you could find opium-addicted tourists to sell their passports on the seedy edges of the strip. "I need to handle this."

"And end up mugged or arrested?" Rajini scowled. "No. Let my brothers swing you one. I'll tell them to hurry. They have the cleanest passports. Don't go to Khaosan Road."

Laney nodded, unconvinced. "I need cash, too. We'll pass the bank—do you want to—"

"Sorry." Rajini looked at her phone. "I have to get back. How about after the weekend?"

"Okay," she said, dismayed.

"After the weekend. Promise."

"Okay." What could she do? Her account was under Rajini's name. She was at Rajini's mercy.

Rajini smiled and chatted brightly as the little tuk-tuk wove in and out of traffic.

Laney half listened, unable to shake the feeling of danger pressing in.

CHAPTER TWO

Macmillan straightened his tie as he strolled past the row of tall, slender torches that illuminated the edges of the outdoor courtyard of the Bangkok Imperiale Hotel Des Roses. The tables were occupied by mostly Asian tourists, but clustered near the front were some of the most notorious arms dealers on the planet.

And he had arrived to screw each and every one of them. With his ears.

Macmillan adjusted his glasses, resisting the impulse to study the faces. He wouldn't be recognized, but it wouldn't do to be remembered. He wore a linen suit—top quality, just a bit rumpled, and his dark blond hair had grown just over his ears, swept back like a proper academic's. His glasses had whisper-light frames, very man of letters, for his Peter Maxwell, PhD, linguistics expert persona. It was easy for Macmillan to play Dr. Peter Maxwell. It's who he had been once upon a time.

In a sunnier lifetime.

Nobody seemed to notice that Dr. Peter Maxwell accepted teaching and speaking assignments in zones of unrest, or that the world's most notorious terrorists and predators were taken into custody in the very cities he visited, often just days after he left.

Macmillan scanned around. A cloud had moved over the moon, casting the back tables in darkness, but then he saw it—the light of a cell phone illuminating a scruffy cheek. He made his way to the far edge of the courtyard and stopped in front of a table occupied by a lone man with sooty hair and glasses. "Nice night for a drink under the stars."

His old friend Arturio—Rio for short—gave him a level glance. "Clears the mind." This format of greeting served as an all-clear signal among the Associates. Not that they needed it; the Associates were tighter than a family; they'd know if something was off from a mere look. But the greeting was protocol. Part of their culture.

Macmillan sat.

"I left a message," Rio said. "The Russians have a hitter on you."

Macmillan crossed his legs, stiff from the sedentary existence of the adjunct professor, teaching and grading. "Good luck with that."

"It could be Anders."

Macmillan shrugged it off. Nobody knew what he looked like—as Peter Maxwell the linguistics expert or as Macmillan the spy. A grainy video had circulated for some years, but it was useless, even to a legendary hitter like Anders.

"People will have guessed you're here," Rio said. "Somebody's out there waiting for you to screw up, old friend."

Macmillan scanned the crowd up front. "Let them fill my belly full of bullets."

Rio gave him a dark look, but he damn well knew: Macmillan would do anything to stop the auction of the TZ-5. He would give up everything. His humanity. Even his life.

In a lot of ways, Macmillan had died long ago. He was just an operative these days. A tool. A charming, deadly overachiever. Nothing touched him. That was part of his power.

"Your belly full of bullets would be the opposite of my plan," Rio said.

Macmillan watched the stage. They were setting up for some singer.

Noise. Great.

The TZ-5 was a disturbingly advanced weapon—a powerful remote control drone with a wingspan of just seven feet and deadly laser weapons, and it could be powered from miles away by lasers. It was configurable enough to take out an entire airport or a single man running down a crowded street. In short, it made US drones look like plastic playground toys. The Association had been hunting the TZ for two and a half years. The man who possessed it would finally be turning up here at the hotel, ready to sell. The highest bidder would get the blueprints and the prototype, exclusively. It would shift the balance of power, no matter who got it. Lots of innocent people would die.

A waiter came over to light the candle on their table and their hands came up in unison. "No thanks." Neither wanted their faces illuminated.

Rio smiled at the waiter. "We'd love another round of tea. And more of those little cakes."

The waiter nodded and left.

Rio shifted his dark eyes to Macmillan. Rio wore a lavender silk shirt under his dinner jacket. Quietly stylish. Quietly lethal. He was the Association's resident assassin.

"Is there a show?" Macmillan asked.

Rio pulled out his mobile and scanned through emails. "Woman singer. An American."

"Not too loud, I hope."

"You won't even notice. Barely-there ballads," Rio said. "Sexy, what you can see of her. Unmemorable. Walking wallpaper." Rio chose his words with imagination and precision. Macmillan liked that in a friend. Rio put away his phone. "What are you carrying?"

"My regular." Meaning a Smith & Wesson Platinum 500.

Rio raised his eyebrows. Meaning, *and? What else are you carrying?*

"Party favor." Macmillan angled his gaze down, indicating the .22 at his ankle.

Rio waited. Eyebrows raised.

"I was just teaching class for God's sake," Macmillan said.

The assassin's hands disappeared under the table. A few moments later, Macmillan felt a tap on his knee. "Take it," Rio said. "It'll beat a metal detector, too."

Macmillan felt the soft leather, the buckle, the ridges of the grip. Rio's favorite Sig. "Rio."

"Put it on. Humor me," Rio said.

Rio often showed affection through firearms. He lent them and even gave them as gifts, the way a mother might dole out mittens and cookies. Macmillan kind of loved that about Rio. He loved everything about Rio. Of all the Associates, Rio was most like a brother to him; they'd saved each other's asses more times than he could count. Macmillan strapped the holster around his free ankle and sat back, eyeing his old friend. "Happy?"

Rio gave him a wry glance then nodded toward the stage. "Take a closer look at the far right table up in the front."

Macmillan stood as though to search his pockets, scanning the front. Six, seven tables of dealers. He noticed the North Koreans in the sea of faces, and even a table of Glorious Light operatives. And he'd never known the Peruvians to be acquainted with Dmitri Turgenov's clan, but they were mixing it up now. With one of the New Tong out of Texas. Macmillan sat. "It's like international arms dealers gone wild up there."

"All flown in over the last two days. Who knew they'd all show so early?"

They were waiting for a man known only by one name: Jazzman.

"They all want to pre-empt the auction," Macmillan said.

That was the worry, that the weapon would change hands before the auction, and the Associates would never see it again. Until people started dying.

"The new thinking is that Jazzman is here already," Rio said, "mingling, assessing his buyers, waiting to unmask himself."

"That's what I'd do if I were him," Macmillan said. "If he's here, I'll find him."

Rio nodded once. A simple, precise reply.

Nobody escaped Macmillan. Back when he had been a rising star in the linguistics world, he could spend entire months studying the way different people pronounced a diphthong like the *ow* in *low*, and draw all kinds of conclusions about what that meant. He could see a universe in a single word choice. He used his expertise to understand people, and by extension, humanity itself.

These days, he used his ability to ferret out scum. Fugitives who'd used plastic surgery to change their appearance. Killers.

The TZ could turn out to be the most prolific killer of all. This was the case he'd been born for.

Jazzman had stolen the TZ in a bloody attack on an independent lab in Panama over two years ago—freelance scientists working on their own designs to sell on the world market. Governments across the globe went on red alert when the news got out that the TZ had been stolen. Nobody talked about it publicly, but contingency plans were made from Washington D.C. to Tokyo.

Then Jazzman and the TZ had simply fallen off the map. For two and a half years, the security community had held its collective breath. There was some hope out there that Jazzman had hidden the TZ and gotten himself killed.

Until last month, when talk of this auction started up. Jazzman was back, and he was hot to sell. The sale was announced during a series of conference calls, during which Jazzman used sophisticated voice distortion software that disguised his gender and his accent during the calls—everything but his word choice.

And that's all they had to go on to find Jazzman. His choice of words.

Worked for Macmillan.

Macmillan had studied the recording extensively, charting the man's errors and idiosyncrasies. He mined his word choices and frequency of use. He got to understand Jazzman's speech habits well enough to be able to recognize him to a 99.5% certainty—*if* he could hear him speak. Not just a few words; it had to be a real conversation.

That would be the trick. To get close enough to the dealers to hear conversations.

Rio, on the other hand, was hunting the old fashioned way. With a very powerful rifle and a list drawn up by Dax, the leader of the Associates.

"How many of them are staying at this place?"

"About thirty so far," Rio said. "Turns out the Shinsurins own this place."

"Ah, Shinsurin hospitality. Ideal for the romantic exchange of weaponry." The Shinsurins were a powerful clan with strong connections to the Chinese business community and the New Tong out of Texas.

Rio speculated aloud on ways to get close enough to the tables of dealers to record their conversations. The

Arabs would be the problem—they weren't mixing with the other arms dealers.

Macmillan didn't think Jazzman was an Arab. English could be Jazzman's second language, but Arabic wouldn't be his first. But he let Rio spin on. He was soaking in Rio's tone, the gestalt of his speech and manner. Rio had lost his wife some years back and he'd turned darker and more nihilistic since. Anybody could see when a man held himself apart from the crowd; Rio was smart enough not to do that. But Macmillan could hear Rio's remoteness in his language itself. More passive constructions. Fewer content words and third person pronouns. The tone, the delivery, even the unsaid. As if Rio was drifting away. Sometimes when Macmillan listened to him, he had the impulse to clamp a hand onto his friend's arm, to be his anchor. Macmillan knew what it was like to lose somebody.

The assassin gave him a steely glance. "I know that look. I know what you're doing."

Macmillan tilted his head.

"Back off," Rio said. "I won't be one of your puzzles."

"Fair enough," Macmillan said.

The waiter set down two teas and a plate of honey cakes. Rio thanked him, smoothing a stray bit of dark, wavy hair back out of his eyes. "Will the libidinous student body survive the week without their eminent guest lecturer?"

"They'll have to parse their tender sentences without my strong, sure hand, I'm afraid," Macmillan said.

A smile in Rio's eyes. He always seemed so amused by the groupies Macmillan got when he was forced to play tousled, self-effacing Doctor Peter Maxwell. Macmillan wasn't one to sleep with students, though. There were classes to teach, papers to grade, books to write, and severed hands to not think about.

Macmillan had a lot of sex, but it was always for the job—just him, gathering intelligence, a shining blond Viking with ill intent.

Macmillan caught sight of various players: The Russian clan leader. The Valdez brothers. Then he spotted Thorne, the notorious Hangman lieutenant. "Thorne's here," he mumbled.

"Party's really starting now," Rio mumbled. Things got dangerous when Thorne came around.

Up on the stage, a boy in a white, short-sleeved shirt set up a microphone stand. Then he set out a stool and pushed two large vases of roses onto either side of it, so that they would frame the singer.

A minute later, a lone woman with a mass of loose, dark curls walked out onto the stage. She had on a pillbox hat with a net that came down to conceal the top half of her face; her dress was a classic little black number, worn with knee-high panty hose, pulled up like tall socks, of all things. She lifted a hand in a wave, smiling at the audience, then she adjusted her microphone with deft movements, pale skin glowing in the torchlight.

His eyes fell to those knee-highs with their crass stripe of too-tight elastic squeezing the flesh just below her knee, the hose itself just a titch darker than her skin.

Macmillan knew, from his extensive experience undressing the opposite sex, that knee-highs like those had been designed for wearing under 1970s pants suits. You rarely saw them anymore what with today's fashions, but such out-of-date garments were still available in Bangkok. This woman was wearing them wrong, like socks. The effect was dirty and delicious.

Macmillan couldn't take his eyes off her.

He wished she would pull off her hat so he could see her face. And good God, he wanted to hear her speak. Her tone. Her words.

Macmillan could feel Rio's eyes on him. He needed to stop staring at the singer. He tore his gaze away and focused on Thorne, who stood up and moved to where the Finns sat. He fought to find something intelligent to say. "Tenacious, painful, annoyingly indestructible. Have to admire a man who lives up to his name."

"Thorne?" Rio asked.

Macmillan nodded. It wasn't like him to get distracted. He'd been feeling a little feverish in the last day or two, maybe that was it. Or maybe it was the hat, hiding her identity.

"I would love to hear Thorne speak," he continued. "Thorne could be Jazzman. Or the Finns. Or Valdez. That whole table is suspect. What I wouldn't give to be that potted palm."

The potted palm stood at the intersection of four tables of arms dealers. They wouldn't be saying anything sensitive out there, but Macmillan didn't care. A rambling conversation about the weather would work for his purposes.

"If we could get a listening device in that potted palm—"

"Wouldn't work," Rio said. "The dealers cluster in different areas every night. And these minimalist tables. Candles and drinks." Nowhere to hide a microphone, he meant. Putting it underneath would be ineffective in this din.

"We should have tech look all the same."

Up on the stage, a boy brought the singer a guitar. She hooked the strap around her neck and tuned a string or two, then strummed a chord. "How's it goin' out there?"

Macmillan straightened. Rio had thought her *unmemorable? Walking wallpaper?*

Nobody answered, but she kept on. "I'm pretty goddamn happy to be here tonight, singing for y'all," she said.

The accent. Florida, or maybe lower Alabama, Macmillan thought.

Again she smiled. "Now my mama always said, Laney, you want to have a friend, you gotta be a friend. And my mama was one of the best friends I ever had, I'll tell you that right off. A little bit crazy maybe..." She tuned a string, strummed. "But a girl'll forgive her mama a whole lot of things if she's just doin' her best."

With that she began to sing in a breathy, husky voice. You could barely call it singing, though there was a certain cadence to it.

The lyrics were unusual; hardly lyrics at all, really, more a list of commonplace things. But as he listened on, it came to him that this was a list of things lost. Lost forever.

Macmillan's throat began to feel thick as he dug into the song. It was relentless, the way she piled up the details. Out-of-ink pens in the kitchen junk drawer. An inside joke. The phone-answering voice of somebody long gone.

He swallowed, chest full of ragged energy.

Stop.

Was it possible his fever was worse than he thought? That sometimes happened in the tropics.

"What?" Rio's whisper was like a shotgun in the torchlight.

Macmillan shook his head. "Nothing." He had to pull himself together. Quickly he set to analyzing the song, breaking it into manageable parts. The objects on the list: commonplace enough to evoke the universal, but specific enough to feel real. Style: folksy, even a bit alternative. Basic singer-songwriter stuff. Yes, she was a decent songwriter. Clever, that was all.

He took a deep breath. Analyzing her did the trick. He was feeling much more under control.

She was clever with words, and he had a fever. Case closed.

"What is it?" Rio asked, scanning the audience. He'd thought Macmillan had seen trouble.

Macmillan waved his hand at the stage. "Please. Couldn't Jazzman have picked a hotel with an Elvis impersonator? Or maybe a Thai act?"

Rio furrowed his brow. "You have a problem with her?"

"Don't you find this song a bit...emotionally manipulative?"

"What do you mean?"

"Designed to pull at people's heartstrings," Macmillan said. "She's a clever wordsmith, but these emotionally manipulative, hyper-nostalgic lists..."

Rio smiled.

"What?" Macmillan asked.

"Heaven forbid the great Macmillan should be made to feel something."

Macmillan crossed his legs. "I feel the urge to put an ice pick through my ear right now. Does that count?"

Rio kept smiling. He stirred his tea in a very *no comment* way.

She went on in that Southern twang. He added a bit of Georgia and West Virginia as influences laid over that Florida accent. She made a little joke using the word pixilated in the old hills way—referring to pixies, not pixels. Something of a magpie with words, this woman. He'd been like that, way back when. Back when words were a pleasure. Back when language was about interacting instead of hunting.

As she sang on, he found himself getting sucked back in. Damn, the list just wouldn't stop.

He put his hand to his chest, wanting to push down the sharp feeling. He flashed on a memory of his fiancée Gwen, standing in the rain in a party dress, laughing. It was then he'd known he loved her.

He fought the memories but they came anyway—that night ten years ago. He saw his parents and sister and Gwen, playing the adjective game as the train rolled through the dark jungle. His father had pantomimed drinking a soda standoffishly. It had taken forever for the four of them to guess *standoffishly*. They'd felt sure he was drinking the soda *impudently* or *superciliously*. Macmillan had guessed *presumptuously*. God, they'd all been such nerds about that game. That was the last time he'd seen them alive. After his father drank his soda *standoffishly*, Macmillan had taken a walk through the cars, stretching his legs, listening to dialects.

He was three cars down when the bomb hit.

He pressed on his chest harder but the emotions wouldn't go down. It was with great effort that he fixed his attention back on the arms dealers. "Blue hat sitting with the New Tong of Texas," he mumbled. "Who is that?"

"We think he's Valdez cartel." Rio pointed out the new Valdez players. "We heard chatter that Jazzman is picking up some sort of package here."

"What sort of package?"

"We don't know," Rio said. "Dax thinks it's unrelated to the TZ. Maybe drugs. We don't know anything."

They discussed the idea of getting other Associates close enough to record the conversations. Macmillan had created a quick and dirty software program they could feed a transcription into. Even if Macmillan was killed in the next five minutes, the program could help them recognize Jazzman from his speech habits.

The Association tended to look to Macmillan for magic. Well, linguistics *was* a kind of magic, a way to see hidden worlds.

Her next song was about a childhood home. Another listing song.

Good God, she couldn't just say kitchen—she had to get in the needlepoint hanging with an ancient spatter of tomato sauce on it, and a dog's nose touching your knee under the table. A darker subtext was in there, too—he'd done enough time in the English lit trenches to take apart a verse. Back in his old life, he used to love getting muddy with a multi-layered text. He'd once engaged with language, heart and soul. Now he mined it for parts. Commodities. Weapons.

His family had been so proud of his career. They'd be sick to see him now, hollowed out by vengeance. All the goodness gone.

Well, they weren't the ones left behind.

Rio was staring at him.

Macmillan forced a smile. "I can't say what I need more at this moment—to stop Jazzman from selling the TZ or to stop this woman from singing another song."

"Mmm."

"What?"

"You know you always joke when you're distressed."

"Distressed." Macmillan spat out the word.

Rio jotted something on the small pad. Noting the dealers' social movements. Funny how unaffected he was by Laney's web of sentimental cues and signs. Macmillan tried hard not to focus on her. Or on those hose, but he found them so powerfully sexy. He found her powerfully sexy. He couldn't see her face, but it didn't matter; this thing was beyond physical. He put the back of his hand to his head.

"You coming down with something?"

"I don't know," Macmillan whispered.

Rio tipped up his head. "Top two floors are where they've got the players—the 17th and 18th, and it's where everything will happen. High security, manned at all time, halls guarded at two sides. They're keeping the 16th floor vacant. Stairwell is no-go. It's going to be a bitch to get ears up there." He went on about the Sawadee Palace Hotel across the street where most of the Associates were staying. It wouldn't do to have them trotting through the Bangkok Imperiale Hotel des Roses lobby. Rio turned to him and smiled. "We could have Associates fan out and listen for people to say *vim and vitriol.* How about that?"

"Hah." Jazzman had used the phrase *vim and vitriol* several times on the conference call, his own personal variant on the idiom *vim and vigor.* "Not a bad thought, except I could see other dealers using it now. As a callback, an inside joke. But did you notice the emotional charge Jazzman had around it? You heard the call—he sounded proud of switching the words."

Rio gave him a look. "I didn't think it at the time but...yes."

"It is, for want of a better word, a *thing* for him," Macmillan said. "Altering idioms. It's something he wants people to notice. My money says he alters idioms all the time. That alone won't identify Jazzman, but it's a damn fine thing to listen for."

Onto another song. *You in the dark alley next to the McDonald's. Paper bags at your feet. You dirty and alone outside the dry cleaners, eyes wild.*

The song was crafted to sound like it was about a down-and-out friend, but Macmillan got that it wasn't about a friend at all. Something else. When he listened to what was actually there, he got that she was talking about dragons. Specific dragons, in fact. He'd walked this neighborhood a lot over the past month and he'd seen them, too, eroding quietly between chain stores and noodle shops. Up on signs. Stone, plaster, lacquer, paint on brick.

It was a little puzzle, this song. So she'd been in town quite a while. Rambling around alone, judging from the degree of observation. Or maybe it was vigilance. Fearful people tended to notice more.

It was clear that she related to the dragons. He suspected that she was a dragon, broken and alone, squeezed into an out-of-the-way place.

Another song—with a shout-out to the 18th century poet Byron, nestled in like an Easter egg. A line from one of his favorite poems way back when he was optimistic, naïve, vulnerable Peter Maxwell.

It was here he came up for air. How long had he been ignoring the arms dealers? He had a job to do.

He forced himself to groan. "The sophomoric shout-out to Byron. Can this night get any more magical?" Macmillan knew he should shut up, but he couldn't. "Tell me she isn't here every night. Please."

Rio adjusted the cuffs of his silky shirt in a way that suggested he was holding back comment.

"What?" Macmillan demanded. "It's just a bit much."

"Why not ignore her like everybody else does?"

Movement up at the front tables. A man in a blue suit approached a group at the center of the cluster. A Somali, he guessed by the way he moved his mouth and jaw as he greeted another man. Language often shaped a person's facial muscles; Macmillan could sometimes tell a person's nationality by how they held their lips between utterances. Could Jazzman be a Somali man? The conversation up there was really flowing, especially between songs. They'd be speaking English—that would the common language.

If only he could be that potted palm.

He and Rio discussed ways to get speech samples. They could wire up some Associates and plant them at intervals across the front of the place before the show tomorrow night. A few of the female Associates could try to get themselves invited into the inner circle, which was 99% male. Associates could fan out and shadow known dealers as they went about their daily business. But they needed more than coffee orders; they needed conversations.

Once Jazzman was identified, the Association would abduct him and get him to reveal the whereabouts of the TZ prototype and blueprints. They had to identify him before he sold.

Jazzman, unfortunately, had a talent for sniffing out agents. The CIA's agent in the New Tong out of Texas had been killed. Interpol's network across the former Soviet states had frayed, the Russian Associate on the original conference call had been killed, as had their China connection. There was nobody friendly inside that auction.

It was up to Macmillan.

Laney was onto another song—a young girl making dinner for her man. *Cookbook full of wishes.* If the scruffy little dog moving his legs like he was running in his sleep, or mama's Irish lullaby didn't get you, the cookbook full of wishes would.

He rubbed his eyes. "Good lord, woman, if you miss your alcoholic hoarder Mama that much, go back to Florida."

Rio turned to him. "That's what she's singing about?"

"More or less. And all the bit about dinner—the cornpone mama meaning so well. The whole Mama song is infused with classic child of alcoholic thinking. It's probably the reason our poor Laney up and married that controlling husband."

Rio stared at him incredulously. "I've been listening to these songs for three nights, watching the tables. They're just...lists of things. You can't be getting all that meaning from lists of things."

"English Lit 101. A poem is rarely about one thing. A rose is more than a rose. A cigar is more than a cigar." Macmillan had always had a soft spot for the poets. Back in his life as Peter, anyway. He broke off a bit of cake. "My guess is that she's on the run from that controlling husband."

"Seriously?"

"Trust me. It's all in there."

"Well, if she is on the run, she's a fool," Rio said. "That hat."

"I know. She may as well tack a sign on her back. *I am in hiding. This is my disguise.* She probably doesn't even realize it."

Rio shot him a warning look.

"Don't worry. I don't do damsels in distress."

"There's always a first time."

Macmillan sniffed. "Let her set herself on fire up there. I only have eyes for Jazzman."

Rio stirred his tea in a *no comment* way.

But Rio didn't get it.

Sure, Rio understood on an intellectual level why Macmillan wanted to stop the auction, but he didn't understand it on a gut level. Rio didn't know what it was like to dig through piles of bodies that were no longer human. Rio couldn't know what it was like to recognize the person you loved more than anything in the world from a barrette clasped to a bloody bit of hair and scalp. Rio couldn't know the horror of grabbing somebody's hand, thinking to pull them out of the wreckage, only to come away with the hand itself, attached to nothing. Rio couldn't know that a severed hand weighs roughly the same as a tennis shoe, or what it feels like to hold such a hand while your world falls away.

Macmillan wished he could stop going back to that goddamn hand. The memory was surfacing too often these days. It was the situation with the TZ, bringing it all back, reminding him of that night ten years ago. The idea of innocents dying, caught in something larger. Back then he'd been a mere civilian. A powerless passenger. But he could do something about this threat.

He would do anything, become anything, to stop the TZ.

CHAPTER THREE

An hour later, Rio left for a meeting across town. Macmillan stayed to finish charting the dealer movements.

Her show ended a bit after midnight.

The crowd began to disperse soon after. He took the opportunity to wander around, catching fragments of language in the air like a hound dog on a scent. He followed a pair of Moroccans and a German through grand brass and wood doors and on into the elegant Hotel Des Roses lobby. He trailed them loosely across the gleaming, pink marble floor under a dark wood ceiling studded with tiny lights like stars in the night sky. Ornate brass banisters marked wide, rose-carpeted staircases up to the reception areas, but the dealers went to the gift area and fell to examining postcards on a spinning rack. Silently. Then, when the conversation started back up, it was Spanish. He needed to hear Jazzman speaking English. That would happen in more widely mixed groups.

He wandered back out to the courtyard. The tables stood mostly empty now except for a few couples in the back and an old man off to the side, puffing on a last cigarette.

And there she was, talking and laughing with a pair of young Thais near the potted palm. She'd pulled the face-concealing net up over the top of the hat to reveal amber eyes that looked bright under lavishly dark lashes and brows. A smattering of freckles covered her nose and her smile had just a bit of the devil in it.

And she took his breath away.

One of the young men spoke in rapid Thai, and Laney clearly followed along. So she'd been there long enough to learn Thai.

The other young man fussed with a leaf on the potted palm. He began to unwrap a wire from its trunk. *A wire.* A microphone. Connected to a laptop.

Macmillan's pulse pounded.

They'd been recording the music! A recording device in the potted palm.

Could it be so easy?

He settled down at a nearby table and pretended to focus on his smartphone. Between the recording and the charting, he would be able to get a speech sample from nearly every dealer who had been out there. He'd be able to rule them out. Or rule one of them in. He'd know if Jazzman had been out there.

He would follow that recording.

The friends left. Laney stayed, zipping the equipment into bags and cases.

She'd take it home.

Well then, she'd take Macmillan home, too.

His eyes fell to her crazy sexy knee-highs. The prospect of seducing her filled him with excitement, guilt, delight, dread, and lots of emotions he couldn't name. Since when could he not name something? It was this fierce sense of push and pull he felt with her—it had him all turned around. Or maybe it was the fever.

He'd do what it took to get alone with her computer. He could copy her entire hard drive in a matter of minutes and she'd never know. He'd seduced dozens of women to get access to secrets. She was just another.

He thought of her up there alone, singing in the background every night being completely ignored by the audience. She had something to say and nobody heard; he found himself annoyed on her behalf on top of everything else.

He needed to disengage. This was about the TZ. He'd be the most despicable gutter dog if it meant getting his hands on the TZ.

He would charm her and steal from her. End of story.

In his mind, he went back over her songs, flipping through them like a Rolodex of her heart. She'd revealed so much; she would be easy to seduce.

He came to the dragons.

Oh, yes, he'd use the dragons. He pushed away a pang of guilt about that. There was a dragon she hadn't mentioned, one she wouldn't know about, right in the neighborhood.

And the poetry—that would be another way in. There was the box in the back of the used English-language book stall at the all-night bazaar, the best place in all of Bangkok to get old editions of classic poetry. A colleague at the university had told him about it. The box wasn't on display; you had to ask for it, like in a speakeasy. You couldn't find this stuff in Bangkok. She'd go crazy.

But seducing a poet wasn't all about lofty ideas and starry nights—that would be the mistake most men would make with her. No poet worth her salt didn't love carnality. A bit of dirt and teeth.

Macmillan was impressing even himself now. It was as if he had a direct line to her.

He stilled when he realized why: Laney was the kind of girl he would've picked out in his pre-spy days, back when he lived as Peter Maxwell. She was Peter's type.

Macmillan's throat felt thick.

Sure, during the last ten years he'd played Dr. Peter Maxwell in and out of lecture halls. He'd played Peter Maxwell the author. But never once had he played Peter Maxwell the man. Not since that night on the train.

He sucked in a breath. He'd do what it took. He'd court her as Peter, get her to take him back to her room. He'd take her to bed if he had to. He'd use every tool in his arsenal to get the TZ under his control. Sex was nothing but a highly useful tool. He himself was nothing but a highly useful tool, a means to an end.

He needed to keep his feelings out of it.

He looked down and flexed his fingers. He could still feel the hand in his palm. The weight of a tennis shoe. The hand, connected to nothing, to nobody. The memory crept over the edges of his mind.

He shut his eyes, fighting the undertow.

CHAPTER FOUR

L aney had watched him all night, way in the back in the dark. She'd told the waiter to light his candle, just so she could get a better look at him, but he and his friend didn't want it lit. Still, the torches had lit him enough.

He put away his phone and looked at his hand, moving it just slightly. Was something wrong with his hand?

He wasn't one of the conventioneers, she'd known that right off. The conventioneers were all dense and dark and grunty, and he was quicksilver bright. Shiny in a way she couldn't explain. It wasn't just his light hair, it was the feel of him. He sat quietly in his chair during the show, focusing hard on the audience—anywhere but her. Sometimes he'd lean forward with something apparently important to say to his friend. His skin was kind of burnished gold, as though he spent a lot of time outside, maybe walking the streets. He wore a light linen sports coat, sort of a tropical colonial deal. Best of all, he wore a T-shirt underneath his white buttoned-down shirt. She liked a man who wore a T-shirt under his button shirt, even in the heat. It showed a certain decorum.

His glasses had just a touch of gold on the rim and sides; it brought out the gold in his hair, which was long enough to be tucked behind his ears. He was so cool, so dapper, so together, she just wanted to kiss him and mess up that hair. She imagined him disheveled, wet with sweat. Hair hanging over her face. Brushing against her cheeks. Back and forth...

Furthermore, she'd spent two whole songs wondering what color his eyes were—something light for sure, maybe gray, blue, hazel. That was one good thing about the net hat; she could brazenly stare at people and they never knew.

She wound the cable around her elbow, thinking about putting the net back down so she could stare at him some more. He was much larger than she'd thought. He'd come off a bit studious back there, but up close he looked so solid and fit in the way he filled out that jacket that she revised her thinking. Maybe he was studious, but he was also an athlete—a boxer. A scholar and a boxer.

Hellbuckets, that was hot.

Then, as if he felt her watching, he looked up. Smiled.

Her heart just about sprung out of her chest. She smiled back. Nodded. "Hey," she said, and went back to her cord-winding.

He got up.

Oh, God, he was coming near. It was one thing to muse about men; it was another thing to engage with them. She still didn't much trust men.

"Need any help with that? Are you carrying all this alone?"

"I'm fine, thanks."

"It's the least I could do," he said. "Your show was...quite moving."

Big, fat liar, she thought to herself. He was just a guy hitting on her. Telling her what he thought she'd like to hear. Pretending like he'd listened. He'd been watching the audience and talking with his friend all night. Still, she was polite. "Well, thanks."

"You don't believe me?"

"No, I appreciate it," she said.

"Meaning no, you don't believe me, but you appreciate my bullshitting about it?"

She stopped her winding and smiled. "Yeah, I suppose that's what I mean."

He tilted his head, looked into her eyes.

And she forgot to breathe. She had her answer. Blue— his eyes were light blue with gray shards and a pale line around the iris, as if to emphasize their blueness. But blue was just a color; the word did nothing to suggest content: humor. Intelligence. Sparkle shot through with challenge. He had a look that said, *I have something wonderful for you.*

"I meant exactly that," he said. "Moving."

"Okay," she said.

"Though I have to say, that song—*You in the Alley?*"

She kept winding. That song listed the junkiest, dirtiest, cheap and chipped dragons in the neighborhood, though it never used the word dragon. Laney didn't like to be obvious, and also, the dragons were a lot of things. Rajini always insisted *You in the Alley* was about old boyfriends.

She sort of wished this guy wouldn't talk about her songs, because he hadn't been listening.

"You left out the best one," he said. "I was curious why."

"The best one what?" she asked.

"The best forgotten dragon."

Her heart skipped a beat. He'd gotten it. She looked up. "Well, aren't you observant."

He crossed his arms, half-sitting and half-leaning on a table top, so calm and confident. Like his posture alone was reply enough.

Did he know the song was kind of about her? She felt exposed, suddenly, at the thought that he might. Even she hadn't realized it when she first wrote it. She'd just felt so horribly sorry for the dragons being crushed by the unforgiving city. She imagined that someday they'd be all gone, and it broke her heart. She'd reflected on it only later, realizing it was how she felt, and Rolly was the city, crushing everything out of her with his hard angles and force. "I'm sure there's a lot of dragons I missed."

"You didn't miss any of the others of that type on Tamron Road or the alleys off it. The song lists out every dragon in this area except the plaster one near the bazaar. I was waiting for it because it's far and away the best. Well, they're all wonderful, of course." He had a whiff of an accent. Like he didn't learn English in America.

She narrowed her eyes. "There's no plaster dragon over by the bazaar."

"Oh, yes there is." He didn't smile as he said it. Nah, this guy, he *shone*.

"That you can see from the street?"

"Yes. Just before Pim Song Palace." A lock of blond hair escaped from its swept-back position and kissed his cheek, grazing the gold rim of his glasses. Her pulse sped. "I was curious," he continued. "I wondered if it was because it didn't fit your thesis, the idea that they're losing the battle."

Her heart pounded. She felt held...invaded...*ravished* by how much he'd heard. As if she'd been undressing in front of a mirror, only to learn it was a two-way mirror, and he'd been on the other side, enjoying her. She almost couldn't believe he was real, this man starting in about secret dragons.

He smiled lazily. "To the left of Pim Song. You'd like this one."

"Because it doesn't fit my thesis?" Funny that he'd called it a thesis. Like he took her songs really seriously. "Does that mean you think it's winning?"

"Well, I think they're all winning, but with this one, it's obvious. When you're a dragon and your habitat is *legends*, the shadow of a high rise, a bed of wrappers, that's nothing, don't you think?"

She felt like bursting into laughter. It was as if she'd put a message into a bottle and cast it into the ocean, thinking that was the end of the conversation.

"I go by there all the time," she said. "If there was a dragon there I would know about it."

"It's not obvious."

"I would've seen it. You're getting your streets mixed up."

And then he put out his hand, strong and golden like him. "A thousand bhat."

Around thirty bucks.

She could touch him now. She very much wanted to touch him. It was the craziest thing.

His lips formed a hint of a smile and he watched her with those blue-gray eyes so full of knowing and humor; the way he looked at her, it made her feel special. It made her feel *seen*. "Are you frightened, little dragon?"

Heat rushed to her face.

Little dragon. She fought to keep her expression neutral. So he had gotten it all—even that she felt lost and walled in like the dragons. It was sexy and scary, and she wanted him to say more things like that to her, and suddenly she felt less lost, less walled in.

Less alone.

And suddenly she was putting out her hand. "An easy thousand bhat."

He took it and squeezed. A shiver of excitement flowed clear through her.

"We're not just betting that it's a dragon," she said. "It has to be the best ruined dragon."

"I understand."

"Meaning I've got to be able to see it from the street and admit it's the best."

He let her hand go with a nod. "Full surrender or nothing."

Twinges curled through her belly. Had he meant that sexy? Because she sure heard it sexy. Her whole body heard it sexy. She swallowed. "How do we prove it?"

"I tend to go with visual confirmation in circumstances like these."

"Meaning go look? Like right now?"

He tilted his head, all playful confidence, and something in her longed to rise up and meet him there. She didn't know the first thing about him, but he got the dragon thing. He'd *connected*. It made him feel familiar from the inside out. You didn't need a man's name when you had a feel for the inside of him.

He said, "You can buy yourself something if you win. You won't win, of course, but you can tell yourself that for now."

"You are so full of it." She smiled, full of such a crazy, good feeling. Maybe she could trust this good feeling. And what the hell, the all-night market was a safe place. She'd wear her hat. She'd bring her Ruger. She needed to go anyway—to pick up a backpack. If she was going to be mobile, she needed to have a backpack with essentials ready to go. She'd be less noticeable shopping with this guy alongside.

She narrowed her eyes. "Fine."

"We'll take a tuk-tuk. I'll carry your things—they look heavy."

She slid her gaze over to see Dok Shinsurin, who was watching her from behind the courtyard bar. *Crap.* "Let me put it in my room."

"You stay here? At the hotel?" He sounded surprised.

"Yeah," she said.

He took hold of her computer bag. "May I help?"

"No, please." She took it from him. "Meet me out in front in five minutes. Outside the doors."

Her stuff felt light as she picked it up. *She* felt light. He seemed to not want her to go. "Five minutes." With that she walked off.

Niwat Shinsurin, the most rational of the Shinsurin brothers, had joined hothead Dok by the bar. She walked over and gave the formal Thai greeting of a woman, "*Sawadee Kha.*" She loved saying it, loved the music of it. "Did Rajini mention about my passport?" she asked Niwat. "I'm getting itchy without one. I know you have a lot on your plate, but I'm feeling like it's reckless that I don't have one. I should be prepared for anything, you know?"

"*Passpoto! Pom Khortot Khap,*" Niwat apologized. "You asked for that months ago."

Yes, she had. The Shinsurin brothers were usually more up on things. "And you have my hotel ID picture. That'll still work, right?"

Niwat nodded. "No problem."

"I just want to say, I would be more than happy to pay for it. I know you pay someone for this sort of thing. I'd have to wait until Monday to get my money—"

"No. You don't pay," Niwat said.

Dok flicked an ash off his cigarette. "You should not be separated from the herd," he said. "It's what Rolly would like. He would like you to leave our fortress of safety."

"I agree," she said. "But you always want to keep all your doors open."

"You do." Niwat shot a glance at Dok. "I apologize. I see our man tomorrow. I'll put it at the top of his list."

"Thank you," she said.

Dok frowned, offended. He was always offended, always ready to fight somebody.

"Our man will require a few days," Niwat said. "You will have your passport after the weekend."

Dok gave his brother a funny look.

"Thanks," she said.

"Who was that?" Niwat nodded his head where the man had stood.

"Just an audience guy." She smiled brightly. "Thank you. Good night."

CHAPTER FIVE

Anders sat at the far end of the lobby of the Bangkok Imperiale Hotel Des Roses noodling on his phone, adjusting the cotton in his cheek with his tongue. The cotton helped create the late-middle-aged Indian executive look he favored on jobs in Asia. Late-middle-aged was key. People underestimated how age let you fly under the radar.

He liked this seat, right at the edge of a cluster, turned just so; it allowed him to see the elevators, the desk, and the only way into the building from the outside courtyard.

The show had ended and bar was closing down. The patrons were returning. Some of them headed up to their rooms, others up the stairs to the lounge. The place had been made over with spare surfaces of dark woods and bold colors, but some decorator had ruined it with a profusion of brass ornamentation—bannisters, planters, mirrors. Not a good look. But he wasn't there for the décor.

He was there to identify and kill Macmillan.

The Association knew about the auction. They'd be desperate to get their hands on Jazzman and his weapon. Which meant they'd have to send Macmillan, the invisible hunter. They always seemed to send Macmillan around when they needed intelligence, details, *more*. You never knew Macmillan was there until well after the shit hit the fan and by then he was gone.

Nobody knew what Macmillan looked like or how he tracked his targets. There was a rumor he was some type of psychic, or even a remote viewer. That would be bullshit, of course, but it made for a good story and it gave the newbies a certain thrill.

Well, not just newbies. Over the years, Anders had seen numerous cartels, factions, and crime families get whipped up into a paranoid frenzy about the Association, and Macmillan in particular.

Anders wasn't surprised by how difficult it was to find the man. He was far more surprised nobody had tried to have the man killed before now.

He spotted people he knew from the Somali contingency, and the German group, too, but they didn't recognize him. Earlier, he spotted the man who had taken out the contract on Macmillan—a Russian in a Greek fisherman's hat. They'd never met, but Anders always vetted his employers.

People like his Russian employer feared the Association because they didn't understand the Association. Most criminal organizations were in it for the money and power. So were government agencies, when you got right down to it.

But not the Association.

As far as Anders could tell, the Association had to be bleeding money, and they didn't have power, or at least not the kind you could wield. Sometimes they seemed to be working for themselves. Other times they appeared to freelance for various governments—usually Western governments, though not always. They were clearly picky, and when you put together all the operations they'd gotten involved in, and looked at what side they got in on, you could see a hero complex in operation. They would be solidly on the "stop the auction side" of this affair.

Which meant Macmillan was here. Hunting. He made a note of an Aussie roughneck type tracking Thorne, the Hangman lieutenant. People looked at Thorne as a dangerous thug, but Anders had seen Thorne be very shrewd.

The Chinese man in the corner seemed overly observant. A blond man had been at the postcard rack near the Germans and the Moroccans; the man had felt wrong somehow, but he didn't look around once. Not a hunter.

Anders was a journalist by training; he could research a mark better than any hitter out there. He wished he could talk about his data mining techniques, but he didn't want his rivals to copy him.

Macmillan didn't exist ten years ago—that was one known fact. Which meant he'd jumped identities ten years ago. Which meant something had happened ten years ago to push Macmillan into the Association, or to alert the Association to his existence.

Possibly both.

Anders had run through the obvious databases and archives, going at reports of brawls, arrests, and tragedies from different angles. He was running through the more obscure databases and archives now, paying special attention to suppressed information.

He was getting some interesting flags.

Anders' clients all believed he was in the assassination business, but really, he was in the research business. That's what made him the best. That's how he'd find and kill Macmillan.

CHAPTER SIX

U p in her room, Laney splashed water on her face, not sure if she should trust the hopeful, happy feeing she had. One guy connects with her songs and she's ready to give up her firstborn.

She brushed her teeth.

Back in Stoley, Florida, back when she was Emmaline living in that overstuffed kit home full of mold and all the junk her mom couldn't quite part with, she and her girlfriends would describe their future husbands. Her girlfriends gave their future husbands mansions and convertibles, but what Laney wanted was connection. She wanted to be with a man so completely that she could say one word and he'd understand everything she meant in it—the references, the echoes, the degree of jokiness, the color, the angle. And then he'd say a word in reply, and they would share their worlds so completely that those two words would be a conversation.

She'd never had anything close to that—not with anybody except her brother at times, but that was different. And as wonderful as Rajini was, as close as they were, they didn't really *get* each other. Being on the run, she felt more distant from people than ever, like she was all alone, walking on the moon.

And suddenly this guy. Another moonwalker, traipsing along beside her.

She brushed her hair and put on a black felt hat with a small brim—a good nighttime hat. It didn't have a net, but it was pretty, and it really changed her look when she pulled it down over her forehead.

She put on some lipstick and paused. The hopeful, happy feeling scared her a little. She'd sometimes felt like, getting out of Stoley, she'd tried to take too much—like a jack-in-the-box popped up too high, and she'd spent the following years getting violently stuffed back down by Rolly. And now, this feeling of hope made her feel dangerously popped up. Like maybe it was safer to stay inside her little box. Like hope and happiness were for other people.

She shoved the cap back on her lipstick. It was just the night market. And it was her birthday, dammit.

And she wanted to touch him again. Because he was beautiful and magnetic.

She locked her door and headed out the side way. The Shinsurins would frown on an excursion like this. Let them assume she'd gone to bed.

She dated now and then, mostly emo travellers, like the German boy who wanted to look at the stars. Or Darrin, the American singer, all sweetness and pop hooks. Like her they'd been in their late twenties, but she thought of them as boys because they were pretty and sweet, and the opposite of Rolly. Even Rolly's face was hard, with sharp cheekbones, as if his hate was trying to bust out of his brain.

In both cases, the boys had up and left town after a few dates. It was probably for the best—any guy she was running with would be in big trouble if one of Rolly's thugs showed up. But they were both so lovely and she'd enjoyed having sex with them, even if she didn't ever orgasm during sex. Rolly had always said it showed she was frigid. Well, with Rolly it wasn't so much a frigidity problem as a being-married-to-a-frightening-and-narcissistic-psychopath problem.

She was a shy orgasmer, that's all, and she had great orgasms on her own. And as she got time and distance away from Rolly, the idea of sex was way more exciting. These days she was a very sexual person—at least in her mind. She was even a little kinky...in her mind. Or did that not count? Was being a little bit kinky in your mind like being a good gymnast in your mind?

She slipped down the stairwell and out the side into the hot, moist, diesel-flavored night, heading down the walk and around the corner to Tamroung Road where four lanes of traffic buzzed up and down like crazy, even at this time of night.

Across the way, a shop girl swept the neon-lit entrance of the 24-hour donut shop, but most of the other shops up and down the street were gated now. Shabby apartments and office buildings soared up into the sky, topped by colorful, constantly changing signs. You saw a lot of this mix of color and concrete grubbiness in Bangkok. Decrepitude and wealth at vivid angles with each other, like shards from different mirrors.

Then she caught sight of him and a smile spread across her face all on its own.

Hopeful.

Stupid.

On she went. He stood to the side of the entrance, talking with a tuk-tuk driver. This man, taking her to see a dragon. She pressed her fingers against the outside of her shoulder bag, locating the handle of her gun. Let one of Rolly's guys show up. She'd protect the both of them. The stupid hope was making her feel brave.

He and the driver were speaking in Thai, she thought at first, until she drew near and realized it was English. Or had they switched to English?

He looked so handsome and tropical in his linen suit, like a character out of a Maugham novel, and he glanced down at her legs with a shadow of a smile that made her belly flip flop. Did he like the sheer socks? Or maybe he thought they were funny like Rajini did.

He looked up at her and her heart sped. He watched her approach with a glimmer of a smile that was like a cord to her belly, pulling, enchanting. He extended his hand as she neared.

She took it. Shivers played up and down her arm as he closed his fingers around hers.

"You went the scenic route," he observed.

"Everybody's always in your business when you live at a hotel. And here I am meeting some guy whose name I don't even know."

He helped her in and let her have her hand back, settling at her side as the driver took off.

"Maxwell," he said.

"Is that your first or last name?"

"Last, but it works for both. It's what people call me."

"Well, isn't that handy." She sat back, enjoying his easy presence. "Business or pleasure, Maxwell?" She asked it half ironically, because it's what *farangs* always asked each other in Bangkok.

His gaze was full of humor, as though he got exactly how she meant it. *Business or pleasure.* A thrill shot through her.

Business, as it turned out. He was teaching linguistics at the University. Not a professor, just an adjunct, there for the quarter. A *subject matter expert*, he called himself. The way he said it, she got that it was a buzzword, and that he didn't quite like it.

"*Subject matter expert*," she said, rolling it around for herself.

"S. M. E. for short."

"But never a *smee*, I hope."

He gave her a sly look. Lordy, his charm could light a burnt-out bulb. "Smee? Don't even utter it. That's how words like that start."

She smiled innocently, thinking she might have to call him a *smee* later on. She was having fun already.

They sped down bright streets full of colorful signs and lights under thick, black power lines strung back and forth like ropy garlands for a strange kind of holiday, or the webs of power line spiders trying to trap the whole damn city.

She rambled on about her life at the hotel, carefully avoiding the whole being-on-the-run business, as they drew near the chaotic night bazaar. He had the driver stop at the west end and they got out.

"I thought your supposed dragon was on the east end," she said, pulling out her money.

"It is." He pushed her hand away and paid the man. "We've got a stop first."

She frowned. A man paying for things and making decisions for her was a little too Rolly-ish. "You've decided to change our plan? Just like that?"

He smiled. "I'm going to spend the thousand bhat I'm about to win from you before I win it."

She snorted as they began to walk. "So sure you'll win?"

"I am," he said.

"Total surrender—that was our agreement." She felt her face heat as she said it.

And when he glanced at her again, she knew he'd caught it, like they were connected. Two travelers on the moon.

And then he said, "That's what I'm expecting."

"Hmph," she said, trying to cover a rush of excitement. Again she imagined the way his hair would look during sex, no longer combed neatly back, but hanging down in his eyes, and him all sweaty, and their bodies mashing wildly. She resisted the urge to kiss him, just out of the blue. She hadn't been impulsive like this since before Rolly. It was something about this guy. She could do it—she was close to doing it.

"Ready?" he said.

"Yes," she replied.

He looked at her for an extra beat, and then he touched her elbow and they headed between rows of colorful stalls stuffed top-to-bottom with purses, puppets, electronics, jewels, and every other kind of merchandise known to humankind, all lit by slender fluorescent bulbs affixed to the undersides of colorful canopies. They wove through the crowds, past hawkers and shoppers and zombie-like tourists stuck in other time zones.

She kept an eye out for Harken. Rajini had been so sure it wasn't him, but Laney couldn't shake the residue of that scare. Looming danger. Eyes watching.

Deeper and deeper they went. Finally Maxwell stopped in front of a book stall, tables topped with boxes of colorful paperbacks, an oasis of calm in the bustle.

He had chosen books. She loved that. Just being in his airspace made her happy. He was hot, he made her feel happy, and he *liked books.*

She studied the side of his face as he ran his finger down the colorful spines of the mostly mysteries and thrillers. She liked the way his smooth cheek swept up to his cheekbone under glasses that were neither square nor round. She liked his strong, straight, simple nose, and the way his linen suit tightened over his arm when he moved his hand to a different box. She had half a mind to touch him, to make sure he was actually real.

Maxwell spoke in a low voice. "He keeps the hard stuff in back."

Hard stuff? She stilled. Was he talking about porn?

He turned to her then, all secrets and danger.

Of course. What else would a vendor hide from public view? Her heart sank. "Oh."

Maxwell watched her eyes, like he found her disappointment amusing. He whispered, "I think you'll enjoy it."

It must be especially shocking, considering they were in the middle of one of the red light districts where you could buy an hour with a girl as easily as a pair of sunglasses. Bringing her out to see a man's stash of dirty magazines or something? Creepy. Probably there wasn't even a dragon.

"The books *are* a bit dirty," he said, then he leaned over and spoke in Thai to the man behind the table. Requesting the box in back.

What a fool she'd been.

She looked around, strategizing her exit, feeling more upset than she likely should.

"But if you keep an open mind..."

"No thanks," she bit out. His obvious amusement pissed her off more than this wasted night. "I come with you. Like a dope, I trust you have something fine to show me..." The man was coming up with a heavy-looking box. She averted her eyes as he heaved it up and onto another box.

"I thought you'd be into it." Maxwell seemed to glow with pleasure. A real pervert.

"Seriously?" She motioned at the box the man had set down, looking over at it, finally. It was full of...old hardbacks. Clothbound editions with gold lettering. Classics. Poetry.

A hush came over her as she moved to the box. English language classics. You couldn't get these in Bangkok.

"Forgive me," Maxwell said. "I thought you were a certain kind of woman, but it seems I was wrong."

She felt her mouth fall open. She didn't bother to close it.

"I'll have him get them out of your sight." He moved to wave to the man and she caught his wrist and electricity flowed between them, and she wanted to laugh and yank him to her and push him and kiss him all at once. She turned back. "Sweet Mary, this is..." *Everything.* Shakespeare, Keats, Coleridge.

She pulled out a fat volume of Romantics and paged through. She only ever looked at this stuff on the computer, or on her phone. Here it was live, heavy with smooth, cool pages and the old book smell.

"I hope you're not disappointed. It's not exactly Naked Cowgirl Party."

"Not funny."

Except it was, a little. She slid her finger over the elegant, old-world typesetting. She turned to the Byron section and read the first line of her favorite. Her blood raced. "How did you think of this?"

"You told me," he said. "Up on that stage you told me."

She turned to him. She was so used to Rolly telling her what she wanted. Even Rajini told her what she wanted. But Maxwell listened. He saw her. He soaked her in, seemed almost to enjoy her, with a kind of sparkle in his eye that seemed just for her. It made her feel happy, bold. And it was mercilessly sexy.

"What're you getting?" she asked.

"Hmm?"

"What book? You're here to get something specific."

"This. For you," he said. "Or choose another if you prefer."

"You don't have to."

"I'm about to take your money. I insist."

"I'll say yes. But only because it's my birthday."

A cloud seemed to pass over his eyes.

"What's wrong?" she asked.

"Nothing." He pasted on a smile. "Happy birthday."

"You think it's pathetic," she guessed. "Here with a stranger on my birthday."

"Not at all," he said softly.

She turned over the book and ran her finger along the roughened edges. "This one." Maybe she could trust him. The idea of trusting him felt like a flower in her heart.

He paid the man. "Come on."

CHAPTER SEVEN

Maxwell touched the small of her back as they made their way through the increasingly wild crowd. The touch felt proprietary. She liked it.

"How'd you know about the place?"

"University colleague. We're all very eggheady over there."

Riiight. To her, eggheady meant somebody with an overdeveloped brain and a weak body, liable to crack and break. Too many thoughts. Maxwell wasn't that. He was an academic, sure...like Indiana Jones was an academic. Like an adventurer academic.

"I thought you were linguistics," she said. "Not English lit."

"You don't get to linguistics by way of math. You get there through language. Some people get there through poetry."

"Like you?"

He scanned the area, ignoring her question. He seemed to be always on alert, this guy. Had he sensed somebody watching them? He pointed to a line of stalls that stretched up to the right. "This way."

"Not answering the question?"

"No, I'm getting ready to savor the moment of your capitulation." His gaze sent a bolt through her. "You can't imagine how I'll enjoy it."

"You think I'll roll over that easy?"

"I do," he said simply.

Her belly tightened. She wanted to roll over for him. Preferably naked.

"Where to?"

"The dragon," he said. "We have a mission to complete."

Oh. Complete the mission. Get on with it. She tried not to feel disappointed, it's just that she wanted this birthday to last. He made her feel big and bold, like her old self. She was tired of being small.

After she found a sturdy travel backpack she insisted they stop at a booth full of strange little wind-up toys. She wound one up and watched him track its movements. She decided that the lovely icy luster in his gaze came from his eyes being—okay, gorgeous—but also from being curious.

After that, she insisted they buy ices and eat them at the little patch of tables at the lit edge of the bazaar. She got lime and he got kiwi, but then they tasted each other's and traded.

His was tastier, and also, it was his. "I would've never gotten kiwi," she said. "Who the hell gets kiwi?"

He turned to her slowly, gravely, as if in warning, and she laughed. And right there, the moment expanded. It gave her shivers to feel it, like a song changing key or deepening in an unexpected way. Or the world getting bigger and taking on magic.

A fellow traveler on the moon.

Suddenly she wanted to tell him everything about herself. Not hide anything. "You never asked me the question," she said. "Business or pleasure."

"Do you want me to?"

"I'm here for neither," she said. "I just thought you should know. I'm hiding out from a crazy ex and his guys. They're a pretty bad bunch. I just thought you should know. Two years I've been fine. I'm not saying we're in danger—"

"Don't worry about that," he said, forehead furrowed. "Are you okay? Do you need help?"

"Oh, I've got lots of help. More help than I need. Just thought I'd tell you."

"I'm sorry," he said. She could feel the sorry in him. He meant it.

"Thanks."

"What happened? You don't have to tell if you don't want, but..."

"No," she said. She wanted to tell him. She'd always been one to bare herself. "I married the guy when I was 18. Stupid. Dazzled by a whole lot of shiny hoo-hah."

"That's very young."

"Not the time of life known for good judgment, that's for sure. I was singing in this shed bar up in the Florida panhandle. I was too young to be in a bar, but you know. And this guy comes in, all charm and polish and money. I didn't have much of a home situation at the time. And the next thing I know, we're flying around on planes and he's fixing up my mama's house and putting my brother through college." She licked her ice. "I guess I felt like I was doing that for my people. It felt good."

"Heady, for an 18-year-old girl."

She loved the quality of his attention, as if he listened with his whole being. "Yup. And suddenly I'm married to him. Rolly. It was nice at first, everything so lovely, and people looking at me like I'm somebody. But little trade-offs, they have a way of growing into bigger trade-offs. It was like he wanted to scrub everything off me. He broke me of smoking and drinking and swearing."

Maxwell's lips quirked. "That didn't quite take, did it? The swearing."

"Hell, no." She smiled. "But it sure took while I was with him, believe me." She picked at the hem of her dress. "Life went way easier when I bent. Like a coward."

He gaze darkened. "You're no coward."

"I *felt* like a coward. The first five years, it wasn't bad. Certainly not enough to leave and make my way in life as an unskilled, uneducated person. But then he started turning, and little by little it got to be where I had less rights than a poodle."

A dangerous glint appeared in his eyes. "And you're okay now?"

"Only because he's doing a 10-20 year bid in an Arkansas prison." Thanks to evidence she'd collected. "Prison only made him madder and meaner."

Maxwell asked a lot of questions—he seemed really to want to know about her plight. She found herself telling him about the scary messages Rolly would send from inside. *You're mine. Only mine.* She'd moved deep into the panhandle, staying with distant cousins, but Rolly's men found her all the same and tried to bring her to him—in prison—and it was only luck that she slipped away. She told him about all the woman-on-the-run tricks she developed, even back in the States. She fled to D.C. and they found her again. She told him how she finally traveled to Bangkok with the help of a dear friend.

"That's not the story of a coward," he said. "It's the story of a fighter."

She looked up at him. She could tell he had something more to say. "What?"

"The hat...I can't say the hat is the best disguise ever."

She frowned. "It's a great disguise."

"No," he said simply. "It's not."

"Is the linguist suddenly an expert on disguises?"

"It's obviously a disguise. You need to change the look of your face, not hide it. Hiding invites speculation."

"Trust me, it's under control," she said. "It's a 1940s look. A torch singer thing."

"Laney—"

"You're just very perceptive. You're the only one on the planet who got the dragon thing. And hey, it's worked for two years, hasn't it?"

And bottom line, the Shinsurin brothers would've said something if they thought the disguise was bad. Who better to know disguises than shady characters like the Shinsurin brothers? Not that she said that to Maxwell.

Something changed in him then—he seemed almost to disengage. He took her paper cone from her fingers and tossed it in the trash bin with a charming smile. "Come on, then. Dragon's this way."

The mission. Back to the mission.

On they went, out of the night market on the restaurant side. Maxwell was still very aware of their surroundings; she might not have noticed if she wasn't the same way. She might not have noticed their circuitous route, either, if she didn't take those, too. Maybe not wanting to meet up with Rolly's thugs. That wouldn't turn out well.

He stopped at the opening to an alley that dead-ended at a cement wall covered in graffiti. "Can you see it?"

"No," she said.

He pointed at a convex mirror mounted high on the side of a building. And there it was, the dragon, reflected in the mirror. Which would mean it was behind the wall at the end. Visible from the street.

"Cheater," she said.

"Can you not see it?" he asked. "Is it not the best?"

He was right on both counts, and he knew it. This one was far more amazing than any of the others. You could see that even from the mirror.

He extended his hand, palm up. Cool, remote, charming Maxwell. "Pay up."

"I want to see it," she said. "Up close."

He hesitated. Was he so eager to get her back? "Okay." He led her in and pulled up a cement block.

She eyed the wall. "Yeah, that might work for somebody who's six feet tall." Like him.

"Get up there and grab the top. I'll lift you."

She hesitated only a moment. Then she looped her purse over her neck and shoulder and stepped up. She felt his solid body draw close, felt strong hands grab her waist. He lifted her easily and she scrambled up to the top.

And there it was, a plaster dragon the size of a small car, fierce and wild and colorful. He hoisted himself up and sat next to her.

"I love how he's guarding the collapsed building parts behind him. Loyally guarding the ruined slabs," she said.

Maxwell looked at her strangely. "Yes," he said simply.

She snapped a photo. There was a misshapen block of concrete next to the dragon's crumbly shoulder. Like a tilted table for the dragon. Scrub trees peeked out from behind discarded doors leaning on the far wall. Somebody had gone to town with spray paint, but they'd left the dragon. "Can we go in?"

"There are spiders in the rocks," he said. "You don't have the best leg covering."

So he'd gone in himself once before. Maxwell. So damn mysterious. "I'll stick to the clear parts." She swung a leg over and hopped down.

He dropped down right behind her, alighting with muscular grace in his crisp tropical suit. No, not an egghead at all.

"What do you think he was for?" she asked.

"I think a restaurant was here," he said. "I suppose they hauled off the big stuff."

Reverently, she approached the dragon, so wide and thick, with a body that seemed to curve in and out of the

72 | CAROLYN CRANE

earth, as though the earth was nothing but water. His wide mouth was open in a silent battle cry.

"So amazing. And just hidden here. Nobody knows."

"I'm sure the neighborhood people know," he said, somewhat remotely, like he was holding himself off from her.

You could see there had been colorful scales all over the dragon's back, but now it was bits of color broken up by dirty gray patches where the plaster showed through.

She turned and caught him looking at her stockings. "How'd you find him?"

"Observant." He strolled up to the beast, like he wanted to get away from her. Maybe avoid the question. Even the way he'd said the word—*observant*—it was designed to end the conversation.

But words and images were her domain. The secret little flourishes at the margins of life. Why did he explore like that? "Looking over walls, it's more than observant."

"Why should looking over a wall be unusual?" he asked. "Is it because of the information age? We're only supposed to accept the presented surface now?"

She smiled. It was a tasty tidbit he'd thrown out. But she wasn't biting. "Accept only the presented surface?" she asked. "Like you want me to do with you?"

He turned to her with that strange light back in his eyes. The linguist was used to running circles around people with language. He wasn't used to being busted.

"*Presented surface*," she said. "That's a whole lot of non-answer. I'd expect a smee such as yourself to do so much better."

"Did you just call me *smee?*"

"Why won't you tell me? What aren't you saying?"

He came nearer to her. "Did you just call me *smee?*"

"I certainly did," she whispered, enjoying the heat of him up close.

"Words like that spread, you know."

She gave him a level look. "Report me to the CDC."

He smiled, seeming to forget himself.

Her heart banged in her chest. "So secretive," she said. "With the walls and the dragons."

"And you owe me a thousand bhat."

"I'm not paying until you tell me," she said.

"Tell you what?"

"Why you didn't stop with simply spotting the dragon. You came over the wall."

"What makes you think there's something to tell?"

She cocked her head. This guy was like a fortress, and if there was one thing she didn't like, it was fortresses around people. Did he let anybody in? "Isn't there?"

She saw the moment he decided to tell. Or decided the truth wasn't important enough to conceal. "It's nothing, really," he said. "Poking around in a new city is habitual. Because when I was young my family moved all over the world—25 countries in 18 years." He turned and picked a rock up off the ground. When he flipped it over she saw it was a divot from the dragon's back. He went over and fit it back into place. "I started this habit of seeking out three secret wonders, I suppose you'd call them, in every new city. Three hidden things to make my own. It made me feel less alone."

She felt a rush of triumph. "And you still do it. To feel less alone."

He seemed to weigh his words. "It's only force of habit now," he said.

Like hell, she thought. He was still a stranger. Still seeking connection. "More than force of habit got you over this wall."

His blue-gray gaze felt heavy in her body. "Is that so?"

"I think you got some slabs of stone of your own you're guarding," she said.

He came to her and touched her cheek. It was just a fingertip, but it felt electric. "Clever Miss Callback." He'd seemed remote before, but now he was very much with her, breath warm on her nose. He slid the finger on down her cheek.

Wild heat bloomed through her. "What made you climb over?"

"I'm not telling," he said.

"I want to know."

He held her with that heavy gaze, turning his attention slowly to her lips, which caused her belly to do a flip-flop. He would kiss her, and he meant her to know it, but still, it came as a surprise, the way he slid his hands along her cheeks, coming to a stop at the back of her head, then he pulled her to him, crushing his mouth over hers. The rough, confident strength of his kiss made her feel warm and glowy, like heated honey.

"I want to know where your other places are," she said into the kiss. But more, she wanted to know him. Hell, she just wanted him.

"I have something better." He yanked off her hat, seeming to forget his program of leaving this place.

"Something better to *show* me?" she asked, voice husky. Her voice was actually *husky*. She put her hand on his chest, feeling the uneven rise and fall of his breath. Cool Maxwell being not so cool. She liked this Maxwell. Maybe she'd get that hair disheveled, too, now.

"Yes, but not like that."

"You have something to show me, but not *like that?*" she teased, like her heart wasn't jackhammering. "You would—"

He kissed her again before she could finish the question, roughly, all whiskers and heat and invading tongue. Like a gate opened. Strong hands gripped her waist, fitting her crassly and perfectly against him.

The kiss felt wild. Disordered. She reached up and untucked his hair, mashing her fingers through it as he walked her back to the chunk of stone. The dragon's table.

She hit it with her ass, but he kept going, pressing into the V of her legs, puzzle pieces of fucking. It's all she could think of now. She wanted him with a mad, mad fever.

"Yes," she said, pulling him closer.

He kissed down her neck and she melted a little bit more. Warm hands slid up the backs of her thighs, up over her panties, taking the dress up and lodging it at her waist. He lifted her onto the rough stone surface and set her there. She would get imprints on her thighs, and she was very okay with it.

"What are you going to show me, then?"

He rested his hands on either side of her thighs. "A favorite place on you."

She swallowed. "Oh, yeah?"

"*Oh,* yeah."

Her heart banged inside her chest. "That's what you're going to show me? Your favorite place on me?" She narrowed her eyes. "Is this going to be the cheesiest thing ever?"

"No," he breathed.

"Cheesy never seems cheesy to the cheeser," she said.

"Is that an ancient saying that you've learned during your stay in Thailand?" He rested his hands heavily on her thighs and slid them down to her knees. His gentle touch contrasted with the rough stone beneath her.

"Maybe," she whispered.

He knelt down and kissed her knee, then he looked up with that pale blue gaze. "I'm going to show you now. Unless you stop me."

Unless you stop me. She shoved her hands into his hair. "I won't stop you."

He kissed her thigh.

Yes. She tightened her fists in his hair.

He looked up, gaze dark.

"Oh, sorry." She loosened her grip.

"No, go ahead, keep hold of my hair. You might want something to hang on to."

Wild energy shot through her. Again he kissed the tender inside of her thigh. She imagined his tongue, warm and wicked between her legs. It was a little obvious for her pussy to be his favorite place on her. But when he kissed her again, warm lips on sensitive skin, she decided it was okay for him to be obvious. More than okay. *Go there*, she thought. *Be obvious. Be totally, stupidly obvious.*

Instead, he moved in the other direction, lower on her thigh, heading toward her knee.

She loosened her grip. *Noooo!*

He flicked his gaze up to hers as he slid a hand down to her sheer sock, touching it. Then he slid his hand back up to the tender inside of her thigh. "You're so pale here." Again he slid his hand down over the nylon part. "And then this nylon. It's absolutely ruthless."

"The nylon socks? Are ruthless?"

He gave her a devilish smile. "Ruthless." He stroked his heavy hand from bare thigh to nylon. She loved the way the sensation changed when he did that. Bare skin to nylon. Nylon to bare skin. Heat built between her legs. She clenched the muscles between her thighs to stop the feeling overload.

It didn't stop the feeling overload.

"The elastic," he said, tracing a finger over the brown band just below her right knee. "These tight elastic bands. Hot and a little bit evil."

She could barely breathe. "The elastic? That's your favorite place?"

"Not exactly." He hooked a finger over the elastic band and pulled it out. Angry pink lines furrowed her skin where the elastic had grabbed tight to her calf for hours. She got the crazy sense that he was exposing a tender secret.

Then he blew. The sudden puff of air was cool bliss on the tortured little band of skin. "Oh, my God," she panted, clutching his hair way too hard. He'd found and invaded the tenderest part of her.

Then he kissed it, lips like silk.

It was such a forbidden place to kiss. And unexpected, too—that made it way dirtier.

"Do it again," she begged, startled to hear her own voice say that.

He smiled up at her, just a little bit evil.

He wouldn't do it again.

She held his hair tighter, every nerve ending taut.

He pulled the elastic out further. What was he going to do now?

She trembled when he leaned in again and dragged his lip along the band of indents. Or maybe that was his tongue. He was like a dirty and unstoppable force of nature.

"This, then," he said. "Would be one of my favorite places on you."

Maxwell. He'd turned her on and taken over her senses, and he hadn't even gotten above the knee.

"I can take the socks off," she rasped.

"God no." He let the elastic snap back over her skin.

She jolted up from the shock of it. "Ow," she said.

"Ow?"

What was he doing to her? "Ow," she said, breathing fast. Maybe she wasn't getting enough air. The moon seemed too bright. She didn't care, because it was good. "Do it again."

With a sly look, he hooked his fingers under the elastic of both her nylon socks now.

Then he shoved her legs apart.

Her blood raced as he kissed up, up, up her thigh, keeping her legs apart, fingers in contact with the dirty, secret tattoo of tortured skin he was so into. Every molecule in her was begging him to hurry now, to kiss her throbbing, heated core.

She sucked in a breath when he paused at the edge of her panties. "Show me another place," she begged.

He pushed her legs apart even further now and pressed his lips to her sex, an exciting pressure through the thin fabric panel. "Oh," she said.

"Is this okay?" he said into her core.

The vibration of his voice nearly sent her over. "Yes. Especially if you talk again."

"Like this?" he rumbled.

"Yes," she hissed.

His low, sexy laugh sent a wave of pleasure up through her. She felt something hard—teeth, grazing her lightly. Then he straightened up, gaze dark, and kissed her belly, her neck.

She grabbed his head. He put her hands back. "Sit on your hands."

"On my hands?"

"Do it," he whispered. He gave her a stern look. He was used to women worshipping him, doing his bidding, she realized. Well, she was all in, dammit.

He drew near, kissing her, clever hands unzipping the back of her dress.

She liked sitting on her hands. It made her heart race extra fast. It made her feel things more. He made her feel things.

He nuzzled her neck as he slid her cap sleeves down over her arms, revealing her bra. The humid heat kissed her skin as he helped himself to her, sliding his hands over her, fingers trailing a whisper of sensation through the lacy fabric.

She wanted him to find more secret places, and to invade each and every one of them. He could have anything.

He drew his hand down her belly, a warm, confident slide that made her inner thighs clench with desire.

"You're so soft," he whispered.

He dragged his hot palm back up, then down again, as though he had to consume every inch of her with his hungry hand. She arched under his touch, shivering in the heat. He seemed on the edge of control, like untamed energy was coming out his fingertips. It was a kind of honesty.

He kissed the swell of flesh her bra didn't quite cover. "This is a good place, too," he said, voice ragged.

"A favorite secret place?"

"It's in the running." He'd pressed his clever fingers under the fabric of her bra now, finding her nipples both at once, toying with them wickedly. She sucked in a breath as he covered one nipple with his mouth, drawing hard between flicks of his tongue. Wild energy pulsed clear through her core.

He slid her dress down further, hands a smooth, unpredictable presence on her belly, then slipped his hand down under the elastic of her panties.

She exhaled as she felt his fingers slide gently over her silken folds. He grunted with a mixture of pleasure and triumph as he delved into her wetness. Her face heated, but she forgot her embarrassment when he pressed a finger clear into her slick channel. "Yes," she breathed. Because, oh, it was heaven.

He pressed in two fingers then, drawing them slowly in and out, letting his thumb play over her sensitized nub, tauntingly, teasingly.

It was hard to stay sitting on her hands. She moved wantonly under his touch, butt cheeks clenching and releasing.

He grabbed her thigh, stilling her. "Wider," he whispered, and then he pushed her thigh a bit to the side, getting her just how he wanted. Electric sensation shot through her when he took one of her pebble-hard nipples between his lips.

"I have you," he whispered into her nipple, which was highly erotic. "You're going to come for me."

"Uh, well," she whispered. "I don't think I will. I never do."

He let go of her nipple. "Never?" He looked at her now, caressing her molten cleft. It was hard to stay looking at his eyes as he touched her, as he had his way with her. She imagined that he could see her feeling what he was doing, which seemed like it should be private. But she also liked the feeling of being open to him and a little bit at his mercy. "Never?" he asked again.

"Not...with somebody," she panted, undulating slightly with him, because it just felt so good. "Not with a guy."

He stroked her, more lightly now. Then he leaned in, put his mouth by her ear.

"Except you're already there." He whispered it like it was a dirty secret. "You can't stop yourself from coming now."

"I can't?" she asked stupidly as he pressed three fingers into her, furthering his delicious invasion.

"No. I'm sorry, you can't stop it."

He fucked her with his fingers, caressing her with his thumb, or whatever—she didn't know, it was just a chaos of pleasure. His kiss on her ear felt hot as she began to move with him.

"Uh," she said, losing her train of thought.

"Nothing you can do will stop it." Like he was some Neanderthal, taking over her body. Well, he was.

But then he stilled.

"No," she pleaded, filled with wild craving. "You have to keep going."

He nuzzled her neck. He might even have been laughing. "I do?"

"Yes."

Then he moved once more, curling a finger inside her, finding her tender nub, starting up again, relentlessly. She couldn't hide from him, not in words, not in her body.

"Like this?" he whispered.

She didn't remember the question but the answer was *yes*. She had no idea if she was saying it aloud because her world was flying apart. Because he was kissing her and manhandling her and plunging her down, down, down into a sea of pleasure until she broke into bits, there on the dragon's table.

CHAPTER EIGHT

Macmillan kept his face pressed to Laney's neck as she came, hoping that she wouldn't notice how he was trembling with the effort to keep control. Not once in the ten dark years since Gwen's death had a woman sparked such a powerful feeling in him. Sex was just another function, like sleeping, or eating, and now this.

The timing couldn't be worse. He needed to get into her room, get the recordings, and get out without her knowing what he'd taken. He needed to be unmasking Jazzman, not having a hoedown with her stockings in a Bangkok alley.

Hoedown. That's the way she'd put it, anyway. Or something equally colorful from her collection of words. She gave her words freely, just like the details of her life. He shifted and kissed her cheekbone.

"Maxwell." She pulled her hands from under her, grabbed his hair, and kissed him. "God." She rubbed her calves on his legs, up and down.

He grabbed hold and caressed her nylon-clad ankles. Those goddamn knee-highs. He was losing himself. "I want to fuck you while you're wearing just these." The truth.

"Here?"

Anywhere, he thought. No, he had a job to do. He tightened his grip. "In your room."

She searched his face, a question in her eyes. Of course
she would feel the unnaturalness of the request that they
go back there now. How it broke the flow. She had a way
of tracking nuances.

"I'll show you another secret place," he said.

"And this must take place in my room?"

"Yes." He pulled her dress back over her. "Turn
around." She jumped down and he zipped her up, then he
handed over her hat.

She took it, still wary. Yes, she had a sense about
things. And in the end she'd understand that he was
somebody she should've stayed away from, but it would
be too late. In the end, Laney was no match for the likes
of him.

This sort of thinking usually gave him a pleasant little
charge. Now it only made him queasy.

She stuffed her hat onto her head and smiled. She
sometimes looked haunted, but when she smiled, she had
mischief in her eyes.

He swallowed. "Let's go."

As they neared the hotel, she had the driver go around
to the back. "Just easier this way," she said.

"I see," he said.

She unlocked a door that was set into a tall, vine-
covered wall, and they entered the pool area. The water
was a dark mirror, and you could actually hear the night

birds over the city traffic. She led him around, keeping to the shadows.

"Everybody's so nosy," she explained, gesturing at the hotel's back face, looming above them. The construction looked late 1960s to him. All concrete, of course, but painted white, and each floor was slightly wider and longer than the one underneath it, making the hotel seem to flare out as it rose up. This type of construction tended to be difficult—but not impossible—to climb. In its most extreme version, it was considered riot-proof.

She unlocked the door and led him into a side stairwell. Who was she hiding him from? The Shinsurins? He couldn't imagine her with one of the playboy Shinsurin brothers. Were they the ones who told her the hat with a face-covering net was a good idea for a woman on the run? Surely they weren't that stupid.

They climbed the steps to the next floor.

She wouldn't be bringing him home if she had a romantic partner; if there was one thing he'd learned from her lyrics, it was that loyalty and emotional honesty were precious coins to her.

That's why he'd been honest about finding secret places in every new city. She required the ring of truth. It was like a toll he'd had to pay to keep the night going.

He'd left out the important information, of course. Like the fact that the story belonged to his former self, Peter Macmillan Maxwell, a man who'd boarded a train in Mexico City with his fiancée and family some ten years back. He'd never quite made it off that train.

Or more, the dark parts of him had gotten off, stumbling around that little village in shock, lying in one of the tents they'd put up for survivors, completely alone in the world. Lost. Grieving. Unable to process what he'd seen. Unable to understand why some terrorist had to kill so many innocent people.

They'd told him that the man responsible, the elusive terrorist Mero, would never be arrested. Nobody knew who he was.

Soon after, he'd learned that the police had a voice recording of Mero claiming responsibility. They couldn't do anything with it, somebody explained. Nobody could identify a person from a phone message.

Well, *somebody* could. Given enough time, enough determination.

Everything changed in that moment. He adopted his hated middle name, Macmillan, and turned his attention to hunting and killing Mero, short for *Merodeador*. The Spanish word for marauder. He would end Mero. Never again would Mero make a family suffer.

Macmillan began his search by studying recent papers on Mexican regionalisms. He created possible geographical profiles—where Mero might be from, where Mero might be living, where he'd gone to school.

Eventually he turned to the man himself. The recording showed Mero to be a stylish, charismatic speaker who displayed many unique language tics. For one, he pronounced words beginning with *S* with great stress and duration, producing the fricative with an intensity that was unusual even for a Mexican. Macmillan recognized it as the kind of thing followers would tend to pick up, and he knew he could track the hyper-fricative *S* backwards, almost like a virus; he'd written papers on that very subject. Another helpful clue: an oddball bit of slang, the word *sumisimo*, which Mero used as a lexical intensifier, like the English word *very*. *Sumisimo* had occurred in none of Macmillan's Internet corpus searches, suggesting it was unique to Mero's peer group.

He moved from village to village, mixing with the people, hunting with his ears. Now and then he'd hear something and plot it on a map.

It was a slow process, but Macmillan had nothing but time and vengeance. Five months in, he was finding more of the markers. The clusters got thicker. He was closing in. He started to hear *sumisimo* and the hyper-fricative *S* more often. Soon he was able to identify ground-zero for them both, a little village at the edge of the jungle, a place of concrete-block homes, piles of dirt, and one roadside stand with a dusty red Coca-Cola awning.

From there it was a waiting game. Mero's voice had a specific boomy quality and he had an unusual way of pronouncing the O sound—produced slightly forward in the mouth, unlike most Spanish speakers. Or most English speakers, for that matter.

Finally, in a rough little bar a mile up the road, he located and recorded Mero himself, a grizzly 50-something man with wide cheeks and tiny glasses. He knew it was Mero the instant he heard him, but he liked to be thorough, so he took it back to his truck and ran it through software, comparing the recordings.

Bingo.

As soon as he had Mero's identity, he wrote letters to every authority and newspaper he could think of, detailing his search and revealing the terrorist's true name and whereabouts, just in case he didn't succeed in killing Mero. He dropped them in the public mailbox and went to the little roadside stand with the Coca-Cola awning to wait for nightfall and work up the courage to shoot a man. He didn't plan to survive.

It was after he ordered his second Coke that he became sleepy. So sleepy. The next thing he knew, he was lying in a cage in Merodeador's jungle compound.

Every day after that, Mero's men would drag him from the cage and try to beat the name of the snitch out of him—they didn't believe a man could be tracked off language alone.

And every night, Macmillan would dream of killing Mero. He felt sure Mero himself would come to beat him one day. Macmillan suspected his best weapon against Mero would be his teeth. He visualized going for the man's jugular and the larynx. It seemed a poetic way for a linguist to kill, sinking his teeth through the voice box, severing the vocal cords, forever stilling their vibration. This was what his PhD had come to.

It was during those beatings that he began to really analyze the way the different guards spoke, the way they produced their words, and he found that it helped him handle the pain of beatings. The more he analyzed, the less he felt. Anything could be chopped up into words, phonemes, sounds.

"Here we are." Laney stopped in front of a door in the third floor hallway. The noise, smells, and lack of carpeting suggested to Macmillan that this was a staff-only wing.

It occurred to him, as she unlocked her door, that she'd spend some time in the bathroom freshening up—women always did. He could have the contents of her computer downloaded to his thumb drive in under two minutes, depending on how fast her box booted up. And then get out of there. He needed to get out of there. She was pulling too much Peter out of him.

She let him into her room. "A little small, but they let me stay here for free," she said.

"It's nice." It had been a hotel room once, but she'd personalized it with colorful fabrics and hats on the walls, and recording equipment all around. The lair of an artist.

She put her guitar in its case and leaned it against the wall. Her laptop, which was covered with shiny stickers, sat on the dresser. She turned to him, smiled nervously, then picked up a shirt and threw it over the chair.

"I didn't expect anybody."

"It's okay." It could be a pit of snakes for all he cared. His gaze fell on a scraggly plant in a coffee cup. Nothing but a stem and a cluster of leaves at the top.

She picked it up. "Amy needs water."

"You name your plants?"

"Just this one. She was growing up from a crack outside the hotel. They would cut it down and she'd keep growing back. She just wanted to live. So, I pulled her out and put her here."

Just a stupid plant, he told himself, but it touched something painful in him, the idea of this plant coming up again and again after being cut down. Laney fighting to keep it alive. "Rescue plant," he said.

She gazed up at him under dark brows, pink lips pursed. "Sounds a bit psycho when you put it like that."

"No." He went to her, drawn to her. Whatever that ex of hers Rolly had done, he hadn't destroyed her spirit.

"Here. Wait there." She thrust Amy into his hands, grabbed a plastic jug, and went to the bathroom, leaving him standing there.

Just a scraggly thing, he thought as the sounds of the sink drifted out of the bathroom. *Hardly alive.*

The click of plastic on the counter. Toilet lid.

Why should he feel all broken up about a plant? He'd been hunting the worst scum of humanity for years. He could kill them with his bare hands and enjoy a nice meal and a joke not an hour later, and now he felt emotional about a plant?

It was Laney. She engaged his lizard brain. No—she engaged his Peter brain, and that was worse; it made her as dangerous as any laser. And what the hell was he waiting for? She was in there freshening up; this was his chance! He set Amy down and went to the laptop.

Before he even could open it, the bathroom door creaked. He turned and pretended to be gazing out the window. *Damn.*

He was getting sloppy.

"I might bring her to the jungle." She splashed in some water. "I should get a proper container, first off. A coffee cup doesn't drain. I keep thinking I should drill a hole in the bottom."

But she wouldn't have a drill.

Her eyebrows drew together as she inspected the little plant. His eyes followed the line of her pale, smooth cheek down to her long, elegant neck, complete with a hard-drumming pulse. Her mind wasn't only on the plant.

She set it next to the window. It would get sun in the morning. "Some rescuer I am."

He needed a new plan. He needed not to touch her, but he would now. He went to her and smoothed back her lush dark hair. She closed her eyes as he pulled it aside to kiss that drumming pulse below the edge of her jaw. "You are exquisite," he said.

"Exquisite sounds like a brooch or something. Something dainty."

"No, you can be exquisite and valiant, too."

He felt her cheek move. A smile. She seemed to like that.

"Now where were we?" She asked, pulling back. "I do believe you owe me a favorite place."

His mood darkened with that. He didn't want to play that game anymore—there was too much honesty in it. "I'm finished with favorite places," he said.

"I'm not."

She backed away. Before he knew it, she was standing on the bed. She liked to be onstage. Probably hated wearing the face-covering net she wore during her shows. It would cut off a full connection with her audience.

She pulled off her hat and threw it at him.

He caught it, wanting nothing more than to lose himself in her, to let the world melt away. A reckless impulse.

"And it's my birthday, so...one more favorite place." She reached around and began to unzip the back of her dress, eyes on him.

She gave him a nervous smile. He got that she was coasting on a heady mix of vulnerability and bravery, and that made her beautiful. And it made him wonder what she'd be like if some madman wasn't forcing her to stay small and silent.

She pushed the sleeves off her shoulders and let the dress fall down over her hips, revealing a pale, freckly belly and long legs. She wore only a pink lace bra and bikini panties now. And those knee-highs.

He forced himself to remain rooted.

"I believe you established a dress code earlier," she said, stepping out of the dress.

"I did," he whispered, cock raging against the confines of his slacks. *Don't move. Keep control.*

She narrowed her eyes. "Come 'ere." She mashed the words together in that Southern twang of hers. There was no word more perfect. *"Comere,"* she repeated making the c extra hard, extra sweet, extra dirty.

He couldn't stand not touching her anymore. Like a sex-crazed zombie, he went to her, straight into her, not stopping until he had his arms clasped around her legs, face pressed into her crotch. Energy and potency rushed through his veins as he lifted her.

"Hey!"

He ignored her protests, laying her out on the bed. "I'm finishing for you," he grated, undoing the clasp of her bra with uncharacteristically clumsy movements.

Peter movements.

He untangled it from her arms and pulled off her panties and stood over her, holding them, drinking in the sight of the light red curls between her legs. Her natural hair color. And the knee highs. She thought they were stockings. It was all he could do to not claw his clothes off and attack her.

"Happy now?" she asked, pulse drumming again in her neck. She ran a foot up his thigh.

"No," he breathed. He'd begun the night as a high-functioning spy on an important mission and now he was a starving man who needed this woman more than his next breath.

Slowly, he pulled his glasses off, faking a level of cool he didn't possess.

Her eyes darkened as he set them on the bedside table.

He would not be a slave to his emotions. He forced himself to unbutton his shirt casually. She crossed her legs, rubbing her panty-hose clad calves together. He found he could barely work his fingers. She knew about the knee-highs now. She was a little bit diabolical, and he loved that, too.

"Do you remember my plan?" he managed to say.

"Yes. And I think you should hurry up and *comere*."

The delicious hard C. So diabolical. "What's my plan?" Finally he had his buttons undone. He ripped off his shirt.

"To fuck me wearing only my socks," she said. The word *fuck* fell awkwardly from her lips. He found he loved that, too.

With shaking hands, he stripped his T-shirt off his sweaty torso, control degrading. Sex was a tool, the price he'd pay for a few minutes alone with her computer. Nothing more.

Control.

He focused in on the word. The delivery.

"The unconvincing *fuck*," he said. "You said it so easily before when you used it as an exclamation. But now that it means something, it's not as easy." His breath felt ragged. "The word doesn't have the right life. Try again."

She narrowed her eyes, going for vixeny. "To fuck me wearing only these."

He shook his head. "Forced emphasis." He knew she heard it, too.

"To fuck..."

"Few can do it. It's the nature of the word."

"Why? You're a linguist. Tell me why I can't say it convincingly."

He was feeling less wild. Good. "When it's a verb—*that* verb," he began, discreetly removing his gun from his waistband and slipping it out of sight. He pulled off his pants and both ankle holsters, and finally his boxers. "When it's a verb instead of an exclamation...when you say it as, what you might call an exclamation, it's an empty word. But when you say it now as a verb..." He was babbling. Her eyes roved over his steel-hard cock and his breath heated in response. He was a furnace, a fire of need.

He forced himself to sit next to her, to touch her arm and nothing else. You never wanted to fuck when you were trembling with need. "When it's a verb it contains more." He slid his finger down her wrist.

She gazed at him warmly. "Like what?"

"Emotional charge, for one. It means a surrender of your body." He fit his hand to hers. It was working; the switch to analysis was calming his rush of feeling. He took her hands and drew them over her head and smoothed her fingers around the newel posts on the headboard. She'd liked sitting on her hands. A whiff of immobilization.

She closed her eyes and drew up her shoulders. God, he could get lost in her.

He swallowed, focused. "It means I want to fuck you so long and strong...one word can't contain that." He slid his finger over the mound of her breast, skin was like silk.

Dimly he realized that he'd used *long and strong* as an adverbial phrase. Christ, he really was at the edge.

He touched her throat again, the place where her pulse beat erratically.

Her voice sounded rough. "I'm on board with all that, Maxwell."

He touched her lips, and she bit his finger. She sucked it in. Her mouth was warm and wet and tight. His cock pulsed. He bent down to kiss her belly, voice lowered to a whisper. "It means...." He kissed her breast.

A shimmer of sweat shone under her arms and across her forehead. He wanted to kiss her all over, worship her head to toe. It's not what he did—ever. Sex was a tool. Nothing more. "It means..."

She opened her eyes. Smiled. "Maybe the linguist can put a sock in it." She twisted her torso and wrapped her legs around him, and that was the end of the fuck disquisition.

He climbed right over her, panting and trembling and mindless, sliding his hands greedily over her silky skin, kissing her neck, tangling his fingers in her thick, dark hair.

"Yes," she said, sighing with pleasure.

He kissed her neck, tasting her like a man starving. When he finally got to her lips, she sucked in his tongue, just as she'd sucked in his finger.

He groaned and melted further into her, cock jumping against her thigh. Down her neck and chest he went, covering her with frantic kisses, on down her belly, caressing and worshipping her, feeling her energy coil as he headed toward her pussy.

If this was any other time, any other woman, he'd tease her a bit. All he could do now was devour.

He slid his fingers under the elastic of her hose, enjoying the dirty, primitive naiveté of it. And now there was her: dirty, primitive, naïve her, and he didn't know how to take it, how to respond without everything cracking open. He shouldn't fuck her like this. He might get lost, he might sail off the edge.

A crinkling sound; she was fumbling with the condom he'd put on the bedside table.

He took it from her. She grinned, watching him with sharp eyes full of trust and challenge. He rolled the condom roughly over his dick, and then he grabbed her legs, pressing them onto the bed and apart.

"Yes," she gasped.

His objectives were long gone; he moved over her now like a man in a fugue state.

She sighed softly as he guided himself into her; she felt like a silky warm glove around his cock. He couldn't believe the pleasure of her, the peace of her. He moved inside her, loving her, fucking her, driven by a rhythm that seemed to belong to some larger force. Electricity. Magnetism.

He pressed his face to her skin, enjoying the spicy, bright scent he'd come to associate with her. Then he planted his hands on either side of her and fucked her anew. She groaned and said his name, sharp and breathy. When he opened his eyes, he found her looking up at him, face half covered by his hair, which was brushing her eyes and cheekbones.

"I'm tickling you," he grated, stuffing it behind his ears with one hand.

"Put it back," she whispered, messing it up, seeming almost drugged. "Like that." Because she loved the little things. She was so raw, so open. She was dangerous and thrilling.

"Hellbuckets," she said as he felt her tightening, filling with feeling. Relentlessly he fucked her until her breathing turned to soft moans. He shut her up with a kiss and kept on, plundering her mouth with his tongue until she was on the edge, until she dissolved into vibrations under him.

His own orgasm came up from nowhere and burst through him, splitting his mind. His cry sounded strangled as his body pulsed with feeling.

He collapsed on her when it was over and quickly rolled off to the side.

She went up on her elbows, looking down at him. "You're all sweaty."

"So are you." He slid his finger along a dart of dark hair that had gotten plastered to her sweaty cheekbone, moving in the direction of the strand so as not to disturb it, filled with a strange pride just for getting her all sweaty. Like he'd branded her or something.

When he removed his finger, she directed a puff of air at it from the side of her mouth, trying to dislodge it. It didn't move. This delighted him unaccountably, which was maybe why he allowed her to lie back and pull his head to her chest. Resting his head on a woman's chest was something he hadn't done for over a decade, not since he'd been with his fiancée, Gwen.

And then she started to hum a tune—*You Are My Sunshine*. The vibrations filled him, soothed him. He had the curious feeling that he didn't know who he was, or what anything was, or even where he was.

He flashed on the image of a medieval map, the known world in the center and ocean at the edges. They used to think that if you sailed too far out into the ocean, you would fall off the edge. He was gripped with that feeling now—of being too far out in the ocean, of nearing the edge.

He pulled himself away from her, feeling seasick.

"What?" she asked.

He looked down at her. He'd done what he had to do to get into her room: he'd given her Peter. Now he needed to get at that computer.

He said nothing; he simply got up and went into the bathroom. His cock had calmed down enough for him to pull off the condom and throw it in the trash. He washed up, hands twisting and sliding in and out of each other under the gushing water. He got lost in it a little bit, washing faster and harder as the memory of holding the severed hand kicked up. Even now he could feel it, resting in his palm, dead and rubbery.

Keep it together, he told himself. He just had to copy that recording.

He shut off the water and grabbed a towel. Her purse lay open on the counter, lipstick and little plastic makeup boxes strewn around it. She'd tried to make herself beautiful. She shouldn't have bothered. She understood a lot of things, but she had no idea what he was.

He hung the towel back up with quick, efficient movements. Anybody could carry out a plan when things went well. The best agents were the ones with the balls to stay the course when things went to hell.

This would qualify. Her chipping at his walls.

He splashed water on his face, getting his focus back. He could have Jazzman's identity within the hour.

The bed squeaked from the other room. She appeared in the mirror behind him and circled her arms around him. Happy, glowing. "That was so amazing," she whispered. "And I mean, so, *so*, amazing."

He looked at the pair they made, two moving parts in the Association machine. He was sorry that he'd reduced her to that.

His gaze fell to her hands on his abs; he counted the moments until he could reasonably dislodge himself.

"You're forgetting something," she said.

"What?"

"That you owe me that favorite place."

"So I do," he said.

"Fine. I'll take a rain check."

He turned to face her, removing her hands. "How about a shower instead?"

Her eyes lit. "Mmmm."

"You start it up. I have to make a phone call."

"At two in the morning?"

"A linguist's work is never done." He lowered his voice. "You go in first and lather yourself up. I want you to be perfectly and completely lathered. And don't think I won't inspect."

She snorted, amused. "What happens if I'm not?"

"All kinds of things will happen."

"Well, with an offer like that." She put a foot up on the toilet seat and peeled off a stocking.

He headed back out to the bedroom, pulling out his thumb drive, along with his phone, just for show. Soon he heard the crash of water. Drawers. Shower door open. Shower door closed.

He strolled over to her laptop and fired it up. The damn thing took its time coming to life. Once he was in, he poked around until he found a file entitled music and photos. Updated five hours ago.

He slid it over. Watched the bar. If the voice of Jazz-man was on there, it would be all worth it. It had to be.

CHAPTER NINE

With shaking hands she texted Niwat as the steam from the shower filled the bathroom. The message was simple. *HELP Man in my room. Rollys?*

He got right back to her. *Coming.*

Thank God for the Shinsurins. Night owls, all of them.

She sent the same text to Rajini, then quietly she put away the phone, still unable to believe what she'd seen when she'd poked her head out to grab an extra towel.

Him. In her computer.

She felt sick—physically ill. She'd felt so connected to him, so brave with him. She'd shown him bits of her soul. He'd made love to her like the world was crashing down around his ears. He was another traveler on the moon, goddammit.

Had he faked their connection? Could a person even do that? Or was the connection there, and he'd simply used it to betray her?

Quiet as a mouse, she pulled on her robe. Then she took her gun from her purse.

Back in the States, one of the thugs Rolly had sent after her had cuffed her to her porch railing, pulled off the wig she'd been wearing, and photographed her. He said he wouldn't get paid without proof of identity.

Maybe that's what this guy was doing, then. Getting proof of identity for Rolly. Why else go through her computer? She looked so different with brown hair, maybe he'd decided he needed her songs and her writings or something. He wasn't lying when he'd said he'd fuck her.

She wiped her palms on her robe and adjusted her grip, eyes hot with tears. The skills she'd developed over months of hard practice down in the basement shooting range had made her feel safer, but what good were they? She didn't think she could actually shoot a person. Not even this man who'd betrayed her so cruelly.

She should've been tipped off by how alert he'd seemed, and how he noticed everything. Rolly would lose it if he knew his P.I. had screwed her, but this guy would deny it. And if Rolly ever did get ahold of her, it's the last thing she'd tell him. Rolly would do something horrific to her in punishment.

She wished Niwat would hurry. What if Maxwell—or whatever his name was—left and alerted Rolly? She'd have to leave instantly—no passport, no money. So dangerous.

The little room felt hazy. She ran her thumb over the grip of her gun.

Maybe he was sending the stuff to Rolly now. She'd be put back in that house—that's what Rolly wanted. A prisoner there until he got out. Forced conjugal visits. Maybe this guy was looking through her searches and emails to see who was helping her.

Rajini.

Rolly would find out that Rajini had helped her. He would kill Rajini.

She couldn't wait for the cavalry. It wasn't just her life on the line.

She sucked in a breath, then crept out of the bathroom. There he was, naked, sitting at her computer. He'd put his glasses back on and even tucked his hair back behind his ears.

She pointed the gun, a two-hand hold, feet planted. "Stand up," she said. "Hands off the computer."

He looked up with a quizzical expression, like she was being amusing at a cocktail party. And then he smiled. That cool fortress of humor and untouchability was back, and she hated it.

His eyes fell to her Ruger. "*Really?*"

The rumble of her own voice surprised her. "Shut up!"

"Fine." He pointed at his clothes. "I'm just going to—"

"Hands up. No fooling, no joking," she said.

His sigh had an edge of humor. She had the crazy sense that he was immune or something.

"Do it."

"A *gun*. I've never liked guns," he said. "Bombs, guns, they're dullard's tools, don't you think? For somebody who has nothing left to say—that's what a gun is. The end of a conversation."

Rage rose up in her. As if he didn't care that she held a gun, as if her reality didn't mean as much as his. He was making her feel crazy, just like Rolly used to. "Hands up."

"You won't shoot me," he said. Like he set the rules.

She forced herself to speak. "The fuck I won't." Where were the Shinsurins?

"You won't shoot a man for putting on his clothes, will you? Shoot a man in the back?" He turned his back to her.

"I will."

He pulled his socks off the small pile of clothes on the floor. Looking for his gun? Rolly's man would have a gun.

Her voice sounded hysterical to her ears. "Hands up or I shoot."

He grabbed his pants.

She aimed a hair to the right of his arm and squeezed the trigger.

Bang. He jerked up, clutching his tricep. Then he turned to her. "So you will," he said.

She'd meant just to graze him. She was pretty sure she'd only grazed him.

But the way he looked at her; it really was like he was a different person.

He lifted away his hand; his palm was covered in blood. He put it back. "Either you're a very good shot or a very bad one.

"Arms up."

"I'm bleeding."

"Do it."

He sighed, and then, of all things, he smiled. Like it was all a joke. "Apparently the cookbook full of wishes lacks a section on hostess etiquette."

Heat rushed to her cheeks. He'd make fun of her song now? "Fuck you." She shot the wall. Concrete sprayed.

Again he smiled and, still naked, he scooped up the flash drive and covered the distance to the balcony, pulling the door open.

"Stop!"

He kept on.

Crap. She'd have to hurt him if she wanted to stop him now. He knew she didn't have it in her. He'd figured her out.

Just then, two figures slid down onto the dark balcony from ropes, grabbing Maxwell as he tried to escape to the neighbor's balcony. Maxwell fought them—it was like a dark whirlwind of arms and flashing eyes out there. Her table overturned with a crash of glass. She heard the *thwop* of punches connecting and a grunt that sounded very Maxwell. Two more dark figures leaped up from below. There was more fighting. The metal of a gun flashed in the moon.

They had guns, and Maxwell didn't.

Laney stepped back as they dragged Maxwell in, naked, bleeding from his arm—and his lip, now, too.

Terse commands and military-fast moves put him on his knees, still naked. A guard bound his hands behind his back with rough precision. It was like an action movie. The door behind her clicked. She turned and jumped aside as three guards burst in from the hall, followed by Niwat and Dok Shinsurin.

Niwat came up next to her. He wore a dark red turtleneck and his jet black hair was parted severely on the side. "Are you all right?" he asked quietly.

"No," she whispered. "I mean, he didn't attack me or anything," she said when she realized what Niwat meant. "Fooled me is all."

Niwat held out his hand. "May I?"

"Oh." She let him have her gun.

Rajini burst in, hair up, makeup off. "Laney!" She flung an arm around her. "Honey!" she said. "Are you okay?"

"I'm okay."

Dok strolled to the far end of the room to where Maxwell knelt and said something she couldn't hear. Maxwell simply stared at the ceiling, bored. Too cool for all this nonsense.

Outrage welled up in Laney's breast when one of the guards going through Maxwell's clothes pulled out a gun and set it on her desk. Stupid to feel upset about that after what he'd said about guns, as if they had some pact of truth that transcended everything. Another gun was set out, complete with holster. And another.

"*Three* guns? Really?" Her voice sounded high. Hysterical. "For somebody with nothing to say. A dullard who works for Rolly."

He finally looked at her, expression hard and remote as he was pulled to his feet, barely phased by the fact that he was naked and surrounded by five heavily-armed men. She was phased by it. She wished somebody would cover him so she wouldn't have to see his cock, like a bouncing taunt every time he moved. *I fucked you and you loved it.*

Dok was in his face, mumbling questions she couldn't hear, questions that Maxwell didn't care to answer, apparently. Maybe he knew when he was beaten. He seemed to have stopped bleeding, at least.

"Rolly knows," she said to Rajini. "Maybe it really was Harken who I saw in the restaurant."

"It wasn't," Rajini said. "You're okay."

"How can you say that? It's over. I have to get out of here. Y'all have done so much—" she waved at the team of thugs. "I'm more grateful than you'll ever know."

"You can't leave," Niwat said.

Rajini hugged her closer. "We won't let you," she whispered. "We're here to keep you safe."

"I have to."

Niwat studied her face. Softly he said, "He may not have made his report to Rolly."

"He made a call. He could've sent an email. He could have partners." Her eyes blurred with tears. "I've been found."

Niwat called for Dok to bring over Maxwell's phone, along with her laptop. "Check your last sent emails," he instructed.

She took the laptop, sat on the bed, and checked. Nothing had gone out.

"The last call he made was hours ago, to a local cell," Niwat said, pocketing the man's phone. "Nothing to the U.S. for three days." The guards had Maxwell lying face down on the floor now.

She kept her voice low. "It doesn't matter. Police will let him have a phone call and he'll call Rolly."

Dok Shinsurin brought over the man's wallet. He pocketed money and credit cards. Then he pulled out a business card and held it up, smirking. *Peter Maxwell, Ph.D., Bangkok International University.* He crumpled it and threw it aside. "Fake."

"Don't let him separate you from the herd," Niwat said quietly.

"I agree. He hasn't made contact with Rolly," Rajini whispered. "Running now would be the worst thing you could do."

"I'm putting y'all in danger," Laney said. "He was probably trying to figure out what name I'm going by and who's helping me and all that. He's going to tell Rolly."

"Do you trust us?" Niwat asked.

"Of course." She glanced at Rajini. It was Rajini she trusted.

"Let us deal with this," Niwat said.

Panic flared in her belly. "I don't want anybody hurt. So if that's what you mean…"

"Agreed." Rajini put her arm around her, eyeing Niwat. "That's a non-negotiable."

Niwat grunted and signaled at the guards, who pulled Maxwell up from the floor and walked him past, cuffed and at gunpoint. Maxwell didn't so much as look her way.

Rajini closed the door after them.

"Wait—where're they taking him?" Laney asked.

"We're going to keep him here as a guest." Niwat said calmly. "We'll learn what Rolly knows."

Laney shook her head. She didn't like any of it. "No."

"This is a business situation," Niwat continued. "For a price, this investigator can be persuaded that it was not you he saw. And if we learn Rolly has your location, we'll set you up with a new identity and money. But it must be done correctly, Laney. Tell me everything that happened."

Her face went red.

"Of relevance," Rajini said.

She told them the G-rated version of the story, all the way up until she caught him going through her laptop. "He was copying something onto that thumb drive thingy."

"Did we get it?" Niwat asked.

Dok fished in his pocket and tossed the thumb drive to Niwat, who grabbed her laptop and settled onto the bed.

"A guest? You won't take him to the police?" Laney asked.

Niwat looked up. "Do you want us to take him to the police? We would if you wanted."

"I don't want him reporting back to Rolly," she said. "But you can't keep him against his will."

Dok said, "We could hand him to the police and the police will hold him against his will. *And* let him call Rolly. Would you like that?"

"Stop it, Dok." Niwat hit a few keys. "This is simple business, Laney. We offer him something better than what Rolly provided. Everyone has a price."

Rajini said, "It's a win-win. Even for this guy."

"I don't know," Laney said.

Rajini whispered, "All he wants is a payday. He'll make extra money and not have to wreck a woman's life. He'll be laughing all the way to the bank."

It made sense, put like that. "I don't want him hurt. And I shot him. Just grazed, but it should be looked at."

"He'll have the best care," Dok said.

Assurances from Dok. Never satisfying. She pointed at the screen. "The recording from the show. That's all he downloaded. Maybe he wanted the recordings from the show tonight as proof. Rolly would recognize my singing."

"Hmm," Niwat said. "Yes. To bring back to Rolly. I didn't realize you were still making the recordings. No more for now. No more recording of any kind."

Her pulse raced. "Maybe I should leave while I can. I don't want a shitstorm here. Y'all've been such a family to me—"

"Laney," Rajini said. "This is not a problem."

"No problem," Niwat added.

"Whatever you pay him, I'll pay you back. I'll find a way."

Niwat closed the laptop and stood. "We'll work it all out."

Rajini stayed on after her brothers left. "Are you okay?"

Laney looked at the closed door. "Five guys armed to the teeth for one naked man? What do they think he'll do?"

Rajini rolled her eyes. "God, my brothers. They just love to parade around their guys and their guns. It's a black market thing. Show of strength. They wouldn't hurt a fly."

"You sure?"

"That would make them no better than Rolly, wouldn't it?" Rajini said. "C'mon, what really happened?"

"Nothing. I mean it was nice until—" she motioned at the little table where he'd sat, raiding her laptop. "He seemed so...my people. I need to take a shower."

"Yeah, you wash him off you. I'm making tea." Rajini was a big believer in tea.

The shower felt good, and when Laney came out, Rajini was sitting in her usual seat with two steaming mugs of tea at the ready. "I'm so freaked out," Laney said, taking her seat. "Maybe I should leave."

"If worse comes to worse, we'll hide you. There's a lot of places to hide a person in a hotel. Especially this one." Rajini dunked her teabag up and down. "So, one second you're doing your show, and suddenly you're at the night bazaar buying books? And then..."

"Yup."

"Back here."

"Yup."

Rajini raised her brows like she did when she wanted more details, but Laney didn't feel like spilling them. God, staying loyal to the feeling that had run between them even after the guy turned out to be Rolly's. "It's official. I go for the worst jerks possible. Still..." She looked up. "Where are they keeping him? What will they do?"

"They'll speak each other's language, that's what." Rajini said. "Business. This is the best thing that could've happened to this investigator. More money and he avoids the police."

"Right but, where do they keep him? In a room? What's to stop him from leaving? Do they tie him up or what? I just need to know."

"You need to trust," Rajini said. "There's nobody better to be on your side."

"I want to know what's happening in the name of protecting me."

Rajini set down her cup. "I'll check it out. Okay?"

"Now?"

"Once things settle."

Laney tried to sleep after Rajini left, but she kept waking up thinking about Rolly and his angular face and angular smile that never seemed happy. Once she woke up with her heart racing, convinced Rolly was right there in her room.

That was the end of sleep. She lay there, listening to muffler-challenged traffic and the night birds and the barking dogs. Folks who'd known her as a young singer back home would be shocked to see her now, half a world away.

They'd be shocked that she'd married a man like Rolly in the first place, no less that she'd let him control her and isolate her for all those years. Well, what people didn't understand about women who got isolated and hurt by their husbands was that they didn't just *allow* it. It was more about making a whole passel of little choices toward the path of least resistance. Eventually it was just about not being killed. Her life got smaller and smaller until she was a little animal, paralyzed at the kitchen table.

It was always such a relief when Rolly's military contractor gigs took him out of town, but even then she didn't dare step out, especially not toward the end, because he had guys watching her. The FBI agent had given her a burner phone during Rolly's last out-of-town trip, and she'd searched the house with him directing her around. The agent said Rolly had been involved in a murder of some sort. It had been nerve-wracking, even with Rolly gone. The agent had said Rolly would never know it was her who'd helped the FBI, but she'd always assumed Rolly would find out. Probably already had.

And now Rolly might know where she was. If not, he was close to knowing. Could the Shinsurin brothers really protect her? Could they reason with Maxwell?

The little bedside clock said 3:35 am.

She put on her robe, went out onto the balcony, and gazed at the sky. It was pinkish at the lower edges from the haze of neon, with a crescent moon high above. She hated that Bangkok's moon was the same moon for Rolly. She felt as if the moon itself was staring at her. Like Rolly was looking through the moon.

She texted Rajini. *Learn anything?*

No answer. Rajini had probably crashed.

What the hell. She texted Niwat. *Anything?*

He texted right back. *You are safe. Rolly knows 0. No problem. :)*

She felt a great gust of relief. Rolly didn't know.

What about the guy? She wrote back.

Negotiating. No problem.

No problem, Niwat's favorite phrase. What did it mean? Were they still in the process of negotiating? Did they have assurances? She put aside her phone.

The whole thing didn't make sense when she really thought about it. Why go through all the trouble of breaking into her room? If he'd really wanted proof of her being her, hell, just record her show with a phone. Snap her photo. It wasn't like she got plastic surgery. But then, why else sneak into her computer? And he didn't deny he was working for Rolly.

She couldn't stand it anymore. She called Niwat. "What's happening?"

"He's contemplating," Niwat said.

A chill went over her. "So he hasn't agreed to anything."

"He will," Niwat said.

"What if he really teaches at the university?" she asked. "You can't just detain him."

"He doesn't teach at the university," Niwat said. "We check out these kinds of things. He had three guns, Laney, including one designed to defeat an airport metal detector. This is not a man from the university."

Niwat had a point there.

"What if he won't cooperate? Maybe if I spoke to him—"

"You cannot."

"I think he'd respond to the human element. Whatever money you offered him, maybe I can persuade him on a moral basis. And I'm paying you back by the way. Whatever money..."

"This is now our affair. A man threatened one of our guests." Niwat's clipped tone meant business. "I promise you, this type of man does not respond to the human element."

She stared out at the moon, unsure how to explain that she *did* think he'd respond. They'd connected. That was real—she was sure of it. Maxwell had used their connection. Maybe she could use it to get him on her side. "But it can't hurt for me to talk to him, right?"

"Leave it to us," Niwat said firmly. "I'm going to sleep now, and so should you."

She stared at the phone after he clicked off.

None of this sat right. This was her life. Her business.

"Sorry, Niwat," she said belatedly to the phone. She threw on some clothes, stuffed her gun into her purse, and wandered down to the lobby.

Her friends Sirikit and Kalaya were behind the desk, full of concern and questions. They'd heard a man was trying to take her laptop. A thief—that was the staff rumor. Good to see the staff grapevine going at full speed.

Sujet the bellboy pushed an empty luggage cart off the elevator and parked it on the other side of the lobby. If anybody knew where they put the man, Sujet would. And Sujet would tell her. They were pals.

She went over. "I know he's still here. Where would they have put him?"

"Laney..." he shook his head.

"Sujet." She smiled.

"Well, he's not in a room, if that's what you're asking," Sujet said. He was proud of being the eyes and ears of the hotel. Five minutes later she'd gotten it out of him: they were holding Maxwell on LL2, the basement under the basement. In the holding cell. Of course.

She'd never actually seen the holding cell, but she'd heard one was down there on the other side of the shooting range. She recalled the Shinsurins catching a group trying to skip out on their bill and holding them down there for the cops. You sure didn't see American hotels with their own private jails.

There were two ways to LL2: the elevator—if you had a key, which she did, or the liquor delivery hatch. You needed a key for the liquor hatch, too; they kept it behind the desk. She knew because she'd gone down there last year, helping one of the barbacks bring up wine when the dumbwaiter was broken. That would be the sneaky way to go.

"Are they with him? Is he alone?"

Sujet furrowed his brow, lips drawn to the side, his look concerned. "You shouldn't cross this line, Laney. Not even you."

She wasn't worried. She had nothing to fear from the Shinsurins except for their rabid overprotectiveness.

"Are they down there with him?"

Sujet glanced at the ceiling.

"They're up top?"

"New convention arrivals. Niwat, Dok, and Jao are entertaining on the 17th floor."

Laney went behind the desk and grabbed a cup of coffee, and when the girls weren't looking she nicked the key to the hatch.

CHAPTER TEN

New York

Dax was alone in the back of the limo when the alert on his mobile came through. Macmillan's earpiece had been destroyed. Dax swore under his breath.

To the naked eye, an Association earpiece looked like a bit of wadded-up paper, like a gum wrapper. Associates typically carried them in their pockets until they wanted to communicate with Dax. It was a good system; bottom-of-the-pocket garbage was never seized in a search.

From what he could tell from the damage readout, this one had been crushed.

It happened. An earpiece could be lost in a fight and stepped on. But what Macmillan was doing shouldn't have him fighting. Or getting killed.

Nearly four in the morning in Bangkok. But Rio would still be up. He called the assassin and sent him back to the Hotel Des Roses to poke around.

The limo pulled up at a curb in front of a red awning. Dax scooted over to let Zelda in.

She wore thick round glasses and a mod scarf over her short brown hair. She'd always been a colorful dresser, even at the agency.

"Daniel Xavier," she said as she shut the door. She'd always liked Dax's colorful middle name, given to him by his very Greek parents in a little row house in Pittsburgh some 38 years back. Daniel Xavier Heraclides.

"Macmillan has gone dark," Dax said as the driver pulled away.

"God help us." Zelda turned her face to look out the window. The buildings flashed by, faster and faster. "When?"

"It could be nothing," he said. He wished he knew who the Russians had hired to go after Macmillan.

"He shouldn't even be out there," Zelda said. "He needs rest."

"I know," Dax said.

Macmillan had been one of their best operatives for years, but Zelda was right—they'd been running him hard. The man needed rest. Except nobody else could hunt Jazzman the way cool, unflappable, high-performance Macmillan could. He was also wildly motivated—the TZ would surely remind him of the Mexican train bomb. In some ways, Macmillan had been living on that train for the past decade, helpless to rescue his people, trying over and over. Like a desperate player in a never-ending nightmare.

No, he'd never gotten off that train. It's what made him such a fine Associate.

Philosophers said that the individual shouldn't be sacrificed on behalf of the many. Dax agreed with that, but he sacrificed good people anyway. He and Zelda did it all the time. How could they help it? They knew things nobody else did, thanks to Dax's ability to see cause and effect.

One ill-advised word in a Prime Minister's speech could branch into two reactions that would branch into four reactions and then sixteen, and not all of them significant, but Dax could see the one branch that would lead to catastrophe.

There was no voodoo to what he did; it was logic. Information. Knowledge. These things were available to everybody. Why couldn't everybody see what he saw?

Dax's mind was dark with webs of cause and effect.

Zelda licked her thumb and swiped it across Dax's jaw. "You could at least wipe the lipstick off before we meet the Colonel."

"What's he going to do? Fire us?"

"Decorum is important, even when you're the smartest man in the room." She licked her thumb again and rubbed his jaw. "My poor Greek boy." She frowned. "Is that a tooth mark?"

He thought back. The one in his office just now hadn't been a biter, but there was the stranger at the restaurant, one table over. They'd ended up in the bathroom. She'd ripped him up a bit. "Probably."

"You can't use sex as medication, Dax."

"Beg to differ." He needed something to ratchet him down, and sufficient quantities of drugs and alcohol only wrecked him.

Zelda rooted around in her purse and pulled out a makeup bag.

"I'm not wearing makeup."

"Then don't let women bite your face. Now sit still." She dabbed a bit on. "Were things up today?"

"By 34%," he said. "I'm going to have to create some losses." Dax ran the legendary Heraclides Fund, a large, successful hedge fund that made investors very wealthy. He'd gotten bored with making money early on; the Heraclides Fund was only a cover job now. These days, Dax put his attention on keeping the balance of power intact. Keeping World War Three from happening. And stopping the most despicable crimes.

He'd met Zelda over a decade ago, back when they were both in their twenties. He used to call the CIA whenever he saw dangerous cascades beginning, and she got assigned to be his handler. Unfortunately, his predictions had been too accurate—Zelda's bosses had started to suspect him of involvement in the disasters he foresaw.

Zelda knew differently. She'd begun to shield him, and to work on her own to prevent catastrophes. Years as an operative in the field had given her tremendous resources.

Forming the Association had been Zelda's idea.

Dax had the foresight and people skills; she ran the execution and the strategy. She stayed the silent partner. Safer for both of them.

It was a dark path they walked. They were hardly better than vigilantes, no matter how noble their goals might be.

"Keep it quiet about Macmillan," she said. "We don't need the Colonel panicking."

The CIA had sent the Colonel to pressure them about the TZ, to stress its importance, something Dax didn't need to hear. A full 87% of the scenarios involving the TZ getting sold ended in biological and nuclear exchanges.

"Rio will find him," Dax said. "Rio is very attached to Macmillan."

"We need Macmillan out of the equation," she said. "As soon as he identifies Jazzman, he's out. He's coming apart."

Dax said nothing. It was true, of course. The only surprise was that it hadn't happened before.

Macmillan had first come to their attention via rumors inside the terrorist Mero's organization—a gringo prisoner who claimed to have tracked Mero with nothing but a voice recording.

It had piqued their interest, to say the least.

Zelda herself had gone into the field to check out the story. She learned about the train bombing, and soon had a name: Peter Macmillan Maxwell, Ph.D. Records showed him losing his family and fiancée in the event. Maxwell had listed a Mexican national as his contact on the medical forms: Alfredo Domingo.

Professor Alfredo Domingo was a Caribbean creole specialist and a friend of Maxwell's; Domingo's seaside villa had been the Maxwells' destination. From Domingo, Zelda learned that Maxwell had new theories on the way slang spread, and apparently he was doing some sort of work on psychological and aspirational aspects of pronunciation. Domingo felt certain that Maxwell could use what he knew to track a man.

Dax and Zelda were thrilled. It had taken them a full year to locate the elusive Mero—and they had resources. Networks.

This linguist had nothing but a recording.

They sent Rio in to kill Mero and extract the man. By the time Rio had reached Mero's camp, Peter Macmillan Maxwell was a walking, talking death wish who could see nothing but vengeance. The man had lost everybody, after all. He'd spent a night helping other survivors pull the dead and dying from wreckage in the dark, bug-infested jungle, and then survived weeks of beatings from Mero's men. In hindsight, they really should've patched him up a bit, psychologically speaking.

Instead, Dax had him thrown into the harshest wilderness survival training possible. Macmillan had turned out to be tenacious as well as brilliant, and quite a talented fighter—one of those men who was good at everything. Dax sometimes suspected Macmillan might have eventually managed to kill Mero on his own.

At any rate, they'd needed Macmillan in the field, ASAP, so they'd wound him up and set him off as a mere shell, disconnected from everything that made a man human.

Dax and Zelda had no use for happy, well-balanced Associates—they tended not to deliver. Darkness was predictable; happiness was not. Happy people had the luxury of simply being. And they had more to lose.

Dax and Zelda worked a delicate dance of keeping the Associates from self-destructing while engaging their demons.

Dax took off his glasses and rubbed his eyes.

"Your head?" Zelda asked.

"I'm fine." He replaced his glasses.

"Okay," she said quietly.

"There's a special place in hell for us," he said.

She straightened his tie as they pulled up to the restaurant. "I'll bring the flame-proof croquet set."

CHAPTER ELEVEN

Bangkok

A Dr. Pepper craving—that was Laney's excuse for her four a.m. stroll. The front desk girls believed her. Sujet didn't, but he'd keep quiet.

Tamroung Road was busy even at four in the morning. Mostly that was because of all the hotels in the neighborhood, but then, Bangkok tended to be restless and vibrant at all hours. It was a nice night, with a slight breeze cutting the oppressive humidity.

She strolled nonchalantly around the corner. The street that ran up the side of Hotel Des Roses had just two lanes, and it was darker and gloomier than grand Tamroung Road. Which suited her just fine. She stopped at a square manhole in the sidewalk—the liquor delivery hatch, the secret way to get into the basement. She'd walked over it many times and never thought about what was beneath until the night of the dumbwaiter crisis.

Voices from the other direction. She slunk into the shadows as a couple stumbled up the street, clasping the key, feeling like a spy, shocked at herself for even going this far.

Oh, the Shinsurins would so unhappy if they knew. Niwat would think she didn't trust them to handle this.

Rajini would feel betrayed. Laney could hear her: *why didn't you wake me up if you were so concerned?*

But Laney was tired of leaving her fate to others.

When the coast was clear she crouched at the hatch. There was supposed to be a locked door below it, and two people were supposed to open the doors simultaneously from either side, like an armored car or something, but Pramod the busboy had told her that it was a big hassle for the receiving guys, so they often left the inner door open. She hoped it was open now.

She unlocked the outer door and slowly pulled it up. She tried the inner door. Sure enough, it fell open—with a loud bang that nearly stopped her heart.

She froze, listening for sounds.

Nothing.

She climbed partway down the metal ladder, easing the outer door down over her head until it snicked closed. Down the rest of the way she went, into a concrete corridor lit by garish fluorescent lights. This would be lower level one, aka LL1. She snuck past the liquor storage area and kept on, passing some sort of mechanical room, and then a door with warning signs about chlorine. The massive hotel pool would be nearby. She found another stairwell; this would lead to LL2—the basement security area that housed the shooting range.

And the detention area.

She headed downward into the sticky, stuffy depths, every nerve on high alert. The stairwell terminated at another locked door; her shooting range key worked, as she suspected it might. She snuck in and closed the heavy metal door, leaning against it, sweating. Shaky.

Past the point of no return. If Niwat caught her here, she'd be turned out for sure. Well, hell, she might have to leave anyhow. She needed to know firsthand what she was dealing with.

She proceeded down the dark hall toward a splotch of light cast through an open door. She froze when she heard the faint strains of voices. Arguing. A woman's voice. No—a TV. A *Wanida* rerun, it sounded like.

She crept in further, then knelt and peeked into the room. TVs lined the walls, but two guards were fixated on the TV in the corner. The Thai soap opera was just starting.

She crawled past and tiptoed on down the hall. She crept around the corner and down another hall to the end. After a few more turns and one dead end, she found an unmarked door with a dirty window in it. The detention area.

She peeked in.

The room was dim, lit only by a buzzing fluorescent bulb in the corner, but she could just make out what looked like a jail in there—bars marking off a square cage in the corner. Too dark to see if anyone was in there.

Was she really doing this?

Hell, yeah.

The door creaked when she entered. She froze like a rabbit, listening.

Nothing. She eased the door closed and just stood there, squinting into the gloom of the cage. Her breath caught when she finally made him out, sprawled in the shadows with his back to her, bright hair faintly illuminated by the anemic light.

Not moving.

Her pulse raced. The Shinsurins wouldn't kill a man just to protect her. *They wouldn't.*

She moved closer, straining to see if his chest was rising and falling. They'd clothed him in pants and a T-shirt that appeared to be soaked with sweat. Surely that was a sign of life.

"Come back for more target practice?"

She jumped at the voice.

"Because you could certainly use it," he added.

"Lord, I thought..." She closed her eyes in brief thanks that he was alive.

"A regular Annie Oakley." Still he just lay there, like a wounded beast.

"I'm not in the mood for jokes. I want to talk about Rolly."

No response.

She looked around and spotted a camera above her head. It probably wouldn't record in the darkness, but she took out a pencil and nudged it up, then moved nearer to the bars. She wished she could see his face. You couldn't connect with a person's back.

"I know Rolly probably promised you a goodly sum to turn me over," she continued. "Probably threatened you to boot."

Still he didn't turn around. She grabbed the bars, frowning at his sweat-soaked back. What were the Shinsurins thinking? Keeping a man in a cage wasn't right. Even a thug of Rolly's.

Rolly's. It still didn't sit right. How could this man be Rolly's? It defied her intuition.

"Look," she said. "I know the Shinsurins made you an offer. And I'm sure they don't want you down here. And I sure don't want it. If only you would agree to keep quiet about seeing me. If you care at all..." *Did he?*

Silence.

"I have a home here, and a life that's a little bit worth living. Maybe I should think about moving on, but that takes time. *Please*, if you would just take the money. I can't go back to him." Oh, God, she was begging. She'd meant to come in rational. She steadied her voice. "That's what I'm asking you. Forget you saw me and we can get you out of here." She looked nervously at the door hoping *Wanida* was enough to keep the guards occupied.

"Don't worry," he said, tracking with her somehow. "They've only come by twice, and they never bother to come in."

He shifted there in the dark, finally turning to look at her. His face and shirt were half covered in something dark. *Blood.*

"Oh, my God! Are you okay?"

"Define okay," he said.

Anger surged through her. This man had been hurt on her behalf? It didn't matter who he was or what he'd done. "This is wrong."

"The keys are right there on the wall."

She swung her gaze around—keys hung from a hook on the wall. She could let him out. "I need to know you won't tell Rolly where I am. You'll get out *if and when* we have assurances of that."

"*If and when* you have assurances," he repeated. Like that was funny.

"What?"

"You really need to specify both if and when? Once the *if* is handled, the *when* is a permanent state."

She gripped the bars. "Well, thank you, *Professor* Devilwell, PhD in asshole arrogance."

"You're welcome."

Carrying on so nonchalantly when he was a beaten-up prisoner in the basement of a Bangkok hotel? Was it just another day at the office for him? "How about if you talk normal like a human?"

"Rolly didn't send me," Maxwell said. "How's that?"

She gripped the bars more tightly. She'd needed to hear that. Everything inside her screamed for him not to be Rolly's. Should she believe it? "Then who sent you? What were you doing copying my files?"

Silence.

"So you have no explanation."

"Look," he finally said. "I have nothing to do with this Rolly of yours. Take it or leave it."

"Why should I? Why should I believe you after all of your lies?"

"Because I'm telling you the truth."

"I need to understand why else you'd copy stuff off my computer."

He grunted, watching her with that implacable gaze. Even lying there in defeat, he radiated power, virility. Slowly he sat himself up. She let go of the bars and stepped back, as if he could get her from in the cage.

"Oh, don't worry." Chains clanked as he lifted his leg. "I'm attached to the wall by leg irons. I hate to say it, but I'm afraid this type of guest service is going to cost the Bangkok Imperiale Hotel des Roses a half a star. With so many luxury hotels featuring featherbeds these days, leg irons on a concrete floor is something I simply can't over-look."

She felt sick. *Leg irons?* Did Rajini know about all this?

He reached behind to grab something. His eyeglasses. They flashed in the darkness as he put them on. "What's more," he continued, "providing a rusty metal can instead of proper bathroom facilities simply doesn't cut mustard with today's traveler. That will cost the Bangkok Impe-riale des Roses yet another half a star."

"You think this is a time to joke?"

"I'll take that as a rhetorical question." Some of his hair fell in his face as he leaned forward and rubbed his ankle under the leg iron. There was blood even in his hair. He was hurt and he covered it by being an asshole.

"I'm trying to talk to you real."

He lifted his eyes to her and leaned back against the far wall.

"Just don't tell him where I am," she said. "I'll give you money. I have money in the bank I can get at in a few days. I'll pay you everything I have. Don't you want to get out?"

"I'm not here on behalf of Rolly."

"Why else would you copy the recording of my show? And the Shinsurins know you're not a guest lecturer at the university, so I don't want a story about that."

"Ah."

"Obviously you weren't there to attack me or rob me. 'Cause you could've, with three guns on you. So much for guns being dullards' tools. The end of the conversation for somebody who has nothing left to say."

"Oh, I meant every word. They are dullards' tools. It's just that my conversation ended long ago."

She had a strange thought, suddenly. "You didn't take my laptop," she said. "That would've been easier."

"Hindsight's 20/20."

This guy, like nothing was serious. Well, screw it—it had been a kindness. "I still believe what you told me about when you were a kid. To have to say goodbye to all the familiar people and places over and over. I know you know what that's like." She paused, scuffing her foot, thinking about their connection. "You know what it's like when you can never go home again."

He groaned, but she could tell from long years in front of an audience how people listened, where they were in their ups and down. And she always, *always* knew when they were tracking with her.

Maxwell was tracking with her. It was a strange feeling, lording over this wounded lion in a cage. Ironic how he brought the bravery out of her.

"You know what it's like to have everything ripped away from you, and to be all alone."

"If you're not going to let me out, then go away." He pulled off his shirt to reveal his muscled torso, gleaming with sweat. He bunched it up under his head and lay across the floor, stretched out on his side.

He was kicking her out?

"I've had a long day," he added.

She watched a bright bead of sweat dribble down over the curve of his bicep, pausing at the lowest point to gleam and fatten. Then it plunked down onto his chest. Twinges kicked up in her belly as it continued downward, traversing the muscles of his chest. She had the impulse to go in there, to rest her hand on his hot, slick skin. Good lord, here was this man, like a wild, wounded animal in a cage, and she was all kicked up about him.

A real letch, that's what she was.

"Maybe it serves me right, you here. I've been feeling things are off. Eerie somehow. I didn't listen to that." She softened her voice to a whisper, trying to hide the sobby feeling trying to climb her throat. The hell if she'd cry. "If you could hold off on telling him. Give me a few days to get things in order and get a running start, and then you can tell him and collect your money. That would work, right?"

A spell of silence widened out between them. Then he said, "Laney, if you have an instinct to leave, you don't have a few days. For that matter, if you think I'm Rolly's guy, why are you here?"

She grabbed the bars. "I know. I don't know."

"Have you ever seen those flocks of little brown birds, the way they'll all fly away at the least disturbance? Most of the time there's no danger. But that instinct, that's their protection, and it's as formidable as claws or teeth. That's how you need to be on the run. The second the instinct hits, you're out of there with whatever you're carrying. You don't wait until it's so obvious that a man in a cell in the basement of a tropical hotel has to point it out to you. No, you fly."

"I'm not ready. I have nothing—"

"If you have two feet you're ready. And, while I'm giving you advice—really, up in front of audiences every night for two years? It's a miracle you haven't been found by this guy and his friends. It really is. If I ever write a book on how not to be on the run, yours would be the color story. How not to be on the run, step one: find a job where you're performing in front of different people from across the world every night, for maximum exposure. Step two: wear a hat with a face-covering net to announce that you're in hiding."

"The hat again?"

"Did the Shinsurins tell you that was a good idea? That hat?"

"It's a 1940s torch singer look—"

"No. It's a piss-poor disguise. Your best long-term solution is to fight like hell to get guest worker status somewhere like South Korea or Hong Kong. If I were you, I'd head down to Koh Samui first. You can get off-the-books employment there." He went on about transport, establishing a guest worker identity. "Whatever you do, get out of here. Change your hair, start over. Guest worker status would let you move around without being at the mercy of others. How long until your fake passport expires?"

She bit her lip. How would he know she had a fake passport?

"Come on. You're not working under your real name. You're getting paid in cash. A free room. But that passport could be flagged if it was stolen. And it *will* expire."

She looked down. "It's expired, but I'm getting a new one next week."

"But your gut is telling you to go?"

"Yes."

He paused, softened his tone. "That means you don't have a week."

"I can't just run off this minute."

"Yes, you can."

"I won't have access to my money until Monday. It's all in a bank. Anyway, what about the point of view that I'm in more danger when I'm separated from the herd?"

"Separated from the herd?" He laughed his rich laugh.

"It's not funny."

"No it's ridiculous. Even if it weren't ridiculous, I separated you from the herd pretty easily, didn't I? The *herd*." He spat the word out with derision. "Where'd you get that idea?"

"The Shinsurins..."

"Ah, the Shinsurins." A smirk lit his face. "The *Shinsurins*," he said with gusto. "Newsflash, Laney. The *Shinsurins* are holding a man in a cell in their basement. In chains. Not always a good sign, as far as trustworthiness goes."

"I know—I didn't think—"

"That they're dangerous?"

"I knew they weren't...upstanding, but they saved my ass. You don't know my ex. Not that I condone—"

"Leg shackles? And as long as I'm dispensing advice, Dok Shinsurin is unbalanced. Be careful around him."

"How about you just make me understand why you were in my computer so I can let you out?"

"I wanted the recording."

"Why?"

"That's all you get. Unless you want me to make something up."

"I want a reason to believe you." Maybe there were other reasons to want the recording. Maybe he was investigating one of the conventioneers.

He shifted, seemed to move with difficulty.

"You bleeding?"

"No," he said. "I've shifted to the coagulation and infection stage. I'm running them concurrently."

"That's not funny."

"No, it's precise. Precision is often taken for humor—"

"Stop it. Just shut up," she whispered. She knew what it was like to be hurt and alone. He had to be a little bit scared. In all this filth and tropical heat, infection really would set in. "Fuck it." She grabbed the keys off the wall. She wouldn't have this, not in the name of protecting her. "You're outta here."

"What if I'm Rolly's guy?"

She paused. "If I'm the kind of woman who's okay with something like this, then I don't deserve to be free from that son of a bitch."

She could feel his eyes on her as she unlocked the cell door. With a deep breath she swung the door open and walked in, stood over him. "I don't want you hurting the Shinsurins over this. Got it? I'm done with the violence. Promise."

"I will not hurt the Shinsurins."

She threw down the keys. "Don't you make me regret this."

"Thank you." He flipped through them. "And for what it's worth, I'm sorry."

"Just hurry up," she snapped. Maybe she was crazy to think he wasn't with Rolly. She'd come down to play on their connection, but the connection was playing on her.

Well, she was a woman who trusted connections. It had served her with Rajini.

He handed the keys back. "The leg iron key isn't on there."

"Shit," she said. "Niwat probably has it. Or maybe the guards. What do you think it looks like?"

"Oh, no, no, no, don't you dare try to get it yourself," he said. "I don't need a key."

"Beg to differ," she said.

He gazed up at her, all brutal beauty, like a god, brought down to earth and chained up. Yeah, even bruised and bloody, he was all that. Her heart pounded, and not from fear. She wanted to sink right down to him, to touch his skin, to feel his heat.

"What?" she breathed. Her voice sounded husky to her ears. Dimly she was aware that he hadn't said anything at all. Even just sitting there, he spoke to her. "What?" she asked again.

The way he looked at her, it was like he knew. "Come here," he said.

Her pulse jumped. And like a crazy woman, she knelt down and touched his chest. She imagined she felt a slight tremor in him as she slid her palm over his slickened skin. "You feel hot." Surely a tropical disease hadn't set in so fast.

He rose up on his knees and pushed his fingers into her hair. She closed her eyes, enjoying his touch. He kissed her lightly on the lips, and she melted into the soft warmth of him.

"Fuck it." She grabbed onto his arms and pressed against him, glorying in the feel of his hard cock at her belly, the curves of his muscles under her fingers, and the hungry roughness of his kiss that sent shivers all over her skin.

She gasped as he moved to her neck, soft kisses followed by a harsh stroke of his whiskers.

"I want to devour you," he breathed, all heat and desperation. "But you have to get out of here." When he pulled away he was holding two bobby pins. "You mind?"

"Seriously?" She narrowed her eyes. "You could've asked."

"I could've."

"You can open locks with those?"

"Most."

"Do it," she said. "Hurry."

"Not until you're gone. I don't want us seen leaving together. The Shinsurins are dangerous, and not just to me. Lock the cage, replace the keys on the hook, and get out of here. I can take it from here."

"There's a back passage—"

"I've got ears. Concentrate on protecting yourself. My plan is a good one for you. Koh Samui. I've heard the Dragon Day Excursions are reliable for illegal border crossings."

"I understand," she said. "Thank you." She put her hand to his cheek, needing to touch him one last time.

He closed his eyes, as though it was too much.

CHAPTER TWELVE

H er cool touch was heaven on his burning skin.
"You're running a fever. It might be infection.
Wait." She pulled lotion out of her purse. "This has anti-
bacterial hoo-hah."

Hoo-hah. Those words of hers. "Laney—"

"Humor me." Before he could stop her, she was inspecting where her bullet had grazed his arm. It was just a
small burn. Impressive shooting, that. With gentle fingers, she began to apply the lotion. Her touch was tenta-
tive, serious. Breath rapid, brows drawn together in
concentration. "This good?"

"Perfect. Thank you."

She moved to the cut on his eyebrow. It wasn't necessary, but she'd shot him, so she needed to make up for it.
A lot of agents got like that after a kill, needing to care for
somebody or something.

And he liked her touching him.

"Don't advertise that you're going," he said. "You can
write letters of thanks and goodbye when you're safe."

"Put out your legs, Devilwell."

Macmillan shifted to sit so that his legs splayed forward. One last indulgence. The basement guards of the
Hotel Des Roses weren't exactly high functioning.

She slid a finger under the large iron cuff, a whisper of sensation. "I can't believe they did this." She really did seem shocked by it. "They've been good to me, but I'm not okay with this."

"I'll survive," he said.

It was her he worried about. He had the wild urge to drag her out of town himself, but that would be madness, because nothing was more important than getting the TZ. Next best thing: he'd get Dax to put somebody low-level on her tail to protect her from afar. It was the least he could do.

What's more, he damn well planned to teach this Rolly a lesson once the TZ was under control. How many Rollys sat in Arkansas prisons? He'd go visit the man himself and make it clear that his days of messing with Laney were over. He'd take one of his Association brothers with him—Rio or Cole, maybe. Somebody to stop him from assaulting Rolly. Or what if Rolly were to die mysteriously? She'd feel so happy and free. He'd find her and help her get her life back. He'd find her in a day. Whoever her ex had searching for her, they weren't professionals.

She rambled about not liking the rust on the leg irons. His skin was raw, but he'd be okay, she murmured. She'd make sure he was okay. It was like a hallucination of bliss, being cared for by her. He closed his eyes and let himself rest in her care, just for a moment. He wanted very badly to kiss her. And there were those knee-highs.

He flashed again on the image of a medieval map, the known world in the center.

Don't fall off the edge.

The far-off sound of a door. Footsteps.

"Hellbuckets," she whispered.

He gestured at the shadowed section of the wall. "Stand there. Go."

She melted into the shadows.

The footsteps slowed outside the cell, and then continued and faded off. A guard round.

She moved back to him.

"Five minutes until he comes back," he said. "It'll be safe to leave right after."

"Timing it between TV shows."

No, she wasn't stupid at all. She moved to the other ankle, pupils dilated, cheeks suffused with pink. She talked tough, but she was all emotion: fear, desire. Everything was there in her eyes.

Eventually the footsteps came back. Again she slipped into the shadows.

She went back to him once the guard was gone. She knelt down. "You need water or something."

He reached up and took a strand of her hair, slid it between his fingers. "I don't need water."

A hitch in her breath.

Macmillan had become accustomed to playing women like instruments, but he wasn't playing Laney like an instrument any more than she was playing him. The music was playing them both now, and the chord between them vibrated with unresolved desire. He let go of her hair and set his hand lightly on her neck where her pulse drummed clear as day.

Her swallow appeared as an ephemeral swell of her throat. He slid his fingers down to the soft place where her swallow disappeared.

"What do you need?" she asked.

He would've atomized it with anyone else, visualizing the intermittent vibration of the vocal folds as she formed the words, the incessant movement of her tongue starting and stopping the airflow. But now there were just her eyes, her breath, and her lips. The feel of her speech.

The feel of another swallow.

"I don't need water," he said to her again.

He slid his fingers up and took her chin between his thumb and forefinger. She was all wild cat eyes and rapid breath, and God, his cock felt hard as granite. He would give up anything to have her again.

He would give up anything. This had to stop. "Go," he growled.

"Let me help you," she said.

"You have. You alerted me to a back way out. You gave me lock picks."

The side of her neck looked flushed where he'd rubbed his whiskers against her, marking her. He liked the idea of something of him on her.

He liked it too much.

"Goodbye," he said. "And thank you." He went to work, bending one pin into a tension tool. He fashioned the other into his pick.

She stood. "What will you do now?"

Go with you, he wanted to say. He grabbed his shirt, pulling the damp thing back on. "It doesn't matter because you're getting the hell out of here, right?"

"But where will you go?"

"Classes resume at the Bangkok International University soon. Somebody has to lecture the students on the wonder of words."

She inspected his face, unsure whether to take him seriously. Then she smiled. "Right." She scooped up the keys and stepped out of the cage. "Good luck, Devilwell."

"ASAP, right? You're getting out of this hotel ASAP..."

"Yes," she whispered. She exited the cage, hung the keys on the hook, and cracked the door, peering out right and left. Then she turned to him, waited wordlessly. Because there weren't words now.

A second later she slipped out the door.

Quickly he set to unlocking the cuffs. He'd lied about letting her get to safety before he broke out. He would shadow her all the way out and protect her if she got caught, but he didn't want her to know. She'd give him away if there was trouble.

He concentrated on the internal geography of the lock, though he felt her still. Hands on his skin.

Three more moves and the leg iron snapped open in an explosion of rust, which dotted the thick goo of the lotion Laney had applied. Her ridiculous lotion.

He got the other open and slipped out. He crept along, cringing at the noise she was making, even as she tried to be quiet.

She unnerved him. Unsettled him. No, that wasn't right. For once he couldn't come up with a precise word.

Her showing up, it was like a visit from an angel. He'd lain there in the shadows beaten half out of his mind but it wasn't until she showed up that he felt anything. As though she drew something out of him.

No, that wasn't quite right.

He turned a corner, following her through a long stretch. The guard room was coming up. He could hear their TV.

She penetrated him. Pierced him. Pummeled him.

No, no. Not right. Things like beatings and pummelings he could stand. But when she was around, it all just meant more. There didn't seem to be a word for that.

He saw her up ahead, flattened against the wall just shy of the door to the guards' room. He smiled as she dropped to the floor and crawled past.

He followed, glancing in, surprised at just how many monitors they had going. He continued on after her, shadowing her all the way up to the next level. She took a hatch that led to the exterior. Probably set into a sidewalk.

He peeked out and watched her round the corner. As soon as she was home free, he slipped out himself and shut the hatch, letting it lock itself.

He straightened up against the wall, which felt cool against his burning skin, and his pulse sounded tinny in his ears. No, he didn't feel right, and he couldn't stop obsessing about her. It was bad—getting the TZ had to be everything. It *was* everything.

Words—he needed something wordy. The elusive word for what she did—he'd work on that. *Penetrated, pummeled.*

He'd discarded those. *Pierced* hadn't worked. He smiled as he pictured her crawling past the guard room with all its consoles.

And then he frowned.

Consoles. Video monitors. Surveillance. Of what? What were the guards monitoring?

Damn. It could be important.

He'd been so out of it, so focused on her, he hadn't taken a hard look. Mistakes like that could get Associates killed.

His shivered in the heat. He was in no condition to go back in.

Nevertheless.

He knelt down and started the process of picking the lock in the sidewalk hatch.

Two minutes later he was peeking into the guards' room. They were still watching their portable TV. Still drinking coffee.

But that's not what interested him. It was the dozen or so flat screen monitors. Each monitor was divided into nine sections showing different rooms of the hotel. People having sex. People talking on the phone. The restaurant, the lobby. A group of arms dealers playing cards in a suite.

The top floors.

He squinted at an icon on one of the monitors. Mute. They were making recordings.

Macmillan stiffened against the wall outside the door. And smiled.

The fox had found the henhouse. He took off his glasses and cleaned them.

Naughty of the Shinsurin brothers to be recording. But such recordings would be valuable to dealers who wanted an edge in negotiations. Even more valuable to Jazzman.

And most valuable of all to Macmillan. Bright energy coursed through him; a feverish eureka. He couldn't believe his luck.

He looked at the clock. He had 35 minutes, if they kept to their usual schedule of rounds. Quickly he headed out.

CHAPTER THIRTEEN

The Sawadee Hotel stood two streets north of the Imperiale Hotel Des Roses. Macmillan tucked in his shirt and smoothed his hair as he strolled between the golden elephants and in through the main doors. No doubt he looked as bad as he felt, but getting through the lobby would be a game of attitude, not appearance.

He felt the clerks' eyes on him as he stabbed the elevator button with a flourish, spine straight and proud.

A minute later he was knocking at room 508. The door opened.

"Nice night for a visit," Macmillan grated.

"Clears the mind." Rio clasped his shoulders, pulled him in, and slammed the door with his foot. "Godammit," he said, settling Macmillan onto the couch.

Just by the way Rio said it, Macmillan knew: they'd thought he was dead. "Surprise," he whispered.

Fedor came to loom over him, big and brutal, all muscles and faraway eyes. "You look like hell."

"I try."

Fedor, aka the dark watchmaker, was a rogue Associate. He hated their leader, Dax. Nobody knew what had happened between him and Dax and Fedor wouldn't tell. But he still showed up now and then. A brother in arms.

"Fix me up," Macmillan said. "I'm going back in. I have ears in there now."

A figure appeared in the doorway to the adjoining room. Douglas. He wore cargo pants, a green tank top, and dark-tinted glasses. Douglas was head of the mission. "Here's to ears—attached to your goddamn head. He grabbed the first aid kit and brought it over to where Macmillan sat.

"I'll take one of everything," Macmillan said.

Douglas felt his forehead, his throat. "What happened?"

Macmillan launched into a rundown of the night, stopping only to detail his symptoms for Douglas—hot, cold. Lack of hunger, lack of focus. Some dizziness. High emotions. He detailed his plan—they needed to buy, threaten, or drug the guards so he could copy the video and audio files.

Rio frowned. "Fedor, you can't break that hotel network?"

"I can break in," Fedor said, "but if I start pulling video and audio files, somebody's going to notice. That's a lot of bandwidth."

"That's why I'm going back in," Macmillan said. "I can review the files and make copies. All these dealers' faces and voices—it's a gold mine. Send me in with one of those thumbdrives," Macmillan said. "One of your thumbdrives with that Linux compression program."

Fedor was already at his laptop. He tapped a few keys. "Got it. I've made some tweaks—I think you'll be pleased. It'll still take time."

"Do we still have an Associate in the kitchen?" Macmillan asked.

"Dishwasher," Douglas said. "But she's only on at night."

"The night guards drink coffee," Macmillan said. "It comes from the kitchen. We need her to dope it up enough to put them to sleep. You think she can do that?"

"Count on it," Douglas inspected Macmillan's ankle. "The guards will be out cold tomorrow night. We'll see about the day guards. What's all this goop?"

"Anti-bacterial hand lotion."

Douglas sniffed. "The Shinsurins rough you up and put lotion on your ankles? What the hell is that?"

"It was Laney who put it on."

Rio raised his eyebrows. "So you got past the emotionally manipulative songs."

Macmillan gave him a warning look.

Rio smiled. "How far past?"

"None of your business," Macmillan said.

"But Macmillan, you always kiss and tell." Rio rolled up the cuff of his silky lavender shirt. "We live for your escapades."

It was true. Macmillan usually made wry little stories out of his sexual encounters. Not so with Laney.

"Did she show you her cookbook full of wishes?" Rio asked.

"That's enough," Macmillan growled.

Rio raised his hands. "Sorry. You haven't bothered to keep the details to yourself for ten years."

"I'm bothering now."

Rio grabbed the rubbing alcohol and some cotton.

"Not too much," Douglas said. "He can't go back down there smelling like a pharmacy."

Rio's eye darkened with concern. "He shouldn't go back in there at all. We have a way in and out now. Let's use it."

"We can't," Douglas said. "If Macmillan escapes, it could spook Jazzman and the Shinsurins. They could shut down the recording or even move the auction. They don't know what he is right now—let's keep it that way." Douglas stuck a needle in Macmillan's arm. "You'll feel like hell for a while. At least you'll be resting down there. Somebody get water. You'd better be up to date with tetanus."

Fedor the rogue smiled one of his rare, blue-eyed smiles that seemed to cancel all the scariness in him. Most Associates preferred to work with him in jungle warfare circumstances only.

"What?" Macmillan asked.

"I have news," Fedor said. "I've identified the biometric security package on the TZ. They're using voiceprinting."

"What? Voice is a joke."

"It's next generation voiceprinting," Fedor said. "I'll send you the docs. It works on ratios of frequencies and ratios of the voice's volume—something like that. Over time spans of milliseconds."

Macmillan smiled. "So they worked out the kinks."

"Can you beat it?"

"With the right tools and the right sample." He let himself relax for the first time in what felt like days as Fedor ran down the details. If Macmillan could get a decent recording of Jazzman's voice, he could override the controls of the TZ. Surely he could get Jazzman's voice from the hotel recordings.

It was all coming together.

Fedor gave him the thumb drive. "You have somewhere to hide this?"

"Yup." Macmillan pocketed it. "I have 12 minutes to get back. Anything else?"

"A nerve center for recordings. In the basement," Rio said. "It *is* convenient."

Douglas dabbed something onto Macmillan's eyebrow, frowning. "Your Maxwell persona would get stitches for this. He would have the best of medical care. A scar here could erode your cover."

Macmillan thought about his Peter Maxwell cover eroding. What if it was blown completely? He'd have to rest. He imagined himself in a little cabin somewhere, fussing with phonemes on a sunny porch. Putzing around in a garden. But no, that's not how it would go. If his Maxwell cover was blown, he'd have to stop playing him.

The thought saddened him.

"You go cool your heels," Douglas said. "Tomorrow night the guards will be drugged. We'll send word if you have a window sooner than that. I need to call Dax." He stuffed in his earpiece.

Fedor pulled a long, thin blade out of his boot. "I'm not here." He tossed it across the room and it stuck onto a dart board that bristled with thin blades, like a cactus with all the needles clustered at the center.

Macmillan stood. "One last thing. Laney has an ex named Rolly. Short for Roland, I'd imagine. Sounds like he's doing time in a Federal Correctional Complex in Arkansas. I want his file. I have to go."

"I'll check him out," Rio said. "We got your back on this." Macmillan nodded. Rio always had his back.

Fedor threw another knife. "Jazzman is going down."

Seven minutes later, Macmillan was back in his lonely cage. It was five in the morning. The guard shift would likely switch around six.

He curled up on his side with one cheek cooling on the concrete floor, wondering what Laney was doing. Packing, hopefully. If she thought Rolly's men were coming, she needed to trust that. It was good that she was leaving.

What's more, the Jazzman affair could get bloody.

He'd get some sleep over the daylight hours. Once things quieted down, maybe after midnight, he'd get to the recording console and figure out if Jazzman had arrived. He'd endure anything to identify Jazzman and stop the auction. To save people from dying senseless, fiery deaths. To stop the pain.

His sleep was full of tortured dreams of trying to save his mom and dad and sister and Gwen. She'd lit up his world with her green eyes and red hightops and somber paintings. He'd loved her with a passion that sometimes bewildered him.

He was back in that dark, smoky jungle, holding that clump of scalp and hair with the barrette still attached.

Finding the stripes pattern of his mother's polyester slacks melted onto skin. He'd recognized them all by bits.

Suddenly he was back pulling the hand from the wreckage, thinking it was attached to a body, but it came too easily. It was burnt near the thumb, wrist stained with dried blood, tendons hanging down like wet yarn. He'd had the impulse to throw it in horror, but he couldn't. It weighed as much as a tennis shoe. He couldn't get over that, somehow.

Another man had tried to take the hand from him. "*Señor,*" the man had whispered, easing the hand from Macmillan's grip. "*Señor. Por favor.*"

It was too late; the hand had seared into his soul.

Later, he dreamed of a smooth weight on his cheekbone, crushing his skull.

He tried to shake it off, but the weight only pressed harder. It was as if he was trapped under something. He dreamt he was under the twisted metal of the train car, and there were hands everywhere.

He tried again to move his head. The weight moved with him, alive. It rolled his head under it.

That's when he awoke. He kept his eyes closed but he was awake.

The sensation was real. It was a boot. On his head.

He hoped he hadn't been struggling too much; it didn't do to betray fear or confusion. Slowly he opened his eyes.

Dok removed his boot, smiling. He held a briefcase Macmillan didn't like the looks of.

"Good morning," Macmillan said jovially, because Dok would want him scared. Dok was that kind of man.

Dok said nothing in reply. That was protocol; take all the control away. He simply set the case in the corner, well beyond Macmillan's reach, and opened it. Lots of metal in there. Knives. Syringes.

"I'm afraid you've gotten my room service order mixed up, my good fellow," Macmillan said. "I ordered the stir fry with prawns."

Three daytime guards entered the cell, one bearing a chair, the other ropes. They set the chair near him and muscled him in roughly, even though Macmillan didn't put up a fight. Macmillan just let it happen. Dok had the physical control, but Macmillan had the psychological control. He had language.

Still, it was hardly fortuitous that the crazy brother had shown up. Where were Niwat and Jao Shinsurin? Dok had been the most violent when they'd first put him down there; if Niwat and Jao hadn't intervened, Dok would've injured him quite gravely.

So why send Dok? Unless they hadn't sent him.

"Not to insult the chef," Macmillan continued, eyeing the case, "But this doesn't look half as delicious."

The guards tightened the knots and slipped nervously away.

Dok put on a set of brass knuckles. Then, quite unceremoniously, he bashed Macmillan on the side of the head. Pain cracked through Macmillan's head, and stars danced in his vision.

"Why did you want the recording of the show?" Dok demanded. "Why are you really here?"

And so it began.

One of Macmillan's tricks with torture and pain was to tell himself that it had already happened, that it was already reality, that nothing could be done that hadn't already happened. It made things easier.

And in truth, everything *had* happened to Macmillan already. He'd died back on that train in every way that mattered.

Dok pulled off Macmillan's shoes, then grabbed one of the small toes. He had pliers. Unceremoniously, Dok ripped off the toenail. Pain flared hot from his foot to his brain. Macmillan kept his face neutral all through it. Sometimes pain was his friend because it shoved something new into his mind, blotting out the image of the hand. The ubiquitous hand, connected to nothing.

Dok worked a thin blade under Macmillan's other large toenail. Too much pain now. Things were getting bloody.

Dok watched his eyes.

Macmillan employed the yogic breathing he'd learned during the wilderness training Dax had sent him to after the bombing. Those months of training in martial arts, weapons, and mental control had been painful and punishing and so wildly irresponsible, it had nearly destroyed him.

And it had saved his life. Dax and the Association had saved his life.

"Did somebody send you?" Dok demanded.

"No, I happened on your establishment myself, though I must say, I hope you're sterilizing your instruments. I've heard of too many pedicure and manicure places with unsafe practices."

An angry tendon jumped on Dok's neck.

"And I can't say I'm sold on the red. Haven't you heard? Pastels are back in this season."

Dok kept on. Question after question. Macmillan concentrated on the words, and when that stopped working, he focused on the sounds, the way Dok manipulated air flow and air pressure and resonance to produce different sounds, larynx to lips.

Macmillan felt his resistance thinning, though. He could give Dok a story for temporary relief, but it was a bad precedent to set. The questioning continued. Macmillan reminded himself that sounds were nothing but physics and biology. Pain was messages in the brain. Nothing meant anything.

And deep down, Macmillan was with Laney.

He relived the way she had come to him in the night like a kind of angel. Oh, she definitely was the type of girl Peter would've fallen for; Peter had always been such a sucker for a poet with a rebel streak. He pictured the care in her eyes as she touched his wounds. He felt back to the way she'd pressed against him as they'd made love. All those years of empty sex, and there she was, a defiant miracle. She'd accused him of being a dragon guarding his own damn pile of rubble. *You're so full of shit, Devilwell.*

She'd be aware of both possible meanings for the nickname she'd given him—they didn't even have to discuss it for him to know that. *Devil* as a verb, a truncation of bedevil, as in, he devils a person rather well. Or *devil* and *well* as nouns forming a compound word: *Devilwell,* a deep reservoir of darkness best hidden. And then there was the way she'd exploited that *come 'ere* once she got a sense of its effect on him. Her up on that bed. Come 'ere. *Comere.*

He groaned aloud when he realized what he was do-ing—going to a happy place. Such an amateur method of enduring pain.

So embarrassing.

"You ready to talk?" Dok demanded.

"Oh, no, that groan wasn't for you. I was thinking about something else."

Pain bit into his toe as Dok shoved in the blade.

More yogic breathing. More words.

Happy places and sunshine and love and all that made you vulnerable; they gave your opponents something to take away. Good Lord, Laney was more dangerous to him than Dok Shinsurin himself. He laughed.

"What's so funny?" Dok growled. He stood over him, holding the blade to Macmillan's ear now. Macmillan ex-perienced a rush of fear. His ears were his stock in trade. But he couldn't show it. He wouldn't.

"It's not a matter of funny so much as absurdity."

Dok scowled. His English was good, but Macmillan guessed he didn't have much use for a word like absurd.

"Never mind, Dok. Funny will do."

Dok hit him in the ribs with the metal knuckles. Mac-millan realized here that the injuries Dok was giving him wouldn't be visible beneath clothes.

So the brothers didn't know Dok was there. Not a good sign.

Another blow to the ribs.

Macmillan went again and again to the feel of her hair against his fingers. He couldn't stop it now that he'd started. He went back to the way her lips tasted, and how it felt to be cared for by her, to make love to her. Those beautiful eyes, and her gentle touch, like a flower of pain.

CHAPTER FOURTEEN

Washington, D.C.

Rolly held his mobile phone so tightly, the tips of his fingers turned white as frost. "Imagine my surprise when your brother told me about the naked man. In Emmaline's room." He kept his voice calm. "Were you planning on informing me? Because it seems to me that I may never have found out if it wasn't for Dok's email."

My brothers could not make him talk. But I will make him sing, Dok had emailed. *He will be sorry for being in her room.*

"Of course you would have found out," Niwat said simply. "We're holding him for you."

"You and your sister were supposed to keep men *away* from her," Rolly said. "Yet a man was in her room, naked, so..." He paused there. It was good to let your people fill in the blanks—it strengthened your messages.

The Shinsurins wouldn't say what the man was doing there. Emmaline wouldn't tell, Niwat had informed him. No doubt because they hadn't asked.

He'd be relieved not to have to depend on the Shinsurins and their lax Thai attitudes.

Niwat speculated that the man was possibly a fan. Wanting her music.

A fan.

"Do I seem like a fool to you?" Rolly asked. "With this timing? The man was investigating the auction."

Niwat protested—worried, no doubt, that Rolly might change venues. Rolly wouldn't be changing venues, though.

"Emmaline probably caught something incidental on one of her recordings," Rolly said. "Or observed something key that she typed into her journal. She's quite the little observer, as you may have noticed."

Niwat had noticed. Well, that was something.

Rolly had learned only too late that Emmaline had been using her observation skills on him, collecting information for the FBI. He'd rescued her from abject poverty and that was his thanks. Two years he'd sat in that cell because of her. Whenever he thought of her spying on him, fingers of anger would crawl through him and he'd want to thrash something, but he never did. You didn't want the other prisoners to see you losing control. So he'd just sit there with that cold energy crawling through him.

"Dok told me Emmaline was talking about leaving," Rolly said to Niwat. "I don't have to tell you how I'll feel if she's not there for me when I arrive."

Niwat assured him that Emmaline didn't have a valid passport, and she wouldn't be able to empty her bank account until Monday. She would not be leaving.

Good. Rolly arrived late Sunday. Less than two days.

"Make sure of it." He hung up. They'd managed to keep her there for two years. He could trust them to keep her until Sunday night.

Harken had suggested having her killed back when her betrayal with the FBI had come to light. Harken didn't understand—Emmaline belonged to Rolly. He was the one who found her and polished her up; he needed to be the one to punish her. It had to be *him* she begged. Every look of fear and every instance of collapse would be for him alone. He needed to personally and thoroughly break her until she would accept anything and everything with gratitude—the kiss, the cock, the fist. He would permeate her every pore, her every breath, her every word. He would possess her so thoroughly this time, there would be no running.

She might resist him at first, but he'd have a zero-tolerance attitude for that. He'd been too lax the first time; that had been his mistake.

This time around, he'd start off with shock and awe; at the first sign of resistance, he'd simply grab the hammer, pin her down, and smash out her upper and lower front teeth. Then he'd clamp her jaw shut and fuck her throat.

A little trick he learned in prison. Nothing broke a person faster than getting their mouth transformed into a 24-hour-a-day-access fuckhole. A psychologist could probably explain why that was, but Rolly just knew it worked, and it would work on Emmaline.

Later, when Emmaline accepted that compliance was her only option, he'd buy her dental implants. The TZ-5 money could buy her the best in the world. Beautiful new dental implants would be a carrot for her. The carrot and the hammer. Shock and jaw.

His body clenched as he imagined her spreading her legs for another man. He was glad the man had turned out to be a liar. It was important for her to see that other men would only use her.

Harken had no idea who the man was. Harken had arrived home from Bangkok just hours ago; with the exception of Rajini, Emmaline was basically alone—Harken swore to it.

Rolly would kill the man all the same. He didn't care who he was; even if the man was Association, it was too late for them to stop him now—the TZ was already in place. That was one of the perks of having such a versatile weapon at your disposal. Let the entire Association storm the hotel. His buyers would welcome the demo.

He threw in his pants and his hat. Sexy white lingerie for Emmaline.

Harken came in with Rolly's boots, shined up for the trip. "You'll feel better when you see her again."

"That makes one of us," he said, throwing in the hammer. He hadn't had the luxury of a hammer in prison. That was prison, always improvising.

He supposed there was a chance she'd show remorse and give herself sweetly over, but he didn't dare hope for that; it was a recipe for unhappiness. Having to use the hammer made him sad. "Doesn't take much to break a docile horse. It's the wild ones where it means something," he said, more for himself than Harken.

Rolly used to enjoy getting into her journal at night while she slept to see what she'd written. From the day he first came across her, he'd gotten a kick out of how she captured things in words, but she never once wrote about him.

It's how he knew he never really had her.

Sometimes when they would have a good day together he would feel confident that she'd write in her journal about him. She never did.

He imagined how her eyes would look when he appeared in her room at the Imperiale Hotel Des Roses. They'd grow big as saucers with a look of surprise that would slowly die. If only she would be still and sweet for him, things would be okay.

He forced his mind off that line of thinking and checked his watch. Flight 5891 to Narita was scheduled to depart that night. He'd handle his business in Tokyo, and he'd be in Bangkok late Sunday.

CHAPTER FIFTEEN

Bangkok

Laney looked down at her suitcase, paralyzed with indecision. Paralyzed, yet shaky. Not the best combo on the menu.

The Shinsurins would have found the cell empty by now. What if they got the notion she'd helped Maxwell?

She hadn't gone down for breakfast or lunch, but she couldn't hide all day.

And what if she'd made a mistake? It was awful of the Shinsurins to hurt him and chain him up down there, but was it equally awful for her to let him out? He'd promised he wouldn't go after the Shinsurins, but what if he'd been lying?

Hellbuckets.

She grabbed a handful of panties and threw them in. Going through the motions of packing, but how could she leave without a valid passport or money?

She collapsed on the bed.

What had she done?

But she'd do it again, that was the crazy thing. She'd let him out of there with glee. No, that wasn't the precise word. She loved that Maxwell always went for a precise word.

171

She'd do it again with a sense of privilege.

So crazy. Maxwell had screwed her and invaded her privacy. And he carried three guns. He didn't work for Rolly, but obviously he wasn't a boy scout.

Still, you had to listen to your gut when you were on the run—Maxwell was right about that. Technically, he hadn't lied to her once. He was right about a lot, even the dragons. In a way, that meant more to her than the rest. And he had that thing with words. In fact, he really did seem like a man who would teach at the university.

He'd thought she should take off ASAP, like one of those brown birds. Well, she would take off. As soon as she got her money out of the bank. And she needed to cut and dye her hair.

Knock, knock.

She jumped nearly out of her skin.

A voice: "Laney?"

Niwat.

She froze.

Had he discovered her part in Maxwell's escape? What if Sujet had said something? She stared at the balcony, feeling like she was in a dream. A three-story leap. Too far.

"Are you okay, Laney?"

He didn't sound angry. And anyway, he could come in if he wanted. He had the master key. "One sec." She shoved her suitcase under her bed. "Hold on." She went to the door and opened it. "Hi."

Niwat smiled. "It's past noon. I didn't wake you…"

"I had my headphones on."

Niwat took a scan around her room; her iPod was not in evidence. "I just wanted to let you know, you have nothing to fear from your visitor."

Nothing to fear? What did *that* mean? "Ah," she said. "What happened?"

He shrugged. "He's willing to play along. A businessman, just as I expected."

She nodded, trying to look relieved. "Good. Wow." How could he not know Maxwell was gone?

Niwat smiled. He wore a yellow turtleneck. Niwat was a turtleneck guy. An odd thing in Bangkok. "Nothing more to fear, okay?"

"Well!" she said, way too energetically. "Thank you. I really do appreciate it."

He hesitated. There was something more. "I'm confident this is the safest place for you," he said, "but I understand you want to be ready for anything. So I came to tell you, I've expedited your passport. It will be ready in three days instead of the customary week."

"Really?"

He looked away. "When I reflected on our conversation, I understood that you felt trapped. And then last night's visitor frightened you, so I requested a rush. How do you like the name *Gia Nordwall?*"

She nodded. "It has a ring to it."

"On Monday, Rajini will go to your bank with you and extract some funds. Soon after, the passport will be ready. There's no place safer for you than with us, but we don't want you to feel trapped."

"Thank you," she whispered.

"*Yin dee khrap,*" he said. *You're welcome.* He smiled. "Nearly full house tonight. Rest up." With that he left.

She sank onto the bed. *What in the hell?* Why would he say she was safe if Maxwell escaped?

Nothing made sense.

Though a passport would make leaving easier. A couple more days. What would two days matter? Or should she flee like Maxwell said? The Shinsurins were far more dangerous than she'd imagined, but did that justify leaving with no passport and barely any money? They'd never been dangerous to her.

And what had happened with Maxwell?

Her brother Charlie would know what to do. She checked her email for the umpteenth time.

Still nothing.

Was he even getting her emails? He'd set up a secret account to email her with under a fake name, and he accessed it from a coffee shop only. They'd been so careful.

She sent him a quick message—*I need your advice ASAP. I need to know you're there!* Charlie had gone through a phase of distrusting Rajini and her brothers, but lately he'd been all about her staying in the safety of the hotel. What would he say when she told him what the Shinsurins did to Maxwell?

Then she got a horrible thought: what if they'd caught Maxwell trying to escape? What if he was dead?

Her heart pounded. She didn't dare sneak down there during the day, but she had to know. She took the elevator down to the lobby and found Sujet at his post near the door.

"Hey," she said. "What's new?"

"No scuttlebutt," he said.

She smiled. She'd taught him that word. He liked funny English words, and they got him good tips from Americans and Canadians. "Have you heard anything regarding the downstairs guest?"

Sujet twisted his lips.

"What?"

"The staff is nervous," Sujet said.

She felt the air go out of her. "How so?"

"Because he targeted you," Sujet said, like it should be obvious. "Also, we thought they would turn him over to the police today, but he's still down there."

"Still down there?" *Hadn't the hairpins worked?* "Are you sure? Did you see him?"

"No, but Pramod was asked to deliver an extra lunch for him an hour ago. And Dok was with the man all morning. It's something serious."

A chill came over her. "Like what?"

"I don't know. Jao and Niwat were running around angry. At Dok. Up and down several times." He nodded at the front desk. "Don't tell Sirikit and Kalaya. They're uncomfortable that a man should be held for so long."

"Right," Laney said.

Sujet's face darkened suddenly. He was looking over her shoulder.

She turned to see Rajini coming up behind her. "Laney!"

Rajini wore a red skirt suit, and her black hair was up in a princess do. "Have you had lunch?"

Laney smoothed her T-shirt. "No."

"Café. Now." Rajini hooked her arm in Laney's. "Sorry, Sujet, I'm taking her."

Laney threw Sujet an apologetic smile over her shoulder as Rajini pulled her to the hotel cafe.

"You get some sleep?" Rajini asked. "How are you?"

"Freaked," Laney said as they settled in to their usual table.

"I bet." Rajini signaled for ice teas.

Rajini wouldn't like that she'd snuck down, but she needed to know what her brothers were up to. "There's something you need to know," Laney said.

"What?"

Just then, the waiter arrived and they ordered their usual—fried rice with prawns.

Rajini bent her head in once he left. "Niwat told you about the passport, right? You'll be Gia. Guess who made that up?"

"Wait...isn't she a dead supermodel?" Laney said.

"Yes, but it's a cool name. Anyway, you can't leave." Rajini reached across the table and grabbed her hand. "I'll die if you leave."

"I don't want to leave, but Rajini—this guy—"

"He's not going to give you trouble. Got it?" Rajini raised her brows in the way she did when she would accept no argument. "Everything's fine with him."

"I don't want to seem ungrateful, but detaining a man against his will? I didn't want him to be hurt, and you're not going to like this, but last night—"

"Laney. This isn't America where everything is so black and white. I get how it seems to you—they're holding this guy. What is that in the US? Kidnapping, unlawful imprisonment..."

"For starters."

They fell silent as the waiter delivered their ice teas.

Rajini lowered her voice. "I get it, it seems wrong to you, but you can't take your American yardstick and impose it on my brothers and people like Rolly and his men. They play by different rules. And don't forget, my brothers are the good guys in this." She sat back. "I can't think of anybody better to deal with some thug of Rolly's than my brothers. These guys—" she flung a hand in the direction of the lobby. "A show of power. It's what they understand."

"Meaning, some brutality is okay?"

"You want guards and fake passports, but no violence, nothing to offend your sensibilities. There's no such thing as a Disney criminal, Laney. My brothers are here for you, just as they are for me. Trust that. Your visitor is perfectly comfortable, in case you're wondering. You need to stop worrying."

Laney knew when she was being handled by Rajini. She also knew that a man chained in a cell wasn't comfortable. She looked down at her tea, re-thinking her big idea of confessing to Rajini that she'd been down there. "Fine. Here's my bottom line," she said. "I don't think he's some thug of Rolly's, and I want him released."

Rajini snorted. "Are you serious?"

"I think he's not a threat to me."

Rajini smiled. "Did you take a degree in FBI profiling when I wasn't looking?"

"I don't like him being held and I want him released. It's not right. In fact, I wouldn't be surprised if he actually does work at the university."

"The university. Seriously? Why would he have three guns? Why would he be in your computer? Why would he tell Niwat he was working for Rolly?"

Laney straightened. "He confessed he was working for Rolly?"

"Yeah. He told Niwat. They're nearly at a deal."

Laney stirred her tea thinking of the man down there. Things got simple when you were on the run. And things like truth and connection got important fast.

Somebody was lying. Who?

"It was the first thing Niwat did—check the university story." Rajini squeezed a lemon into her tea. "Leave it."

"You know for a fact he checked it. The university story. And you're absolutely sure he doesn't work there."

"I'm absolutely sure that he doesn't work there," Rajini said. "I saw proof. Do you need to see proof? Is that what you need?"

No good would come of saying yes to that question. "I want him released."

"It's not your call. The man entered a guest's room under false pretenses and was stealing something. It's out of your hands."

"The whole reason they kept him was on my behalf."

Rajini gave her a look. "Let this be, Laney. It's out of our hands. The man is fine. They'll make a deal, and that's that."

Laney dumped sugar into her tea, heart racing. Rajini was a master at stonewalling disgruntled guests. Laney didn't appreciate being on the other end of that.

At all.

She was thankful when their food arrived. She ate quickly and left, telling Rajini she needed to practice a new song.

Back up in her room, she sat on her bed, all jumpy and paranoid. It was getting to be like the old days, not sure who she could trust. Eyes everywhere.

Just then, she spied Maxwell's business card on the floor. She picked it up and uncrumpled it. Peter Maxwell, Ph.D. A local number was on the bottom.

What would happen if she called it? Who would answer?

She grabbed her phone and punched it in. It rang a good ten times followed by a series of clicks—the phone transferring to another phone. A woman's voice: "Bangkok International University."

She asked for Peter Maxwell.

Hold please. Again the ringing. The operator came back. "He's not there." She told her to try back. No, she didn't know when Maxwell would be in. His hours and class schedule were on the website.

The website. *Hello.* How had she not thought to Google him?

She went to her laptop and put in Peter Maxwell and linguistics. The number of entries surprised her. He'd even written two books.

Well, she could go around with business cards saying she was Lady Gaga; that wouldn't make her Lady Gaga.

Then she found an image from the back of one of Maxwell's book covers.

It was a low-res, black-and-white photo, but it looked a whole lot like the guy down in the dungeon. He had different glasses, but the same blond hair. The same face shape—a sort of masculine diamond; a movie star face shape. Pleasing. Perfect.

You couldn't tell for certain if the Maxwell in the photo had gray-blue eyes, but the glint was right—that mix of arrogant humor and lively curiosity. Even in a basement cell in Bangkok, he'd had that glint. But she couldn't be sure from just the picture. Could the man in the basement have chosen this identity because they were lookalikes?

Rajini had told her flat out that he wasn't a teacher at the university. That she knew it for a fact. That there was proof. Maxwell said that he did teach there.

Who was lying?

The answer to that question seemed massively important. It would tell her everything about who to trust.

The Bangkok International University wasn't far. According to the website, Maxwell was teaching in a weekend program. His Saturday class began at three. Less than an hour.

She'd get the truth. She was done being handled. Doner than done.

Bangkok International University was located in Dusit, the government area of Bangkok, which was lusher and less cramped than the business and tourist-oriented areas. The central school building was a large, mostly glass structure with colorful art showing through from the inside, like candy in a case.

School was in session, with students from all over bustling around. She asked directions and finally made it to a shiny, modern lecture hall where adjunct professor Peter Maxwell was to be guest lecturing. She raced up the steps, hoping to catch the real Maxwell in action. She arrived at the doors just in time to face a wall of students—mostly women—coming out.

"Is Professor Maxwell in there?" she asked one woman.

"No. We have a TA this week."

"Is he sick?"

The woman shrugged. "They said he won't be in."

Mildly helpful. She thanked her and went up to a pair of women. "Did Professor Maxwell say anything about where he's gone? I really need to find him."

"Hah," one of them said. "Get in line." She had a French accent.

"Others are looking for him?" Laney asked.

"Who doesn't want to run into the good professor?" the French woman said.

Laney stuffed down the flare of possessiveness. She pointed at the book in the French woman's hand. "May I?"

The French woman handed it over.

Laney pointed at the back picture. "Does Professor Maxwell have different glasses from these?" Laney asked.

"Yeah. Less frame. Less big and clunky."

"Goldish? Thin gold on the sides but mostly glass?"

"Yeah," the first said.

Like the ones worn by the man in the cell. She was getting a bad feeling about all this.

"What color are his eyes?"

"Have you met him or not?" the American said. "'Cause if you'd met him, you'd know."

"Blue-ish silver," the French woman told her. "Quite piercing."

"Is his hair longer now than in this picture?"

"A tiny bit longer," the American said. "Tucked behind his ears. Why?"

Goosebumps climbed the back of her neck. "I just need to figure out if I've met him," she said. "Does he wear a white T-shirt under his button shirt sometimes?"

The French girl smiled. "You have met him, my friend."

And Rajini had lied.

Maxwell did work at the university. And a man chained up in a cell was not comfortable. She felt her world shift off its axis.

Her best friend. Lying. She'd opened her heart to Rajini.

"Does he have any kind of specialty?" Laney asked.

"Syntax, I'd say," the American said.

"Phonetics, too," the French girl said.

"He kind of does it all," the American said. "We've been mostly talking about slang and jargon in this class, markers that set people apart. And the unsaid."

The French girl nodded. "He has many controversial opinions on the unsaid."

"Like what?" Laney asked, walking alongside them, still reeling. *Her best friend.*

"Linguistic microexpressions," the French girl said. "It's a kind of language tic that can spread..." She went on, and Laney nodded like it made sense to her. Some of his work, they told her, had forensic applications.

"He can arrest me any day of the week," the American said.

Laney thanked them and headed over to the university bookstore, mind racing. Obviously the man in the cell was Maxwell.

I'm absolutely sure that he doesn't work there. I saw proof. Do you need to see proof? Is that what you need?

Rajini had lied. Or was she being lied to herself? But then, what was the proof?

And if the Shinsurins were lying about this, what else?

She thought about calling the police about Maxwell, but how could she be sure the Shinsurins didn't own the cops the way Rolly had?

Fear crawled up her neck. Cut off from her brother. Unable to trust the Shinsurins. Alone in this far-off place.

Except for Maxwell.

Crazy to think of Maxwell as her sole ally in this place, considering what he'd done, but he was her people. He'd never technically lied to her. And he seemed to care about her safety. They were both in trouble. Both with some-body to run from. She highly doubted he'd return to fin-ish teaching the class.

It was there that she got the idea to break him out.

It was Saturday. Without access to the bank, she didn't have enough money to go on the run—she didn't even have enough for a train ticket, but if she broke Maxwell out, he would help her—she felt sure of it. He'd owe her. It was the perfect solution.

A good eight hours before she could even think about going down.

She bought his newest book. Yeah, that was definitely him on the dust flap. She sat on a couch in the student lounge and started reading. If she hadn't known the au-thor and the man in the cage were one in the same, she'd sure know it from reading the book; even the sentences sounded like him. He seemed to know everything about words and the way different people used them.

He went on for pages about the sentence "The car ran over the dog" without ever talking about what it really meant—a dog, dead in the street, which was a very sad thing. It seemed a kind of madness to her, to obsess over how the sounds all go together and not the meaning. She didn't agree with it, and it made her excited to discuss it with him. And just to see him.

She wouldn't be leaving without him this time.

CHAPTER SIXTEEN

Anders sat in the lobby reading the Bangkok Post. Whenever he utilized a newspaper as a prop, he thought of his father, who would sometimes joke around by putting a hole in whatever newspaper he was reading and looking through it at young Anders. An eye in the newspaper. Hilarity ensued.

These days, scrolling through a smartphone was more usual, and it allowed you to reposition yourself naturalistically, as if for better reception or light. But sometimes Anders genuinely wanted to read the paper. What's more, he was feeling happy and confident about finding Macmillan now that he had a photo. And a name.

Hitters coming up in the business disdained anything scholarly, as if ignorance was impressive. As if the mind had nothing to do with the gun. Fine with Anders. It meant less serious competition.

He'd gotten his research chops in college, and he sharpened them every chance he could.

It was thanks to his research chops that he now had the identity of Macmillan, aka Dr. Peter Maxwell, PhD.

Though the name he'd used with the police after the San Juliano train bombing was Peter Macmillan Maxwell. At which point his identity had split in two—Macmillan and Maxwell. He now had current photographs of him, courtesy of his good friend, Google.

It was beautiful.

Maxwell was in Bangkok for a guest teaching post. Linguistics. That would be how he hunted. Speech. Words. Anders almost hated to kill him.

Almost.

And he'd seen the man just the day before, wandering through the lobby. Right there. Macmillan hadn't come through for a day or so, but he'd be back. Meanwhile, he'd start discreetly questioning the staff. Somebody would be able to point him in the right direction.

It was as good as over. Simple point and shoot now.

CHAPTER SEVENTEEN

She stopped at the drugstore on the way home and picked out a tall bottle of water and some hydrogen peroxide for his wounds, then she grabbed a protein bar, a chocolate bar, and a pack of paper clips. In the movies guys always used paperclips to pick locks. If those didn't work, she'd damn well find the leg iron keys.

She grabbed a box of condoms. Just in case.

Ten minutes later she was pushing through the revolving door of the Des Roses lobby, only to spot Niwat and Jao standing at the desk, looking sternly in her direction.

Hellbuckets.

The two of them beelined over to her and pulled her into the lobby waiting area. "Where were you?" Niwat asked.

"Shopping." She lifted her bag in answer, then quickly lowered it when she thought about what she had in there. "What's wrong?"

"We were worried," Jao said. "Considering your visitor."

"Right," she said, blood racing. "So unbelievable."

Niwat seemed to be studying her bag a little too closely; she looked down and was horrified to realize you could see through it. Maxwell's book was partly visible...as was the side of the condom box.

Casually, she twisted the bag by the handle, sure they could read her nervousness. "I just wanted...chocolate and stuff."

"You know you can always ask the kitchen for anything," Jao said. He was the biggest of the brothers; he had a crew cut and a wild passion for Thai boxing. "You should stay close to the hotel. Just for now."

Her heart pounded. Were they being...too intense? She didn't know Thai culture enough to get nuances like that. "You're probably right."

"If you go out again, one of us would be happy to escort you," Niwat said.

"You guys have done so much," she said. "I don't want to drag you all over."

"It's no problem," Niwat said.

"Even if it's bra shopping?"

This got them tongue-tied. She put all the sunniness she could muster into her smile as she began to back away. "Just kidding. Later, gators."

She could not get into the elevator fast enough. With shaky hands she stabbed the button for the third floor five times. She tried to keep her sunny face but her heart was banging clear out of her chest, and it seemed like forever until the doors closed.

She just needed to last through the night until she could grab Maxwell and get out. It was dangerous to set off without her passport and money, but a partner would make all the difference. She wouldn't be alone.

Her show went off normally, aside from her nervousness, which she felt like everybody could see.

At one in the morning, Laney finished packing up as much of her life as she could into her sturdy new backpack: expired passport, toiletries, money, the condoms, hats, and whatever else she could think of.

She slipped into the lobby and up to the front desk, thankful no Shinsurins were around. A few patrons sat around in the lobby. The night guards stood watch at the door. Would they let her out? She decided to sneak out the pool exit.

She chatted with Sirikit until she saw her chance to grab the key to the liquor hatch.

Minutes later she was down on LL2, slipping past the guards' room. They were asleep when she passed, thank goodness. She headed deeper in, and quietly let herself into the cell room. There he was, stretched out on his side on the far end of his cage, hair tousled. They'd given him a brown shirt.

"Maxwell!" she whispered.

He sat up—stiffly.

"Are you okay?" she asked. "I couldn't believe when I heard you were still here. I should've waited to make sure the hairpins worked out." She grabbed the keys from the hook.

"What the hell are you doing here?"

"What does it look like?" She did her best to project cheerful confidence even though he didn't sound at all happy to see her. "I brought paperclips. Assorted sizes.

Those'll work better than the hairpins, right?" She un-locked the cage.

"You're supposed to be gone. You need to be gone, dammit!"

"Lucky for you I'm not. We have to get you out of here. We'll help each other."

"No. Laney..." He sat awkwardly, feet tucked behind him. "I'm fine."

"Right. I don't think so." She entered the gloomy cage, knelt in front of him, and started digging in her pack.

"You have to get out of here."

"I'm not leaving without you."

He grabbed her wrist. "Go. I don't need your help. You understand?"

"Save it for someone who might believe it." She yanked her hand away and pulled out the paperclips. "We need to hurry, so don't fight me on this. Everybody's lying to me but you. So you're getting out whether you want it or not." She extracted two of the best-looking paperclips and extended them to him on her palm. "Start your picking, Devilwell," she whispered.

He stared down at them for a long time, saying nothing.

"I'm not leaving you here again. Nothing you say'll change that."

A bit more time passed, and then he looked up at her. And her blood froze. He wore that empty smile he'd had on when she held him at gunpoint. The smile that put a wall between them. "Unbelievable," he said.

"What?" she asked, hating the waver in her voice.

"I use you in every way possible," he began smoothly. "And then I decide to give you one decent bit of advice about being on the run and you can't quite go with it, can you? Here you are, bothering me and dabbling in things you don't understand. Trying to help me when I neither need nor want your help. You really are a fool."

She paused only a moment. "I get it." She began to unbend a paperclip. "You don't want me in danger or something, so you're being jerky. Chivalry noted and rejected."

"Is that what I'm doing?"

"I think it is."

She felt his eyes on her. "And this is the expert assessment from the woman who thinks a cornpone hee-haw singing show is a capital way to hide?"

His words were a punch in the gut. "Excuse me?"

"Cornpone hee-haw singing show," he repeated. "It's rather precise, don't you think? Hardly needs a supporting cast."

"I know what you're doing," she said.

"You don't know the first thing about me."

"I know you think words are your bitch. Just some shell game for you to play. Making things real that aren't, or putting a new face on things you don't like. But guess what?" She fixed him with a good glare. They were close enough to kiss, but that wasn't in the air now. "When a man is chained up in a cage like a circus tiger, then it's the right thing to help him. And doing the right thing is always the right thing. And I'll tell you something else: when a dog gets run over by a car, it's a goddamn tragedy, not an exercise in phonemes. So take the fucking paperclip and unlock yourself."

He laughed that beautiful laugh.

"You think it's funny?"

"Oh it's not funny so much as delicious," he said. "I see you read my book."

"That's right. A whole lot of bunk designed to hornswoggle folks."

"What a coincidence," he said. "That's what I was planning on calling my next book. *A Whole Lot of Bunk Designed to Hornswoggle Folks Two.* What do you think?"

She didn't like his tone. "Sounds about right."

"Feel free to leave a one-star review on your way out."

She worked on unbending the other paperclip. "You're coming with me."

"I'm not going anywhere."

"Why not? You think you can't get out of those leg cuffs with the paperclip? 'Cause if you can't, the guards are asleep right now. I'll go in and find the leg keys."

"Don't," he growled. "Do you have any idea what Dok would do to you if he found you down here?"

A chill went over her. Niwat wouldn't hurt her, but Dok...he had a point about Dok. "Get picking then, Devilwell." She held the paperclip out to him, willing her hand not to shake. What if she'd been wrong about everything? What if she was really and truly alone?

He just looked at it. "I'm not going anywhere."

"Then I'm not, either." She set it on the ground in front of him and stood, pulling the candy bar from her backpack. Casual as could be, she slung the pack over her shoulder, leaned against the bars, tore off the wrapper, and took a bite. "Mmm."

Maxwell watched her eat with a strange expression— she couldn't tell if it was hunger or loathing.

Please, she thought. *Don't make me go alone.*

She took another bite.

CHAPTER EIGHTEEN

She was killing him. Just like that first night.

She'd called herself cowardly, but she was nothing less than a warrior, standing over him, waiting for him to free himself even though she was scared shitless. Laney and her supplies and her attitude and her unshakeable moral compass. It was perfect that she'd insulted his book. Of course she'd hate that chapter. She had no time for his various reductions, just like Rio. She thrived on emotion. Connection.

He wished he could tell her the truth—he was a spy, and all he wanted was to get back to the console room before the drugged guards woke up.

He couldn't. The truth would endanger them both.

The farther she got from him and the hotel, the safer she'd be.

He swallowed, steeled himself. He had to make her run.

Do it, he told himself.

"Question, Laney. Has it ever occurred to you to wonder why I never asked you to go to the police?"

"I figure the Shinsurins are buddies with them."

He closed his eyes. He wanted to move his feet into a position that wouldn't make his toes feel like they were on fire, but he couldn't let her see them. The last thing he needed was her pity.

"Or maybe I have more to fear from the law than from the Shinsurins," he said.

She simply took another bite. "We both need to get out of here. You're coming with me."

"How do you know I'm not a killer?" he asked.

"Because I know."

He gave her a cold smile. "It's sad. You're pretty, but you're not very well-educated. Though I do love the socks."

She just looked down at him. She had to be nervous. "I'm not buying what you're selling, Devilwell. I'm done being fooled by people."

He didn't have to fool her—that was the grim truth. He'd died in that train. He'd lost everything that made him human.

"Come here," he said.

She frowned.

"Come *here*." Before she could move away, he lunged up on his knees, grabbed her wrists, and yanked her down to him. Her candy bar flew.

"Hey!" she tried to pull away.

He forced himself to tighten his grip, hating that he might be hurting her. Everything in him raged in protest. "Look in my eyes. Ask me if I've killed."

She struggled. "Let me go."

He gave her a shake. "Ask me. You say I'm not a liar. Don't you want to know?"

Fear in her eyes. "Please—"

"Ask me!"

She glared. "Have you?"

"Yes. I've killed fourteen men. Eight by gunshot and three by slitting their jugulars. Did you know that slicing a man's neck takes roughly the same amount of pressure as slicing into a papaya? I bet you didn't know that."

Fear in her eyes. He could see what he'd become reflected there; he was a hunter, a killer, a tool of the Association.

"I know what you're thinking, Laney. That's only eleven. And you'd be right. There was another man I killed by smashing his skull with a twenty-pound free weight. Then there was the time I jammed a wooden spear clear through a man's neck. I whittled the thing myself. I even shot a man in the back of the head once."

"I don't believe you," she whispered, glancing at the door.

"I think you do."

The man he'd shot in the back of the head had been dying painfully. It had been a mercy killing, but the others hadn't been about mercy.

He transferred her wrists to one hand and grabbed her hair into a ponytail, forcing her to look into his eyes and see the truth of his words, the bleakness in his soul. It made him want to die.

"Let me go," she whispered in a small voice.

He twisted his fist in her hair, using it to control her head like reins on a horse. She drove a knee into his thigh, sending bolts of pain up and down him.

He barely noticed. He couldn't be deeper in hell.

"Please," she whispered.

He twisted harder, pulse racing. "There was a whole stretch of my life—weeks on end—when I sat awake at night fantasizing about killing a man by ripping out his throat with my teeth." The truth. It was how he'd thought to kill Mero, way back when he was imprisoned in the terrorist's compound. "I visualized it in my mind just like an athlete would—the way I'd angle my head for the best canine penetration."

Her eyes changed. Turning away from him finally.

"I thought that would be poetic for somebody as linguistically inclined as myself," he continued. "What do you think?"

She tried to push away.

He held her more tightly. "I could do it to you right now."

She stiffened as he kissed her throat. She'd find it creepy. Well, she should. This brave, beautiful woman— she should think twice before asking a man like him to run with her. Before opening her heart to him. Before clawing down his defenses. She finally found her devil in the well.

"You're right about words being my bitch. About my using them to cover unpleasantness. It's how I fooled you."

Pain shot through his groin as her knee connected with his balls. He let her go and she sprung away.

"Go to hell." She picked up her pack and backed out of the cell, keeping a wary eye on him. She pulled the door shut. "You can go to hell."

He was grateful for her anger. Grateful it was over.

She hung the keys up on the nail. Even from where he sat, he could see her hands shaking. She left without a backward glance.

Macmillan quickly unlocked his leg irons and stole out after her, shadowing her through the tunnels, past the drugged guards, and all the way up to the hatch, just to make sure she didn't get caught on her way out.

He quickly unlocked the hatch after she closed it, peeking out, watching her walk down the side street, shoulders slumped.

He spotted a van on the corner. That's where the Associate's admin would be, ready to tail her. *Leave,* he pleaded in his mind. Get away from this place.

Everything he'd said to her would be worth it if she'd get away from the menace of her ex-husband and the looming danger with Jazzman. And stopped visiting him!

She reached the main road and turned out of sight. He lowered the hatch, locked it, and made his way back, toes like fire.

She'd wanted him to leave with her. It was like having a first class plane ticket somewhere beautiful that he could never use. But he could take it out and look at it sometimes, run his finger over the flight number, the seat number and think, *what if.*

He entered the console room and sat next to a drugged guard, grateful for the weight off his feet. Beyond the toes, he had an egg of a bump where Dok had smashed the side of his head, possible concussion, bruised and possibly broken ribs, and the cut eyebrow. And her gunshot graze. But at least his fever was gone, thanks to Douglas's shot.

All in all, he was holding up. He didn't like to think what condition he'd be in if Niwat hadn't arrived to pull Dok off him.

He checked the files. Still compressing and download-ing. He'd been downloading the files when he saw her coming—a mile off, of course. He'd had to scramble back into his cage and wait for her. He'd had to do that two times over the course of the night when people walked through. He'd lain in his cell, holding his breath both times, sure somebody would try to wake the guards.

Nobody had.

He clicked through the video feeds until he spotted her at the front desk, talking to the night clerks. She looked agitated. Did she know how her eyes gave her away? The Shinsurins would see her growing distrust there.

"Leave!" he whispered at the screen.

He'd find a way to protect her if things got ugly with Jazzman, but she'd be far safer if she'd leave. She probably had everything she needed in that little backpack.

Laney stepped onto the lobby elevator. He switched cameras to the elevator interior. The defeated look on her face broke his heart.

"I can't go with you," he whispered to the screen. *"I can't let more people die."*

She hit the button for the third floor. Back to her room.

"No," he whispered. *"Don't go to bed!"*

She got off on the third floor. He watched until the elevators doors shut behind her. There were no cameras in the staff wing—not much money in blackmailing maids.

He didn't need a camera to know she was in for the night.

He told himself she'd leave tomorrow, in the daytime. Even that would be hard for her. It's why she wanted him with her. She'd trusted him and he threw it in her face. God, it had been years since he'd felt so wrecked over a woman.

A decade, to be precise.

Forcing his mind back onto the mission, he slipped a phone from a guard's pocket and called the Associates at the Sawadee Palace Hotel with an update. It felt good to talk to his guys. They were restless—heaven knew what their room service bill was coming to. They were planning an excursion to record the few arms dealers who weren't at the Hotel Des Roses. They'd play the recordings for him over the phone tomorrow night if he hadn't found Jazzman by then.

Good.

He erased his tracks, slipped the phone back, and started reviewing the audio files. The dealers at lunch, the dealers in the elevator, the dealers in the sauna. The Indian gentleman who sat in the lobby for hours on end, vaguely familiar but his speech patterns were nothing like Jazzman's. One by one, he ruled out the guests of the Hotel Des Roses.

It took just two hours for him to conclude that Jazzman hadn't yet arrived.

Another hour for compressing and downloading all of the relevant video and audio. He didn't need that to find Jazzman, but he wanted everything he could get for a database he had in mind. Photos of arms dealers along with extended speech samples from each would be a goldmine for the Association. Or, he'd turn it into one. He'd create software that would help identify speakers by their voices, and he'd do a diction program, too, to help identify the authors of emails and manifestos.

There was no such thing as a linguistic fingerprint, but in a closed group—a hundred of the world's most notorious arms dealers, for example—you could get pretty close. He'd create rules for each individual. The technology tools he envisioned would be a hands-down intelligence coup, the kind of thing he could spend years on, and exactly what he'd be doing if his old life hadn't ended.

The thought of his old life filled him with sadness. His emotions were bubbling too close to the surface these days. Sleep—he needed sleep. He stole a few of the seaweed crackers out of the bag on the table. Sleep and a real meal, that's all he needed.

CHAPTER NINETEEN

Laney watered Amy for the last time. She really had meant to plant her somewhere decent, but there wasn't time. She had to get out. It was Sunday—the banks were closed. She'd be vulnerable without money or a passport, but she would survive. She had two feet.

Her train was to leave at three. The ticket would take all her money, but she needed to be a brown bird.

She rubbed her wrists. She'd always been able to count on Rajini, but her friend had lied to her face.

I'm absolutely sure that he doesn't work there. I saw proof. He's perfectly comfortable.

Lies.

Was Rajini just protecting her brothers? Covering for her brothers? Still, Laney couldn't have it. Didn't Rajini understand that Laney depended on her with her life?

Her thoughts went to Maxwell.

Maxwell hadn't lied. His words had felt like dark confessions.

She looked back at Amy. If she gave the plant to Sirikit, that would show she was leaving. She needed to be a brown bird. The walls were closing in on her. The whole city.

A knock at her door. "Laney!"

She stiffened. *Rajini.*

Three hours until she had to be at the station. She decided that it would be smart to hang out with Rajini now. They'd have tea or something, and then Laney would take off. She'd write a letter to Rajini later on. Explain. Maybe get some answers.

"Just a sec." She arranged things to look regular.

"I have a bone to pick with you," Rajini said from the other side of the door. She sounded mad. Or was that fake mad? Sometimes she couldn't tell with Rajini. Laney steeled herself and opened up to find Rajini standing there with her hands on her hips. Fake mad.

Laney managed a smile. "What's up?"

"Lobby. Now."

Nervously Laney searched Rajini's face. "What's in the lobby?"

"A surprise," Rajini said.

It was too late to get out of it unless she wanted to do something totally dramatic, like run. That would accomplish nothing.

Her thoughts went to Maxwell. Maxwell wouldn't crack; he'd go along with it. Hell, he wouldn't just go, he'd go with a joke and an easy smile, confident he could handle whatever came up.

"You know how I feel about surprises," Laney said smoothly, grabbing her purse and following her ex-friend into the elevator. "You're being very mysterious," she said as the doors slid shut.

Rajini raised one eyebrow. "I'm not the only one."

"You think I'm being mysterious?"

"I think you've been very mysterious."

What did *that* mean? Did Rajini know about her visits to LL2?

Laney smoothed her hands over her simple black skirt, which she'd paired with a simple dark top. Comfy, un-memorable traveling clothes. Except the knee-highs. She planned to put on glasses and a hat when she finally set off. Not the net hat, though. Maxwell had a point—it was a disguisey hat.

"Are you doing a knee-high intervention?"

Rajini snorted. "I should."

"What's the surprise?"

"You'll see." Rajini watched the floor numbers flash on and off as if it was the most fascinating thing ever. Maybe it was something good, Laney told herself. Maybe her passport was ready a day early.

The elevator dinged and the doors opened onto the lobby. Rajini hooked her arm in Laney's. "Come on."

A group of men congregated in the corner of the lob-by. Laney couldn't see their faces, but they had the dark feel of the convention guys. The influx of shady men all week had added tension to the atmosphere, a silent hum that ratcheted up her nerves.

Rajini pulled her past them and up to the front desk where Sirikit and Kalaya stood.

"Is there a special delivery for Laney?" Rajini asked Si-rikit.

"There's a very special delivery for her," Sirikit said solemnly.

Kalaya nodded. "Yes."

Everybody was acting weird. Laney gripped the counter. "What is it?" Whatever it was, good or bad, she wanted to get it over with.

Sirikit reached below the desk; she seemed to be fumbling with something.

Sujet wandered over, expression blank, just as Sirikit pulled up a cupcake with a candle on it. "Happy Birthday, Laney."

"Oh, my God," Laney clapped her hand onto her heart, relief blasting through her.

Rajini grinned. "You sneak. I can't believe you didn't say anything!"

"You guys!" Laney felt so relieved. *Her birthday.* "How'd you know?"

"How could I forget?" Rajini said. "We had drinks at the Baiyike Rooftop bar last year. Many drinks, if I recall."

"Go. Do it." Sujet pointed at the cupcake. "Make a wish."

She'd remembered.

Laney made a wish for her brother to be safe and blew out the candles.

Rajini clapped and smiled at Sirikit. "Anything else down there?"

Sirikit pulled up a wrapped box. "From all of us," she said. "But it was Rajini's idea."

Laney unwrapped the box and pulled up a necklace—a tiny silver elephant on a delicate chain. "Oh, thank you!" She and Rajini had admired it together a month ago. She hugged Rajini, and then Sujet, and then Sirikit and Kalaya over the counter. She would miss her friends so much.

"Turn." Laney turned around and Rajini clasped the necklace at the back of her neck. "Why didn't you say anything yesterday? I could tell something was bothering you."

"Well, you know…" She turned back to Rajini, eyeing her significantly. It was *Emmaline's* birthday, that's why. She was Laney on her fake passport. She should celebrate Laney's birthday, not Emmaline's.

She saw when Rajini realized. "Oh. Well." Rajini gave a defiant shrug. "Happy birthday, sister."

She loved Rajini in that moment. Rajini and her sassy energy. She'd miss her.

"Thank you." Laney patted the necklace, feeling like a traitor. Sneaking out after Rajini had helped her for so long. But how could she trust her when she'd outright lied? *I'm absolutely sure that he doesn't work there. I saw proof. He's perfectly comfortable.*

If she wasn't on the run for her life, it wouldn't be such a big thing.

"The elephant. For good luck," Sujet said.

Laney smiled. "Good."

Sirikit split the cupcake in fifths.

She'd write them all letters once she was safe. These people had been so good to her.

New guests were arriving. The staff flew into action.

"You want to watch a movie?" Rajini asked.

"I'm kind of tired," Laney said, wandering back in the direction of the elevator with her friend. Rajini insisted on riding up with her.

Back in her room, Laney checked her email while Rajini made them both tea.

Laney's heart lifted when she saw Charlie's secret email name in her inbox. "He got back to me!" Laney said.

Rajini came over. "I told you he'd email."

"Thank goodness."

Rajini watched her expectantly as she read.

"A nice, long letter," Laney mumbled, reading. He apologized for missing her birthday—he'd had the flu, but he was much better, and she should email right back with her question. He told her what a comfort it was that the Shinsurins had her back. A comfort to know she was safe within the walls of the hotel. He went on about politics, current events, and something about the auto repair shop that he'd told her before.

The further she read, the more worried she felt.

"What's wrong?"

"Something's up with Charlie. He's been weird all month, but he's weirder now."

"Weirder how?"

"It's hard to explain." Laney reread the letter. "Weirdly cheerful. Talking about politics. Telling me stupid stuff he's already told me. Like he forgot he told me."

"People sometimes do that."

"Right. Still." Laney wrapped her arms around her chest. "Email sucks. You can't see a person's face. You can't feel them."

"May I?"

Laney handed over the laptop.

Rajini read the email for herself. "This is way nicer than what my brothers ever wrote when I was away," she said after a while.

Laney snorted. She could hardly imagine Niwat or Jao chatting on email, even though they loved Rajini, and she loved them back.

"Maybe he was in a hurry. It's a nice letter."

"Too nice. Too...something," Laney said. "What if he's sick? Or Mama? He'd be stupidly cheerful like this."

Rajini rolled her eyes and handed the computer back. "Honey," she said. "After we go to the bank tomorrow, I'm taking you for a manicure. You are way too over-wrought."

Was she being overwrought? Something wrong with Charlie. Two hours until the train. Walls closing in. The Shinsurin brothers turning out violent. Rajini lying—to protect her brothers, maybe, but still lying. Though their lies were more dangerous to Devilwell than to her.

She looked at the letter again. Devilwell would be able to tell her what was up. He saw more in words than what was there. That was his job.

She looked up to see Rajini examining her. "Honey," Rajini said. "I have a recommendation."

"What?"

"I know you said you didn't want to, but..." She pulled a small box from her purse. A DVD. My Fair Lady. Laney's favorite.

"Oh," Laney said. "I can't."

Rajini stuck out her bottom lip. "Why not?"

Laney was starting to forget about why it was so important to be a brown bird. What could another day hurt? If she held out just one more day she could leave with a passport and money. And maybe make Maxwell look at Charlie's emails.

She sat back. "What the hell. Put it in."

CHAPTER TWENTY

The guards who came on Sunday morning at six a.m. were inconveniently awake and alert the entire day, though they did bring Macmillan a bowl of rice around dinner time, which he gobbled up hungrily. Ten more and he might actually get full. A number of people tramped past, but happily, Dok didn't show up.

The night guards came on at ten.

Things calmed at midnight. Soon after, the kitchen boy delivered the hopefully-drugged coffees. Even if Macmillan hadn't heard him bring them past, he would've smelled the aroma. He waited twenty minutes, then freed himself and headed back to the console room, pleased to see the guards flopped back in their chairs. They'd be out for hours.

He set the video feeds to the basement entrances so that he'd know if anybody was coming and started compressing and downloading the files from the day. While that was happening, he started to search the video to see if Laney had left. She was absent from the lobby the whole morning.

Good.

Macmillan was just allowing himself to hope she'd taken his advice and gotten out of there when the camera

captured her heading across the lobby floor with Rajini
Shinsurin.

They stopped at the front desk to talk with the clerks.
Macmillan groaned when the cupcake was brought out.

Her birthday.

Then the gift come out.

"*No!*" he whispered at the screen. "*Don't get sentimental
on me, Laney!*" A lost cause. A little birthday fete would
mean the world to Laney. The feeling of being buoyed by
the love of other people. Of belonging. A sense of family.
She would let it color her judgment.

The little group laughed. Laney was saying something
funny; he didn't have sound, but he found himself smiling
all the same. She felt happy with these people, especially
the girls behind the desk. He remembered what that was
like, to live in that country where people were your
meaning and your security. He watched the little group as
an exile might, longing sharp as a knife.

He fast forwarded the lobby tapes.

The next time the cameras picked her up she was
heading through the lobby with her guitar, ready to do
her show. She stopped to talk with Niwat. Niwat would
see right through those fake smiles.

There were no cameras in the courtyard, but he fast-
forwarded the lobby feed until he saw her heading back
up, presumably to her room.

What are you doing?

Preparing for her flight, of course. Getting her ducks
in a row—passport, money. Which is what got people
killed. He'd do his best to protect her if things got bloody

with Jazzman, but this ex-husband and his men were the wild cards. Quickly, he got back to work. The sooner he identified Jazzman, the sooner he could get out of his cell and help Laney.

He started sampling the speech of the newly arrived guests. Many of them had ended up in the mezzanine lounge. Thorne really was the social butterfly; two of his Hangman pals had shown up, and they argued about soccer with the Finns. Thorne punched one of the men. A fight ensued.

Thorne would lead Hangman someday—everyone knew it—and then things would really get wild. Dax would surely have him taken out by then.

The restaurant recordings revealed that one of the Saudis had some of Jazzman's speech characteristics, especially with his articles, but Jazzman switched p's and b's in an unusual way that ruled the Saudi out. What's more, this Saudi didn't have facility enough with English to be Jazzman. Changing up idioms for effect—like saying "vim and vitriol" for "vim and vigor"—was for more fluent English speakers.

He ruled out some of the newly arrived Somalis, too, as well as a contingent from Canada and some of the New Tong out of Texas.

At two in the morning, real time, he spotted Laney heading into the lobby.

She'd twisted her thick, dark hair into a bun and donned slim eyeglasses. Another one of her sad little disguises. With her prim, dark shirt and skirt she looked like she was going for a clichéd librarian look, but then there were those knee-high nylons.

She settled herself down at the community computers and got to work. She seemed to be printing something out. He touched the screen. The bigness and sweetness of his feelings for her made him uncomfortable and he thought to force his focus away from her, just to get back under control, but he found he didn't want to.

Activity in another sector finally distracted him. A small army of maids stripped the bedding off the bed in the honeymoon suite on the 17th floor. The bedding looked clean—why strip it off? Special request? Special treatment?

Macmillan's heart raced. Was Jazzman about to arrive?

A bottle of scotch was set out next to two lowball glasses. Two champagne flutes appeared. Flowers were brought in. Did Jazzman travel with a female companion?

New activity on the rooftop lounge, which was a kind of open air patio at one end of the sprawling roof. It had been unused all this time, but here in the middle of the night, a crew was hosing down the tiles and setting up the bar. White canopies, presumably for shade during the day, were unfurled under the moonlight. The far end of the roof was just a lot of open space but the crew was clearing off equipment and setting up lights around the perimeter. Landing lights. A helipad. That's where the weapon would go.

Macmillan sat up. Jazzman was on his way.

The rooftop bar. It was brilliant. If they got some live music going, it would be impossible to hear the negotiations. He glanced again at the honeymoon suite. It seemed a bit obvious for Jazzman to stay there, but Dax said Jazzman would want superior accommodations. Dax was always right about such things.

Dax also predicted that Jazzman would stash the codes and schematics somewhere in Bangkok as a kind of insurance policy before he sold the weapon. The buyer would get access to the information after Jazzman was safe.

But with this kind of surveillance, Macmillan would surely identify Jazzman before he made any deal. Once they had him, they'd do what it took to retrieve the whole package: the weapon, the schematics, and the codes.

A door creaked. Somebody was coming in the back way.

Macmillan sprung up from his seat and hurried back to the cell room, trying to keep the pressure on the balls of his feet instead of his toes. He snicked the door shut and clapped the leg irons around his ankles.

Quiet steps approached.

Laney.

Damn.

He shut his eyes and lay down. The outer door opened and closed, but there was no clinking of keys being taken off the hook. She wouldn't be entering the cell. At least there was that.

"Back for more?" Macmillan said after he'd sensed her standing there a while.

"I need your opinion on something. Your professional opinion. I was reading your book some more, the part on how you can draw conclusions about a person's mental state from his sentences and such..." She paused.

He opened his eyes. There she stood just outside the bars, clutching a sheaf of papers. "In the market for some bunk designed to hornswoggle folks?" he asked. "I have the best there is, you know. Once you've been hornswoggled by me, you won't want it from anybody else."

"I just need your professional opinion. I'm worried about somebody and I have his emails here..." Her quiet words were laced with desperation, papers clutched to her chest. The emails had been written by somebody she loved. Not Rolly, then.

That was Laney. A warrior for the people she cared about.

"If you valued my opinion you'd be long gone," he said.

"Why do you care so much if I take your advice?"

"I need the people around me to do my bidding. It's in the killer job description."

"How about you just give me a professional goddamn opinion on something?"

A professional opinion. He'd give her anything. He flashed again on the medieval map. She would pull him right off the edge of the world if he wasn't careful. "As you see, my business facilities in here are substandard. And you know what this means. Yet another star off for the Hotel Des Roses—"

"Shut up! God, I get that you don't want me around, okay? I need your help."

"I'm done helping you."

She clutched the sheaf, standing at the edge of the patch of light cast by the bulb over the door. "These are emails from my brother, Charlie," she said in a small voice. "He's become...weird, and I'm worried about him. I want you to read between the lines like you do and tell me if you think he's depressed or in trouble, maybe hiding something, or just what you think."

He sighed as though bored, but really, he couldn't tear his gaze from her, because she was standing there with her emails and her despair and her stockings and he was half in love with her.

"You know that stuff you said in your book about the Chinese amulet in the import store? How you can tell more about the place where it was made from the box it was shipped in and the way it was addressed, the packing material..."

"I'm familiar with it."

"I know in your book, you'd run this on the computer," she said. "Compare it to a giant corpus. And make those comparative tables of yours. But I'm pretty sure you can do it without."

"Aren't you the attentive reader." He eyed the sheaf. It would take him an hour just to read through, getting the lay of the land. A proper analysis would take even more time. Did she mean to come back down for the results later? Tomorrow night? Like hell he'd give her an excuse to stay yet another day, and he had to get back to the console.

"Your professional opinion."

"I can give you my professional opinion this instant," he said. "My professional opinion is that you're being a fool. Here you are, sensing trouble, and you come down here asking me to analyze emails? Get out of my sight."

"Can't you just read these?" She knelt and slid the thick sheaf into his cage, watching him warily, as though he might break his chains and come right through the bars. "Just tell me if you think there's something wrong."

"Something's wrong."

"You have to look at the letters."

"No, I don't. You wouldn't be down here consulting with somebody like me if you didn't know in your heart that something was wrong. You want me to give you some comforting explanation—*he's just a bit blue; his favorite team is doing poorly.* Or, *he has a hurt finger, so it's merely hard for him to type.* Well, there isn't one. He's your brother, you don't need me to tell you when something's wrong." With his foot he shoved the papers back out, scattering them across the floor. "Furthermore, my professional opinion is that something in your environment tripped your instinct, but you're looking for excuses not to leave, because deep down, you can't bear to be alone. That's what will get you caught in the end."

She gathered up the papers.

"You're a wet dream for a killer like me," he continued, dying inside. "The kind of person I love to hunt."

She looked disgusted when she stood again. *Good.*

"You'll be somebody's papaya very soon," he added.

She looked like she was about to cry. She muttered under her breath—a colorful insult, no doubt, then she stuffed the sheaf of papers down deep in the garbage pail and stormed out.

Relief swept through him. Surely she'd leave now.

He shook off the leg irons—they hadn't been locked—and he let himself out of the cage. He grabbed the emails from the garbage on his way out. She'd shoved them under some newspapers, but it was still conspicuous. He shadowed her up to the surface yet again. Even in his bare feet, it was painful to move so quickly.

When she was safely out, he brought the emails to the console room and hid them at the bottom of the office trash.

Nothing more was happening in the suite, but Laney appeared on the lobby feed, chatting with her friends at the front desk. At one point she moved behind the desk and discreetly returned the key. Trying to be sneaky, trying to keep them out of trouble. How had she lasted so damn long on the run?

He glanced at the trash can where he'd buried the emails, hoping her brother was okay.

Focus.

Macmillan borrowed one of the drugged guard's phones and left a message with their mission leader Douglas about the activity in the honeymoon suite and the roof—they needed to get eyes on those areas from the outside if possible. After that, he went through the recordings, listening to the new arrivals speak and ruling them out. Three-thirty in the morning his downloads were done. She still hadn't left.

The vaguely familiar-looking Indian businessman lurked in the lobby, as usual. At one point he buttonholed the bellboy. It was out of range of audio, but money passed between them. The bellboy seemed animated, frightened. The man made a beeline to the elevator bank. Hit the down button. Either working out or hitting the business services room.

He turned his attention back to the honeymoon suite. Still nothing. His mind whirled as he flipped through the feeds. There was something he wasn't seeing. Something *more*.

What?

As a linguist and an Associate, Macmillan had always made his best discoveries when he'd stepped away from a problem. He stood and stretched. Checked the guards' breathing. Took off his glasses and rubbed his eyes. Finally his gaze fell upon the dustbin where he'd stuffed Laney's sheaf of emails.

Why not.

He grabbed them and sat, riffling through. Emails in chronological order, all dated. He kept an eye on the consoles and set to work.

First he scanned over them as a group, getting a feel for the brother's language, looking at pronoun usage and various points of markedness. The writing in the early letters seemed quite balanced, the words of a man in control. Laney's brother cared a great deal for her.

There were bits of Laney's letters included at the ends of Charlie's letters; these he read for context, though he found it difficult to stay analytical; he felt like he was falling into her words, her reality. She described the bustle of Bangkok in bright, fresh terms, and seemed greatly concerned about the amputees who sold dried fish on the streets. Everything touched her—the dragons, the architecture, the people she worked with. Her sense of humor came into full bloom with her brother, but her despair and her longing for connection was keenest here, too, and Macmillan had the uncanny feeling that he was touching her across time and space. Certain texts used to do that for him, give him the sense of camaraderie with another soul. He'd thought that was gone from his life.

But this thing with Laney was more. He'd gotten used to having nothing to lose, but she was pulling him back into the frightening, beautiful madness of caring. He thought about that pretty butterscotch gleam in her eyes, but when you really looked, you got that they were the eyes of a rebel. She didn't accept the presented surface; she plunged her poet's fist right through.

Stop. Focus.

He forced himself to read on, and quickly decided that she'd been right to feel uneasy. Charlie sounded like a loving, conscientious brother in the earlier letters, but there'd been a shift about a month back. The later letters contained the right phrases—*I love you, sis,* for example, but it wasn't the same. He spread out the two batches of letters. On the right he had the before-the-shift group, on the left he put after-the-shift. He took out a pen.

Layout and sentence length were similar in the two groups, but the earlier batch doubled the question and exclamation marks, mirroring Laney's letters. The later ones didn't. He circled instances. He then turned his attention to the function words—meaningless helper words: *will, and, up, or,* etc. He quickly crossed them out in two random *before* samples, leaving only the lexical words, those that carried meaning.

Macmillan turned his attention to the *after* batch, striking out the function words. On comparison, he found that the lexical density after the shift was markedly lower.

Low lexical density often indicated deception.

Something else: receive was spelled correctly in the *after* letters, but not in the *before* letters.

But that wasn't the most troubling difference. There was a single space between sentences in the *before-the-shift* group; the *after* letters featured a double space between sentences. How had he not seen that right off? A double space was something somebody who attended school before the advent of word processors would use, or somebody who'd had an old-fashioned English teacher. It definitely wasn't a habit you changed one day; particularly not going from one to two spaces.

It was then he knew: the emails had been written by two different people. She'd been emailing with an imposter for well over a month.

He went to the content. The earlier letters asked lots of questions. *How are the S's treating you? Any sign of R? Are you getting any fresh air? Tell me your fave new food!* The later letters were controlling: *Stay put. You are so lucky to be in a safe haven. Such a comfort to know you are safe within those walls.*

Was it that ex of hers? Rolly? Except the man wouldn't have email access from prison. One thing was clear: the imposter wanted her to stay put—more and more urgently as time went on.

Somebody was coming for her. Rolly or one of his men.

But no, no, no...there was something else, something about the sentence construction. The new writer was trying to mimic the brother, even going so far as to lift entire phrases, but Macmillan felt something else in the sentence rhythm. Something familiar.

Damn.

He went back over, scanning for a different set of markers now. In two separate instances, the new writer used the word *that* with proper nouns when no article was called for. *That Brittany Spears is a whore. That Mayor O'Hannon will burn in hell.*

It was something Jazzman had done in the conference call. He'd done it only twice, and yet...

Macmillan sat up and quickly riffled back through, focusing in on the packing material of the language. He found a certain construction—*Would that you were here.* Then, *Would that I had a bike*—construction that was rare among English speakers—fussy, even. Jazzman had used it and it was one of the things that had made Macmillan suspect Jazzman might be a native German speaker, or had perhaps learned English in a more formal setting. He found two more instances of it in after-the-shift emails. The rate at which the imposter used it well exceeded any corpus.

Could it be?

She'd said Rolly had entered prison just over two years ago.

Two and a half years ago, the TZ-5 had disappeared, along with whoever stole it.

Heart pounding, Macmillan went back to the date the imposter took up the correspondence. It was right around the time Jazzman had held the conference call announcing the auction.

Energy blazed through him the way it always did when he hit on an outrageous new theory.

Were Jazzman and Rolly the same man?

Laney had told him Rolly had cops who'd do his bidding. Men working for him even from prison. Could the Shinsurins be among that group? Had he simply parked Laney with the Shinsurins until he could get out of prison? Had he arranged the auction using the name of Jazzman, and then killed her brother and taken over his email account?

He looked up at the honeymoon suite and his blood froze. Champagne in the ice bucket.

For Rolly. For Jazzman. Two glasses.

Jazzman and Laney. The package.

Alarm swept through him like wildfire. He sprung up from his seat.

Laney.

If he was right, Laney was in grave danger. He had to get her out of there. Protect her. He couldn't sit around and wait. Anyway, if Rolly was Jazzman, Laney could confirm it.

He stripped down to his T-shirt and stuffed his bloody brown shirt in the garbage. Gently and quickly as he could, he removed the largest guard's jacket and put it on. He took his utility belt, trying to keep his movements smooth—the drug would be wearing off soon. He grabbed a hat, tucking in his blond hair, wishing the Shinsurins had given their basement guards guns instead of just pepper spray and radios. Bare feet would be conspicuous as hell, but his toes were too wrecked for boots.

It was then he heard it—just a whisper of a movement down the hall. Too stealthy to be Laney. He looked at the monitors. The Indian businessman. Was he lost? What was he doing on LL2? When he caught the dull glint of a gun he realized where he'd seen that face.

Anders. Just feet away.

No weapons. Too late to run. Macmillan stuffed his hair firmly and completely under the hat, pulled up his collar to cover his hairline, and took a seat, resting his head on the desk, face down, just like the other two guards. He forced himself to be perfectly still even though his every instinct drove him to tear out of there and get to Laney. Because he'd die before he reached the street. Anders was a true pro, a man who'd fought before he could walk, and he'd be armed head to toe. Macmillan had nothing but pepper spray. And he was raised a scholar, not a killer. He'd come to killing late.

Macmillan's heart pounded. He was unarmed against a superior killer. He needed luck. Surprise. Something.

He felt Anders come in and move past him. He peeked out the corner of his eye to see Anders standing over the guard without the jacket, Sig P229 with silencer in hand. Anders took hold of the guard's hair and yanked his head up, then let it bang down. It was a wonder the man didn't wake up. Lucky, too. Anders would kill the man if he woke up.

Anders picked up the coffee cup and sniffed, then put it back down.

Macmillan could follow the track of Anders' thoughts exactly. He'd been to the empty cell. He'd figure Macmillan had gotten the guards drugged so that he could escape. There was no reason for Anders to think Macmillan would stay. And his hair wasn't showing.

But there were only two coffee cups for three drugged guards. Anders would notice that. It would be even worse if he noticed Macmillan's bare feet. Macmillan wished he could move them deeper into the shadows under the desk, but he didn't dare.

His mind clouded with images of Laney, hurt and scared. The way her eyes would look. Laney running, caught. Beaten. Worse. He felt like a volcano was in him.

Tap.

Anders had discovered the video feeds.

Macmillan felt his body clench.

Tap.

Anders was using the feeds to determine where and when Macmillan left. Who he'd been with.

Tap.

Tap tap.

Silence.

It began as a tickle of awareness. Maybe a subconscious realization that the keyboard taps had been too far apart that last time. A sense of stillness that hadn't been there before.

Tap.

Anders had noticed his feet.

Tap.

Macmillan's heart raced; he didn't need eyes in the back of his head to know when a gun was on him.

It was at that moment, that very moment, that one of the guards groaned. A chair squeaked. "*Aao...aao...*"

Macmillan slit his eyes enough to see Anders swinging the weapon around to the guard. He'd shoot. He'd shoot all three of them.

Macmillan yanked the pepper spray from his belt and exploded from his chair and right into Anders, spraying the assassin in the eyes and knocking his arm as a wild shot went off.

Anders coughed and gasped, blinded.

Macmillan grabbed Anders's arm and brought his knee up into the killer's elbow with crushing force. He heard the bone crack as the gun clattered to the floor.

Even blinded, even with a destroyed elbow, Anders kept coming. He landed a left-handed blow on Macmillan's throat—just a hair to the right and it would've been lethal.

Macmillan hit back, coughing, eyes watering from the spray, barely able to see or breathe himself.

Anders fell. Macmillan was on him with a final blow that knocked him out cold. Macmillan cuffed Anders' wrists to different metal fixtures and raced off with the man's Sig shoved into the utility belt, trying not to think too hard about the fact that he didn't finish Anders off.

He should've killed him, but something in him had shifted back in that cell, back when he'd told Laney about the men he'd killed. He hated the man he showed to her that night.

Two minutes later, Macmillan was slipping out onto the dark sidewalk, throat raw, eyes stinging from the pepper spray. He melted into the shadows to avoid a trio of drunks helping each other down the block, then he picked the back gate padlock and crept through the pool area, sidestepping empty lounge chairs until he reached the pergola.

Stealth was key now; if Jazzman was on his way, the Shinsurins would be out and about with the guards on high alert.

He scaled the back of the hotel; not easy with each floor wider than the one below it. When he hit the third floor he began to move sideways, balcony to balcony, using the railings as monkey bars until he got to hers.

Room dark. He swung his legs over.

The patio table and chairs they'd knocked down during the fight had been put back right. She'd mentioned sitting on her porch in those emails to Charlie. She needlepointed out there, and watched sunrises. She'd made herself a life here. Of course it was hard to leave.

He picked the lock on her sliding door and slipped inside, shutting it quietly behind him, standing perfectly still as he let his eyes get used to the dark.

She slept on her stomach, sheets tangled around her legs and waist, her back a pale expanse of white undershirt, hair a dark mass to one side of her head. Face calm in sleep.

He needed to tell her about her brother and get her out.

Her brother.

He felt suddenly as if he was looking down at a version of himself the moment before his life went dark. There was a time when he would've given anything to go back to that blissful, ignorant *before*, to spend just one more minute there.

She stirred.

"Laney," he whispered—gently. It wouldn't do to alarm her.

She turned, reflexively pulling the sheets up around her, eyes wide.

He clapped a hand over her mouth before the scream could come out. "Shhh."

She tore at his fingers, kicking him. Confusion in her eyes. Fear.

No way could he carry her out of there; he needed her cooperating. "You're okay. Just don't scream."

She kept twisting.

He grabbed her wrist. "You're okay. I'm not here to hurt you."

She stilled, nostrils flaring, in and out, in and out.

"I'm taking away my hand," he said softly. Slowly he removed it.

She sucked in a breath, preparing to scream. He clapped it back on.

CHAPTER TWENTY-ONE

She tore at his fingers. He was suffocating her! He'd escaped dressed as a guard and snuck into her room! She tried to bite him.

"Okay, I deserve this," he said. "What with the papaya bit and all."

She struggled and thrashed, but he was solid as a mountain. She stopped hitting him and brought a knee into his ribs.

"Oof." He seemed to collapse a titch, but he didn't release her; instead he climbed over her further, straddling her, which prevented any more knees. "Sorry," he said.

Sorry? He was on her. Holding her down. Suffocating her. Her heart beat wildly.

"I'm here to help you, but you need to calm down."

She tried again for the rib but he had her legs and arms pinned.

"I read the emails," he said softly.

She glared at the monster, unsure what to do.

"One question. Shake your head yes or no."

She watched his cool blue eyes. Some part of her wanted him still. Some part of her liked him there on top of her. So screwed up.

He sucked in a ragged breath. "Did you ever hear Rolly use the word *vim* with a word other than *vigor?*"

"Mmm!" She struggled against his hand. Was he crazy?

"*Vim*," he repeated, "unaccompanied by *vigor*. *Vim* and something else." Like that was the problem of the universe.

"Mmm!"

"I'll know it if you're about to scream. Before you do," he warned.

"Mmm-*mmm*," the best *okay* she could manage.

He removed his hand.

"Get the hell off!" She tried to push off his heavy bulk. "You give me your answer on the letters or you get out of here. 'Cause I'm not talking about Rolly."

He didn't budge. "Think. Does he like to modify sayings?"

She stilled. *How did he know?*

"It's not a difficult question. Yes or no."

"Yeah, he used to change around sayings. He thought that was real clever. Why?"

"Did you ever notice his b's and p's sounding alike? And like shots. *Panorama. Banana.*"

"Am I supposed to be impressed that you listened to a tape of Rolly or something?"

His face darkened. "Does he ever over-explain and trail off with the word *so*. For example, *This new blender is powerful. The best in its class, so...*" He continued, "Or, *I don't like tomatoes. They taste like hell, so...*"

"What the fuck?" She wriggled underneath him. "Get out." It was a nightmare, hearing Rolly's talk coming out of Maxwell. "Get out."

"Did he take trips to Panama just before he went inside?"

She narrowed her eyes. "Yeah."

He got off her. "Get dressed. We're out of here."

She felt shaky. "I'm not going anywhere with you."

"It's me or Rolly," he said.

"Rolly's in prison."

He tossed jeans at her. "I examined the emails. Do you know who you were emailing with? It didn't feel familiar?"

Ice crackled through her veins.

"It wasn't your brother," he said.

"Yes, it was."

"Not for the last five weeks. The change occurred about five weeks ago. Am I right?"

She hadn't told him that. "You so full of it, Devilwell—"

He spoke right over her. "Did you ever notice Rolly's fondness for *that* as an intensifying article with proper nouns? For example, he'll say *That Laney drinks beer* when he could just as easily say, *Laney drinks beer.* It's common to only 4% of the population. It occurred twice in recent emails from your brother. *That Brittany Spears is a whore. That Mayor O'Hannon will burn in hell.*"

No. She'd known something was off, but...Rolly? "They don't let prisoners email."

"No," he said. "They don't, do they?"

Every nerve on her skin prickled up. "You think Rolly's out. No way, my brother would've found a way to warn me if...oh, my God!" She felt the blood drain from her whole entire soul. "My brother."

"Come on. I'm getting you out of here."

"No," she whispered as the world careened around her. "I know my own brother." Her eyes misted up. "It was my brother, he's just depressed or something."

"Did you notice how very, very badly he wanted to make sure you stayed put in the last few weeks? And the sentences. The music of the language."

"You're messing with me."

He grabbed her shoulders, looked into her eyes. "You feel language the way other people can't, Laney. It's why you showed me the emails. *Would that we had Twisty-Kreme here.* That's Rolly talk, not Charlie talk."

"Oh, my God." She shook out of his arms, feeling like she might throw up. Rolly inside her brother's emails like a spider in her brain.

"He could be down there, Laney. In the lobby," he said.

She went to her dresser and pulled out her gun. She looked at Maxwell. "I know you're right. But that doesn't mean I suddenly trust you."

"Let's get out of here and you can decide on the trust part later. Grab what you need and let's go."

"He's not dead. I'd know if my brother was dead." She shoved her wallet into her backpack along with her phone, her iPod. "Crap, I think I might throw up."

"Ignore it."

Her brother. She stuffed in her clothes from the day before.

"Put on your jeans, a dark shirt, and sneakers. Now," he said. She couldn't believe how calm he was. "What's Rolly's full name?"

"Jerry Lee Drucker." She pulled on her clothes as Devilwell took out a phone and called somebody, mumbling something about Jerry Lee Drucker and Jazzman. She was glad for the icy cool Devilwell. He was the ally she needed now. He would kill.

Another thought hit her and she spun around. "The Shinsurins are in on it."

"Most likely."

Rajini.

She shoved on a shoe, mind whirling at the betrayal. She knew he was right. It was then she caught sight of his bare feet—they were red, crusted with something dark. "Oh, my God! Your feet!"

"It's nothing. Go. Other shoe."

She slammed on her other shoe. "All this time I've been like a bird in a cage. Like a stupid singing fool."

"Not like a stupid singing fool. Like a survivor."

"A survivor who sings cornpone songs." She stood.

"Well, there's that."

She hauled off to hit him. He caught her arm and yanked her up. The air felt thick and wild—at least to her. "Put everything out of your mind but doing what I say," he said calmly. He shoved her pack at her. There was still room in it, so she nestled Amy in and slung it over her shoulders. "Charlie's not dead. I know you think so, but he's not."

"Ready?" Like he didn't believe it.

A sound at the front—the doorknob jiggling, followed by the clink of keys.

With lightning speed, Macmillan moved across the room, shoved a chair under the knob, then grabbed her hand and pulled her out onto the porch, into the steamy heat of the night.

"Jump onto my back. Now."

He turned and offered his back. She did as he asked, wrapping her arms around his neck and her legs around his middle.

A hiss of pain. "Avoid the ribs if possible."

She shifted her legs down. "Are you hurt?"

"Hold on. I'm climbing sideways."

She held on, trying not to look down as he climbed over the railing. A little wall jutted out between porches; she and Sirikit next door used to lean over and talk to each other, but she'd never imagined traversing it. She clutched him harder as he straddled the wall. He grasped the railings on both sides before he swung them all the way over.

A pounding from the inside of her room. Trying to get in.

"Crap," she said as he scooted down and swung around the wall to the next porch, then to the next. Like the whole hotel was a jungle gym.

Sweat poured off her face and palms. "You're getting slippery," she said.

"Just hold on," he said, moving like a monkey to the next porch.

"Where are we going?"

"The Sawadee Palace," he panted, moving to the next porch. "I hear it's excellent. I understand there's not a leg iron in the place."

A gunshot blasted out. The sound was so loud, it almost rocked her right off his back.

"Ignore it," he whispered.

A man screamed, then moaned. A chorus of street dogs set up barking.

"Hellbuckets." She clutched on harder.

"We're okay." He kept on. Senseless, muffled words came from the direction of her patio. He got them around to the next patio.

"Let's go in and run out the hall," she said.

"Bad idea." He straddled the next wall.

Bang. This bullet hit nearby. Maxwell sucked in a breath.

"They're shooting at us!"

"Not to kill. They're forcing us in."

"Maxwell! You're bleeding!"

He examined his arm when they got to the other side. "Ricochet spray. Skin deep." He climbed over the rail and let her off on a porch. She felt grateful for the solid surface. "Stay back." Maxwell leaned out and shot back.

"They know where we are, now." She gave him her gun and he tucked it in his waistband.

"That's why we have to go down. They won't expect it."

"It's three stories!"

"Just to the porch below."

"How?" The building's V-shape made going down as hard as going up.

"I'll jump down. All you have to do is lower yourself and I'll pull you in."

Maxwell hopped back to the outside of the rail and climbed down, so that he hung by his fingertips from the concrete slab that composed the floor of the porch. He began to swing, and then he disappeared. She heard the thud of his landing, then a voice. "Hang down and I'll grab you. Hurry."

She scrambled over the rail and paused, fixated on the rocks and bushes below. A person would die, falling that far. And her hands were so sweaty!

"Hang down," Maxwell said. "You can do this. I'll grab your legs."

She could hear voices inside over the neighborhood dogs. Somebody pounding at the door. Other voices even nearer. Somebody had been sleeping in there. She crouched on the outside of the porch railing.

Shouts in Thai. A crash.

She wiped her hands on her shirt, then crouched on the outside of the bars and lowered her legs. She felt Maxwell's arms close around her knees. "All the way down," he said.

A deep voice. "Oh, no, you don't."

She jerked her gaze up to meet Rolly's angry eyes. He leaned over the railing. She gasped, grip frozen on the bars.

"Emmaline." His warning tone. Her stomach clenched and curdled as he clapped his hands around her wrists, fingers like iron vices.

"No!"

"Yes," he growled, face hard under his dark flat-top.

She began to struggle, but guards appeared on either side of him. They grabbed her arms and started pulling her up, right out of Maxwell's grip.

"No!" She twisted and squirmed. "Maxwell! No!" They pulled her all the way over the rail and onto the porch. Rolly looped an arm around her neck.

Movement out of the corner of her eye. She saw fingertips on the edge of the slab.

Maxwell.

Strong hands clamped the railing. Forearms bulged with muscles as Maxwell's head appeared. He was heaving himself up.

One of the guards leveled a gun at him.

"Maxwell, watch out!" she screamed, trying to get at the guard.

"Do it," Rolly said.

He aimed right at Maxwell's head.

And shot.

Maxwell disappeared.

A crash below.

She stared at the place his hands had been, dizzy with shock. Maxwell. Gone. Shot. She felt like the whole world got turned upside down and shaken out.

She tried to twist away from Rolly, who hauled her up to his angular face, fingers gripping her upper arms, lips curled, eyes angry. He pinned her to the rough, nubby patio wall. She breathed in the stink of his acrid sweat—booze sweat, she used to call it. She'd forgotten about that smell. He'd put on a lot of muscle in prison. And she couldn't move.

Maxwell gone. Dead.

"This could have been so much easier," he whispered, rage and pain oozing out of him. "Come on, now."

"Hell, no," she whispered.

A wild look passed across his face and he tightened his grip. "You're my wife, Emmaline." Pain in Rolly's eyes. He would hurt her now. She felt the old fear creeping its icy fingers over her. "You're my wife, Emmaline."

Futilely she kicked at him—she needed to get away and get to Maxwell, if only just to touch him one last time. Maybe he hadn't died instantly. He'd be alone. Afraid.

Tears fell from her eyes as Rolly wrapped both hands around her neck. She stopped kicking and clawed at his fingers as he dragged her inside and through the dark blur of somebody's room. She stumbled along, choking.

They emerged into the bright hallway and moved clumsily through the jumble of people. She strained for air as they entered the elevator—she and Harken and two guards. And Rolly.

"Deal with her hands," Rolly said, releasing her. She coughed and sputtered, and in a flash she was pinned to the elevator wall, cheek rubbing against the carpeted panel, her hands bound behind her back with something sharp and cutting.

She stayed there, eyes squinched shut, tears flowing as the elevator rose.

Maxwell. Gone. You didn't survive being shot in the head and falling three stories.

If only she'd been braver. If only she'd hurried when he'd asked her to. She'd frozen instead.

She vowed never to freeze again.

Rolly dragged her into a room, shut the door behind them, and pushed her up against it, choking her again. "You're wearing black. I like you in white. First thing, we're going to put you in white." Then he claimed her mouth in a suffocating, stinking kiss.

She bit his lip. He jerked away and she kicked him in the balls—and connected. He stumbled away and she tried to open the door with her hands behind her back. She'd escape or die. She'd never freeze for him again. Ever!

He grabbed her hair and threw her to the floor. Without her hands to break her fall, she fell on her shoulder and banged her head—hard.

He turned her onto her back and placed his boot on her chest, pressing until she could barely breathe, until her shoulders felt squished behind her. He had a hammer.

"Go ahead, kill me," she said.

"That's not exactly what I had in mind, Emmaline."

"Emmaline's gone. I'm Laney."

He just frowned.

"I'll kill you," she said. "I'll never stop trying."

"You'll stop trying," he said calmly. "You'll see."

Laney's heart banged in her chest. He was going to do something with the hammer. Maybe break her hands. Or her feet? His cock was hard in his pants. She fought back the urge to beg him for leniency. Never again.

Just then there was a knock at the door.

"What?" He barked, not taking his eyes from her.

"It's important." Harken's voice.

"Better be."

Harken came in and handed Rolly a phone.

"Yeah," Rolly said into it, eyes roaming up and down her body. He frowned, then a slow smile spread over his face. "Decisions, decisions," Rolly said. "Seems there's a body on the hotel grounds that needs to be gone before daybreak. What should we do? Throw it to the dogs, or put it in the trash?"

She glared, fighting back a heaving sob.

Rolly watched her. She knew what he was looking for—a kind of death in her eyes. The point where she stopped fighting. Once upon a time she would have crumbled for him, just in the interest of self-preservation. She realized with some surprise that now it wasn't even an option. She'd go down fighting. She'd fight him to the death. She'd do it for herself—and for Maxwell.

Rolly flicked his gaze away, listening to the caller. "Handle it," he said. "You don't want me to have to come out there."

She bit back the tears. She hadn't known Maxwell that long, but the way they fit together—it felt ancient, like they'd been connected for eons, like showing up in each other's lives was just the tip of things.

He'd tried to rescue her, and now he was dead.

Rolly handed the phone back to Harken, who pocketed it.

"Leave us."

Harken left.

Rolly picked up the hammer. "Now, where were we?"

CHAPTER TWENTY-TWO

Macmillan awoke to the feel of his shoulders being wrenched clear out of their sockets and excruciating pain in his toes as he was dragged over what felt like cut glass. He groaned.

"You awake, buddy?" Douglas. "Can you walk?"

Macmillan tried to speak as Fedor and Douglas let him go. He gripped Fedor's arm, swaying.

He straightened his glasses. They were in the alley behind the Des Roses pool, heading for the street. "Laney," he grated.

Fedor looped his arm around his shoulders. "Come on."

"I have to get back there."

"You can't," Douglas said. "Place is full of muscle. Shinsurin's and Jazzman's both. How do you feel? Anything broken?"

"Nah." Macmillan's thoughts raced back to the scene on the porch. He'd let go of the rail just as soon as he saw the tendons in the back of the guard's hand activate, escaping the bullet by milliseconds. He hadn't counted on blacking out. He'd meant to slip back in.

"How long was I out?"

"Minute or two," Douglas said. "Good job, by the way. You did it—you identified Jazzman. Jerry Lee Drucker.

We've got Associates assembling. Don't worry about Laney, we're taking him down."

"Did you aim for that pergola?" Fedor asked, urging him onward. "Those fucking vines broke your fall."

"You were there?"

"We heard the gunfire," Douglas said. "Figured you were involved."

They came to the corner of the alley.

"Hold up," Fedor muttered. He moved to the end of the alley, checking the street.

Macmillan tried to focus through the pain. *Keep it together,* he told himself. "I have to get back in there."

"I can't let you do that. We'll draw him out and take him the right way," Douglas said. "Look at me."

Macmillan looked at him.

Douglas pulled up his eyelids, one after another. "You have a concussion. You'll feel more stable in a bit. But your feet—bare feet—"

"Give me your piece. I have to get her out of there," Macmillan said.

"Don't be an idiot." Douglas grabbed his shirt. "Jazzman isn't going to kill your girl. Look what he went through to keep her on ice. We need her right where she is, occupying his attention."

"I have to—"

"No!" Douglas shook him, face close enough to kiss him. "You busted open his identity, Macmillan. You did it—you just saved a shitload of lives. Do you want to jeopardize that? This situation couldn't be more perfect—Rolly will be focused on her."

"No—"

"Yes," Douglas barked. "We're almost there. You remember what you always say? Anybody can carry out a plan when things go right. We Associates have the balls to stay the course when things go to hell."

Things were definitely going to hell.

"We almost have it," Douglas said. "We'll win."

Maybe. But Macmillan felt like he was still back in that dark jungle, unable to get to the people he loved. All he could see was the fear in Laney's eyes when she talked about Rolly. And now Rolly had her. He tried to shake out of Douglas's grip.

"Don't make me fight you," Douglas growled. "This is my mission and I won't let you fuck it up, got it?"

"*Yut! Aao, yut!* Stop!" Guards were pouring down the alley from the other direction.

"Fuck me," Douglas said. "Let's go." Douglas and Macmillan slipped out onto the street, practically running smack into Fedor, a pack of guards hot on their ass.

The three of them were across the street like a shot. They hit the ground and rolled behind a car. Pain speared through Macmillan's entire body. Still woozy.

Fedor crawled under the car on his belly, shooting.

Macmillan pulled out Anders's Sig. He peeked over the car trunk and took some shots at shadows. His aim was all off. Still dizzy. Douglas shot from the other side.

"Do we have backup? Where's Rio?" Macmillan asked.

"On a job," Douglas said. "Everyone else is twenty minutes away. We can take them. Jazzman doesn't need to know we have a small army in town."

Fedor pulled back. "Small army out *there*. Hold up." He reloaded, switching guns.

"I have to go back there."

"Not possible," Douglas said.

"I'll grab Laney and bring down Jazzman myself," Macmillan said. "The TZ's biometric security is all voice. *Voice.* I can crack into that, but I have to get her out of there first. I have to go back for her."

"How about you break the security after we have Jazzman?"

Fedor holstered up. "Let's scatter."

"Agreed," Douglas said. "Two directions along the cars. Fedor, you go up, we'll go down. Let's get to the truck and get out. Go, Fedor."

Macmillan took a shot at a darkened doorway as Fedor ran to a nearby car, then Fedor covered him and Douglas as they moved.

Somebody shot from a fire escape above and they rolled under a truck. A nearby pop and a hiss. Another pop and a hiss. Shooting out the tires. The truck body lowered.

"Dammit," Douglas said.

"Now or never," Macmillan rolled out and started shooting. They ran, covering themselves with wild shots. Amazing how a firefight cut your wooziness and pain. They slipped around a corner.

Douglas slid to the ground. "I'm hit."

"Where?"

"Belly. To the side, though..."

So maybe it had missed organs. "Keep up pressure. I've got you."

A guard came around the corner, clearly not expecting them to be waiting there. Macmillan grabbed him and head-butted him. The man crumpled in his arms. He kept him upright, using his body as a shield, shooting at the rest of the oncoming guards. The guard he held jerked in his arms.

Shot.

Macmillan felt the man's blood warm on his own face. He shot again and again. Their attackers dropped and scattered.

He had to get to Laney. Macmillan pulled the dead man back around the corner, lowered him to the ground, and knelt by Douglas. "Where's the truck?"

"Too far."

"Like hell. Are you putting pressure on it? Are you able to do that?"

"Of course."

Macmillan ripped off part of the guard's jacket and folded it into a pad for Douglas to hold. He pocketed the guard's gun and crouched. "Grab around my neck."

Douglas looped an arm around Macmillan's neck as Macmillan grabbed his legs and shoulders. He stood with Douglas in his arms, fighting to keep his balance. "The truck. Where?"

"Three blocks north."

Macmillan took off, arms straining, head pounding, toes screaming. He saw sparkles on the dark pavement ahead and knew he'd be going through glass, but he couldn't stop. He rounded a corner and a truck roared up.

Fedor.

Macmillan ran around to the passenger side, opened the door, and heaved Douglas in.

"Come on," Douglas urged. "Get in."

"I can't do that," Macmillan said.

"Are you crazy?" Douglas barked.

No. He was sane for maybe the first time in years. People he loved had been on that train, and he couldn't save them. He could save Laney.

He would save her.

"This is you fucking up the mission. This is you declaring war on Dax," Douglas bit out. "This is you ending things with the Association, Macmillan."

He shut the door with a glance at Fedor. The dark watchmaker wouldn't oppose him. Macmillan slapped the top of the truck and Fedor squealed out.

Macmillan melted into the shadows. Seconds later, a pair of cars sped up the dark street after them. Macmillan leveled Anders's piece and shot out the tires.

One. Two.

Convenient to have that silencer on there. They might not guess he was still out there. He wiped his face and squinted down at his bloody, torn-up feet.

The pain he could bear, it was the footprints that would sink him.

He ran back to where the dead guard lay. Nobody had found him yet. In another hour the city would wake up, and the cops would be all over this.

He pulled off the man's boots, conscious that he'd taken this man's life. That this man had people who loved him waiting at home. It was a Peter Maxwell thought.

Bad time to have Peter Maxwell thoughts.

He shoved on the socks and then the boots. The pain was fire and ice.

He grabbed the guard's gun and checked the magazine. Mostly full. He stowed it and slipped through the dark sidewalks until he reached the neon-lit strip across from the hotel. Alarms had been raised. He recognized two of the Shinsurin brothers flanked by guards. He could get by the clerks, but not the Shinsurins. He reversed course, considering the liquor hatch. Finally he decided to scale the back porches again. A stupid move.

Which is why they might not be expecting it.

He slipped into the pool area and hid behind a fat palm. A lone guard was out there smoking. Macmillan threw a rock into a dark corner and waited for the man to pass by. As soon as he was near, Macmillan jumped on him, covering his mouth and cracking his gun out of his hand with a neat arm destruction, then he smashed the man's head into a post, and locked him to the fence with his own cuffs. The man was out, but he gagged him all the same and rushed off.

He headed to the side and began to scale the drainage pipe. When he got to the fourth floor, he stole into a room and out into the hall, taking the stairwell all the way to the roof.

He pushed open the door; nobody up top, as he'd expected. The night was curiously still so high above the din of dogs and traffic, and the sky was growing pale in the east. Flocks of carrion-eating birds flapped energetically around, as if they knew about the killing that had happened, the killing that would come.

Douglas had a point; he was throwing everything over with this move. Macmillan told himself that he could save Laney *and* stop the TZ. It didn't have to be an either/or.

He looked around for something to use as a rope. Bar towels. He ripped a few of them in half and knotted them together. He tied an end to a post and lowered himself to the honeymoon suite balcony two floors down.

The curtains were drawn, but they were filmy. He could just make out a figure sitting on the edge of the bed, bathed in the blue glow of a TV. Too large for Laney. Rolly? One of Rolly's men?

Macmillan pulled Laney's gun from his pocket and took Anders's piece from his waistband; his next moves were critical; he had to be perfectly quiet so as not to alert the man—or the guards who were no doubt roaming the hall. He slid the balcony door open just enough to get a view in—along with the barrel of his gun.

It wasn't Laney or Rolly sitting there; it was a bald man. And there, curled up in the far corner, knees hugged to her chest, was Laney, wearing some sort of white negligee. Her eyes widened as she spotted him.

"Hey, Harken." She stood up. "I'm hungry."

"Wait 'til Rolly gets back," the man grumbled, eyes glued to the tube. A .22 lay next to his thigh. He could snap it up in an instant.

She moved toward the man, stopping at the dresser. Her cheekbone and throat were bright pink. Rage surged through Macmillan.

The man turned his attention to her. "You're not to leave that corner." He moved his hand to his gun. "Get back."

She flicked her eyes to Macmillan.

Damn.

The man—Harken—jumped up from the bed, grabbing his gun. At that very instant, Laney flew at him with something silver in her hand; she was a blur in a white negligee—with a hammer. She brought it down onto the man's head with such crushing force, such a loud *thwock*, even Macmillan winced.

Harken staggered into a lamp. Macmillan rushed in and caught the man and the lamp. He righted the lamp and eased the man down quietly. Blood poured from the back of his crushed skull.

"Laney! Are you okay?" He went to her, wrapped her in his arms.

She gaped at the man on the floor. "Is he dead?" She was fraying—he could tell by her voice.

"He's out of commission, that's the important thing," he whispered into her hair. "Where's Rolly?"

"I don't know. He got some calls a while back and left. Thank heavens."

Calls. Probably about what happened out on the street.

She looked nervously out at the porch. "We have to get out."

"Don't worry, you're not going out that way again. Who is this guy?" he asked.

"Rolly's right hand man. Is he dead?"

"Yes, but we'll pretend he's not." He pulled Harken's body into the chair and sat him there, upright as possible. He had her put on her shoes and socks, and then stand behind Harken in his chair, holding her gun to his head. "Hit the ground when they enter."

She slung on her backpack and waited, gun to the man's head. He didn't like that she'd have to stand there staring at the crushed back of Harken's skull, but there was nothing to be done about it.

Macmillan slipped to the side of the door. "A little help," he grated out.

The door opened and three guards came in, all focused on her with her gun. They called for her to drop it. She ducked.

Macmillan picked them off with Anders's Sig. One, two, three. "Come on!" He and Laney ran out into the hall. More men were coming. "The elevators! Go for the elevators!"

CHAPTER TWENTY-THREE

Laney ran for the west elevator bank with Macmillan right behind her.

She hit the button and turned to see Dok and three of Rolly's guys barreling toward them. You could always tell Rolly's guys by their frothing thuggishness.

A ding behind her. The elevator doors squeaked open.

Maxwell took off his glasses. "Hold these, hit the button for the 15th floor, and keep it there, got it? If I'm not down there in five minutes, you get out whatever way you can."

"What about you?"

He punched the first of Rolly's guys, knocking him out cold, then swung an elbow into the jaw of another, sending him backward with a sickening crack. "Do it, Laney!"

Laney backed into the elevator as another guy flew at Maxwell. Maxwell fought with small, fierce movements that ended with the guys on the floor. She couldn't believe what she was seeing; he was like a force of nature.

She stabbed the button.

A gunshot sounded as the doors slid shut.

She didn't dare to breathe as the elevator lights flashed to the 16th floor, then the 15th. It was all she could do not to make it head back up, to help him. But what could she do? Her help would probably only hurt him.

The 15th floor hall was empty, thank goodness. She held the door open to keep the elevator there, blood racing, ears ringing. She couldn't get the image of Harken's bloody head out of her mind, the wound had been dark with globs of blood and she didn't want to think of what else; it made her want to throw up, standing there behind him in that chair. She couldn't forget the way his skull gave in under the hammer—it was like a physical memory, living in her hand, her arm. Yes, he would've killed Maxwell. It didn't make it any less horrible.

She inspected a scratch on the left lens of Maxwell's glasses, straining to hear sounds, anything that would tell her what was going on. He'd broken her out and fought so gallantly, but even a machine like Maxwell couldn't survive a full onslaught of Rolly's men. He wasn't a machine. He wasn't a monster.

She had the urge to cry for him.

A gray-haired man with a suitcase approached. She felt naked in her lingerie. "Down?" he asked.

"No," she said. "You can't come in."

He looked at her accusingly. "I need to go to the lobby."

"Take the other elevator."

He pushed the down button, then frowned at her. "You wait out here for the next one."

Laney showed him her gun. She didn't point it at him or anything. You didn't need to do that with regular people. The man backed away. She could hear him calling somebody on his cellphone as he left her line of sight. Heading down the stairwell, probably. Alerting the desk. Crazed woman with a gun.

Her blood raced when she realized that the sounds above had ceased.

Hellbuckets. Where was Maxwell? He'd asked her to wait five minutes. She'd wait a hell of a lot longer than that.

Muffled thumps from high above.

What did it mean? She ran her forefinger over the dots on her gun grip.

A bang on the elevator ceiling. The panel opened. Feet in boots appeared. Maxwell! He lowered himself in.

"Oh, thank goodness," she said.

His hair was half in his eyes, and a sheen of sweat and grime covered his face.

"Thank you," she said.

"End of a small hall. Highly defensible. It forces them to attack one at a time." He plucked his glasses from her fingers and put them on, then stripped off his guard's jacket. "It's dirty, I'm afraid but you're so obvious in that."

"Thanks." She pulled it on over the white negligee she'd been made to change into, trying not to think too hard about what the stains were. His brown shirt was ragged and bloody, and he sounded slightly out of breath as he ripped wires from the elevator panel. But the bleakness in his eyes was what scared her.

Because he'd killed more people. She thought about his confession. *I've killed fourteen people.* It was probably more like twenty now.

She put her hand on his arm. "Thank you." There was nothing to say but that.

The elevator started going down, all the way down past the lobby level, past LL1 and all the way to LL2. You needed a key for LL2. Unless you were Maxwell, apparently.

The car stopped with a jolt in the pit of the hotel.

"Come on, then," he said. They raced through the basement corridors. "They won't expect us to be down here."

"The night guards!" she whispered.

"They'll be drowsy," he said.

They ran through the lower level maze.

You could hear a mobile phone ringtone as they neared the room. One of the guards was stirring, the other fast asleep. A man lay on the floor, cuffed to a pipe. They hurried on.

Minutes later, they were emerging out the liquor hatch into the balmy haze of early morning. Shouts echoed around the neighborhood.

"This way." He pointed. They set off running.

"No Sawadee Palace?"

"Too much heat," he said.

They headed up the back streets toward the canopied entrance of a vegetable market, closed for the night.

"Through here," Maxwell said, pulling her around the sawhorse barrier over the protests of a vegetable seller setting up shop. They raced through the narrow lane between tents. "Out here," Maxwell whispered. They snuck behind a generator and slipped out the side, onto a small, dark street.

"Walk normally, but keep to the shadows," he said.

It was hard to walk normally when all she wanted to do was run, but she trusted Maxwell. His shirt hung open, and his chest glistened with sweat, rising and falling as he breathed.

"You used to have a white T-shirt," she said.

"You know how white shows stains."

He wouldn't have made the joke if he could see the blood on him. But he had a point—thank goodness the material was dark.

On they went. One block, then another. He seemed to be limping. She eyed his boots. "Are you sure you're okay?"

"I'm *fine*," he whispered. "Smile."

She smiled at a man pulling aside the gates of a café.

They turned onto another street. Two motorbikes buzzed by. A few cars zoomed up and down. People on the early shifts, she thought. The entryway lights of a massive apartment complex flickered off as the rosy sky brightened.

"That old blue Mercedes heading this way," Maxwell muttered. "It keeps showing up. Probably Rolly's guys."

Pulse racing, she bowed her head and turned her eyes discreetly to a car with smoked-glass windows.

"Don't look! Good God, stop looking so alert."

"Stop looking *alert?*" She felt madly, painfully alert. How could she not be? Rolly'd had her. She'd killed Harken with a hammer. And her brother...

"Think of something else." Maxwell said. "I can believe they've found us."

"Rolly always has good help," she said.

"They'll be waiting for backup," he said casually, as if to model the mood he wanted out of her. "Stay cool."

He didn't understand: she couldn't just disconnect like that.

"If they think we see them, they'll come out after us," he added.

The car slowed, blocking the vehicles behind it. Honks filled the muggy morning.

"Not good," Maxwell muttered. "See that alley? Get ready to dart in." Then, "Now!" They darted into the alley and ran. They turned onto another street, then another, heading into smaller, more out-of-the-way lanes with uneven sidewalks and shabbier storefronts, all still gated against the night.

Maxwell stopped in front of a rusty gate and guided her into the shadowy corner. "Be small." He crouched and started fussing with the lock. Laney peered inside at what appeared to be an abandoned shop, nothing more than a gaping garage-like stall, empty except for tables and crates stacked in the back. Maxwell swore, and then he smashed the rusted old lock with the butt of his gun and lifted the gate a couple of feet. They scooted under. Once they were inside he pulled it back down.

"Back here." He led her to the back of the space, where he arranged the crates into a small wall. They hunkered down behind them in the dark.

Laney leaned up against the concrete block wall. "I'll never be able to repay you for this. For everything. Two times now—"

"Don't," he said softly. "You don't have to."

"No, I was going to die back there. A death worse than…"

"Than death?"

"Yeah," she whispered.

"A death worse than death. You've been spending too much time with that Rolly."

"That's not funny."

"I know."

She checked in her backpack and almost wanted to cry when she saw Amy in there, coffee mug, dirt, and fragile stalk still intact. Amy the fighter. Amy had survived the trip.

"Got a phone in there?"

She handed over her phone. He set to taking the back off and pulling out the battery, then he put it back together and made a call. There he sat, wounded and fierce and magnificent beside her, conversing in half sentences and grunts the way you do with somebody you know very well.

She peered out at the street through a gap in the small wall of crates. No doubt Maxwell had intended for there to be a gap. He thought five moves ahead on everything.

Traffic had picked up now that the sun was up, and the air was threaded with diesel, curry, and incense. People walked by now and then, most in Western clothes, but you saw the occasional splash of orange robes or a brightly colored sarong wrapped around a person's waist.

Her mind felt electric with crisscrossing threads of thought: her brother in trouble or worse. Rolly out of jail and after her. The Shinsurins. And had Rajini been in on it?

"Rajini saved me," she said when Maxwell was off. "We were friends in the States and she helped me when I needed it most. Why would she save me just to betray me?"

"How long were you friends?"

"Just a few weeks, but..." Shivers crept over her. "No way was it all arranged, if that's what you're getting at. No way was she playing me from the start."

He looked down and started texting. "She was, Laney. The Shinsurins work with your ex. Think about it."

Thinking about it made her feel sick. She'd poured her heart out to Rajini—she'd confided in her.

Maxwell shifted his feet as he typed, moving them carefully one way, then another, brow furrowed. At one point he winced.

"Your feet—"

"I'm fine." He shut off the phone.

She didn't know what to do with this man who seemed to think words could cover everything, this man who lay injured on cell floors making jokes about how many stars the hotel should get instead of saying, *Help me. Hold my hand. It hurts.*

"All that jerky attitude in the basement. You could've told me what you were doing. You could've let me in."

He gave her a look.

"And I know he's not dead," she said. "My brother's not dead."

He just squinted at the half-ripped down Orangina poster on the concrete wall opposite them.

"I bet you anything Rolly did some computer shenanigans where he took over the account from Charlie and locked him out. Maybe he's been fake emailing to Charlie just like he's been fake emailing with me. Maybe Charlie's out there thinking, *this doesn't sound like Emmaline.*"

"That's one scenario."

"*One scenario*," she repeated. "Thanks a lot, Devilwell. I wasn't sure if that was one scenario, so that's real helpful."

"I won't insult you by telling you that's what I think. If you want a companion who will say everything just the way you want, I'd suggest a ventriloquist's dummy." He pulled the back off again. "Though I can't recommend them in firefights."

"He's alive, dammit."

"Laney—"

"Don't bother," she snapped. "You like a precise word. Like dead. Can't get more precise than dead."

"No, you can't." He whispered this like it stung. It surprised her; he seemed so impenetrable to her with his hard fortress and his cool humor. She had the urge to tear his walls down, to get inside. That man she'd connected with at the night bazaar hadn't been fake. Had he?

"What are you doing?" she asked.

"You could be tracked. I don't see anything obvious, but..." he replaced the back. "Stay there." He crept away from their post behind the crates and slid through the shadows along the wall to the gate. When a truck passed, he hurled the phone onto its bed.

Her phone. Gone. Just like that. She hugged her knees to her chest, trying to blot out the sound of the hammer connecting with Harken's head, the way the vibrations had traveled up her arm as his skull gave way with a crunch. She'd taken a life. And her brother might be dead, her home was gone, her best friend had been her enemy all along. All exploded in a flash of violence.

"I hated that phone anyways," she said when he came back. "I didn't need that phone." And then she began to laugh. It wasn't even funny, and here she was laughing like a lunatic.

The next thing she knew, she was sobbing—great, heaving, all-consuming sobs.

She felt strong arms wrap around her. "Laney."

She pushed her face into his neck as he pulled her in tight. "I'm sorry," She sobbed into his solid frame.

"No, it's okay. It's okay." He held her tightly, rubbing circles on her back. It felt comforting to be held by him, to have him rub her back. Just a stupid thing like that. "Shhh," he said.

"It's more than one scenario," she blurted out. "It's my brother."

"I know," he whispered into her hair, tightening his hold, rocking her slightly. "You're right."

"He could be alive."

"Yes."

"Why can't you say so?"

Such a long silence passed, she wasn't sure he heard. Then, "I don't want to give you false hope."

"He might be alive. How is that false hope if we don't know?"

"You're right, that's just me," he whispered. "Just me. Bottom line is we don't know."

Just me. She tried to imagine Maxwell full of hope for something; she found she couldn't. "Sounds like you had some experience with false hope."

He said nothing.

"Tell me," she said. "Let me in."

"Don't," he said.

"You have to let me in."

"No, you have to trust me," he said.

"How can I trust you if you won't let me in?"

"This is not the time," he said.

"This is exactly the time—"

He pulled away, finger at his lips. Had somebody found them? He put his attention back to the front.

A ratcheting sound. The gate. Somebody out there.

Her blood raced.

He put his lips to her hair. "Breathe."

The sound stopped. There was shouting. Then nothing. So they'd only pulled it up a little bit and then left.

She squeezed her eyes shut as the moments ticked on.

"It's okay," he whispered after a bit. "Somebody's out searching the neighborhood."

"What are we going to do?"

"My people are coming. That's who I called." He pulled the magazines out of the guns—hers, the one with a silencer, and the one he'd taken from Harken. Just one bullet between all three.

"Crap," she whispered.

"You can get a good deal of mileage from an empty gun." He was animated, alert. "Tell me more about Rolly. He's military?"

"Army Major. Then he went into military contracting. Moving parts and solvents. What's going on? What'd he do?"

"Let's just say, he's moving some very dangerous parts and solvents." He kept an eye out front, quizzing her about Rolly, his guys, and his travel habits. He drew a picture in the dirty floor with a nail and asked if she'd ever seen any such tattoos on Rolly's guys. She'd seen one of them, a clawed snake.

She knew what he was doing: he was keeping her out with all these questions. Staying on the surface, but she wouldn't believe that man from the first night was an act. She wanted that man back. She meant to get him back.

A dog barked outside the gate and Laney stiffened. Soon there were two dogs, maybe three dogs.

"Strays," Maxwell whispered.

"Strays telling everybody in the neighborhood we're in here," she whispered back.

"Dogs bark," he squeezed her hand. "At cats, at rats."

"And people." The barking grew louder.

"Don't let them smell your fear," he whispered.

"How am I supposed to do that when they won't shut up? They're causing my fear."

"Take control of your thoughts—take it back from those dogs."

"Right."

The barking kept on, biting into her nerves, growing more and more frenzied, telling the world they were there.

She shut her eyes. "I can't."

Footsteps. A sudden car honk made her nearly jump clear out of her skin.

"All just sounds," he whispered. More footsteps. The barking calmed, then started back up. Maxwell tipped the gun up. "All just sounds."

"We have to drive them off."

"That'll make it worse."

"We can't just sit here."

"We can and we will." He rested a heavy hand on her arm and fixed on her eyes. "The dogs' vocal cords vibrate, sending pressure waves through the air," he said coolly. "Nothing more. You understand?"

She nodded. *Waves.*

"If you make it into parts, it's easier to deal with. Sound alone can't hurt you."

Something clicked into place, then. "That's what you do," she said.

"What?"

"You rob the meaning out of things by cracking them into pieces."

He twisted up his lips, as if amused, an expression that didn't quite reach his eyes. "Cracking things into pieces lets you understand more."

"Maybe so, but that's not what you're up to. I think you chop things up to control them. It's what you did in your book. And with these dogs. Nothing but waves, my ass."

A glint appeared in his eye. "So I chop them into bunk designed to hornswoggle folks, you mean?"

"Your jokes. All your words and your jokes, they keep you on the surface. You pretend like there's nothing underneath, but guess what?" She jabbed his chest with her finger. "Guess what?"

He wrapped his fingers around hers, eyes dangerous. "What?"

"There *is* something underneath."

He drew her close and whispered into her ear, "Are you putting that in your one-star review?" His lips caressed the shell of her ear as he spoke, sending sparks all through her. "You can't know how I'm looking forward to reading it."

"I will write it," she said, breath going shallow. "'Cause it's not enough for me. I'm a dissatisfied customer, Devilwell."

"Dissatisfied?" He tightened his hand on her finger and pulled her closer. "In every way?"

"Yes," she said, face heating.

He pulled away and gazed into her eyes. She knew what he was thinking—the night of the dragon.

His gaze intensified, like he might kiss her.

Her eyes dropped to his lips. "I want what's underneath."

"Too bad." He let go.

"I won't accept—"

He raised his eyebrows, nodded his head toward the front.

"What?"

He put a hand to his ear.

Silence.

The barking had stopped. Relief flooded through her. "Oh."

"You see? It worked. We thought of something else. And now here's my guy." Maxwell rose and moved up along the shadowed side of the stall toward the front where a dark figure stood. If she hadn't known somebody was there, she wouldn't have seen him. The brief flash of glasses could've been the reflection of sunshine off chrome.

The ratcheting sound was nearly imperceptible when he pulled the gate up. A man slipped in. Maxwell's guy? He seemed to have gotten there awfully fast.

Maxwell and the man clasped each other's shoulders with affection. Together they slipped back along the wall and behind the crates next to her, stealthy as ghosts.

Maxwell introduced the man as Rio.

Rio had short dark hair and glasses and inky eyelashes—he could get a job as a model in a heartbeat, she thought, though the way he moved told her he was every bit as lethal as Maxwell. And these two had clearly exchanged stealthy-walking recipes.

"That was fast," Maxwell whispered as Rio pulled a wig and a cap from his bag.

"I'm not here," Rio said with intensity, handing him a knit cap. "I was in the neighborhood saying goodbye to an old friend and I heard it over the line."

"Ah," Maxwell said, like that was hugely significant.

"Yes," Rio said simply.

"How's Douglas?"

"He'll be fine, but you have a problem. Dax is sending a few Associates to get you two to a safe house."

"What's the problem?"

"I believe you're looking at a Seattle-style exchange."

Maxwell stiffened. "What about my angle? We can get Jazzman's real voice now. I can break that security and take control of the TZ. I just need some quiet, some samples, some—"

"You're being pulled out."

Maxwell sucked in a breath. Laney realized she'd never heard Maxwell surprised, but he was surprised by this. "He can't pull me out."

"I thought you'd want to know," Rio added.

"Damn right I'd want to know." Maxwell grabbed a wig and shoved it into Laney's hands. "Put this on. We're leaving." He pulled the knit cap over his head, tucked in his hair, and grabbed the gun Rio held out to him, pulling out the magazine and shoving it back in. He handed her gun to Rio and Rio gave him another. They were like a NASCAR pit crew, these two, with their guns and bullets.

"What's a Seattle-style exchange?" she asked.

"A bad idea, that's what." Maxwell shoved Laney's gun in her bag. "Let her have your Sig, Rio. She shoots."

Rio pulled a black weapon from his ankle holster and set it in her hand. It was heavy as hell. "For you," he said. "Be ready for its kick and it'll treat you fine." He looked into her eyes like he really wanted her to get that, to be safe.

"Thanks," she said.

"You good with that one?" Maxwell asked.

"I'm good," she said.

"I'm parked a block down," Rio said. "Blue Toyota. I saw Little Hussein's men roaming around five minutes ago, but the coast was clear when I came in."

"Little Hussein's men," Macmillan said, as if it meant worlds.

"Dax isn't the only one thinking about an exchange," Rio said. "And it's only going to get worse. Every dealer out there wants to be a hero for Jazzman."

"All the decent holes'll be staked out," Macmillan said.

Rio nodded and they went on, gathering stuff up.

Laney looked at her socks and tennis shoes and the dirty hem of the white lingerie, hating that these men were excluding her, talking over her head. She'd lost so much, felt so alone. She needed Maxwell to let her in; couldn't he see that? She needed to know somebody else was with her—not some military type or whatever he was, but another soul.

Another walker on the moon.

Moments later, Maxwell and Rio headed out; she was to wait at the front, watching from the shadows, ready to duck under the gate and slip into the car when it rolled by.

They ambled down the sidewalk with the loose walk of fighters, soft and relaxed, but with a kind of weightlessness, as if they could spring into furious action at any instant. She had the sense of them as a duo, like they'd been through things together. They both had that warrior intensity. That high-functioning intelligence.

Fighters. Could that be all there was to him?

CHAPTER TWENTY-FOUR

Macmillan caught Laney's gaze in the rearview mirror as Rio sped down the dawn streets. He owed his old friend big-time.

"Nice job, by the way," Rio said. "It's definitely him. Jerry Lee Drucker, age 39. Released from federal prison five weeks ago on a dubious technicality. He was in Panama during the time frame."

"What time frame?" Laney asked. "What's going on?"

Macmillan turned to her best he could without excruciating pain. "Your Rolly has a dangerous weapon in his possession. He's in the process of selling it off to the highest bidder. And it's nobody good."

He saw when the recognition came over her. "You've been hunting him all this time. That's why you know so much about his talk."

He nodded.

"What does this weapon do?"

"It can do anything," he said. "It can locate and kill one person on a crowded sidewalk, or it can level an entire building or part of a city."

"Like a missile?"

"It's more like a small plane the size of a rider mower," Rio said, "but flattened out, like a sting ray."

Macmillan said, "The problem with it is that it has laser weaponry, which hasn't been feasible in an airborne weapon up until now because of the energy demand. But this weapon is powered by a network of lasers on the ground, which makes it very dangerous. If Rolly wanted to, he could destroy the White House, then he could turn it around and fly it back to Bangkok, exploding any jets that have the bad fortune to catch up with it. All remotely."

"And you're trying to get it."

"Yes," Macmillan said. "The weapon, the schematics, and the location of the ground lasers."

"And he wants to sell it," Laney said. "That's the convention at the hotel. All those guys."

"I guess you could call it a convention," Macmillan said. "Though it's more of an auction."

"Was an auction," said Rio. "He's a bit more focused on you two at the moment."

They careened under a massive bridge and came out between gleaming new buildings hung with sales banners and vines of riotous flowers. The shopping district.

Macmillan turned to Rio. "Now that we know his identity, we're good. There will be voice recordings of Rolly in that basement by now. I can get down there—"

"You think you can get down into that basement ever again? The hotel is tighter than the Pentagon right now. Recordings offline, everything locked down and guarded. Top floors are no-go. You think Jazzman hasn't guessed who you are?" Rio turned to meet his gaze.

"I know," Macmillan whispered.

"Our people are not happy," Rio whispered.

Macmillan nodded. Any Associate worth his salt would've left Laney there to occupy Jazzman's attention.

Rio said nothing. They hit a traffic jam. Horns honked and motorcycles wove in and out through the knot of cars.

"I can do this," Macmillan said. "I can take it by voice. I can't believe he won't give me that opportunity." Few people in the world had his level of voice expertise—using Jazzman's own voice to fool the biometric security and get control of the weapon could prevent bloodshed.

"It seems certain people aren't in the mood for subterfuge and science," Rio said. *Certain people.* Meaning Dax. "Certain people want the sure thing," Rio added.

"Certain people need a little faith," Macmillan said coolly, but in truth, it was a blow to the gut that Dax had lost faith in him, that he'd shut him out of the mission.

Laney sat in the back seat twirling a dirty twisty-tie back and forth in her fingers, staring out the window with a furrowed forehead. Worried. Thinking about her brother, probably. It was all he could do not to clamber back there and hold her.

She wanted to think the best. To hope. It was a kind of bravery, and he loved her for it. He'd do it his way, no matter what Dax said. And hell if he'd let her get used as a bargaining chip.

Ever.

That's what a Seattle-style exchange meant—to exchange somebody as part of the payment for something when you knew it would go bad for that person. Dax meant to buy the weapon himself, offering Laney as part of the payment.

It was cold logic that Dax was operating on, but Macmillan was working off fire and passion now.

Maybe his efforts to save Laney had unbalanced the mission and set countless arms dealers after her. Well, he'd save her from them, too. He'd save the whole goddamn world, because just watching her twirl a twisty tie made him feel hopeful. And every one of her crazy words filled him with unspeakable joy. And the way she held her lips when she was angry made him happy, and so did her filthy mouth, and all that energetic red hair she hid under that brown dye. There was even something about those songs of hers, much as they nettled him. No, it was more that they pierced him…pummeled him.

A text tone cut the silence. Rio glanced at his phone, then stowed it away.

"What?" Macmillan asked.

"The TZ is on the roof of the hotel."

"So it really is happening."

She turned to him. "What does that mean?"

"The TZ is the weapon. Rolly has his toy out and he may be inclined to demonstrate it. He could hold the whole damn city hostage if he felt like it."

"In a way, he already is," Rio pointed out.

"Ah," she said softly.

"Would you consider him a hothead?" Rio asked. "A vengeful person?"

"Both," she said.

No wonder Dax wanted a sure thing.

The traffic snarl was breaking up.

He turned back to Rio. "I don't need the hotel recordings. His voice is out there in other places. I don't need much to crack the weapon's security. Prison phone calls—those are recorded. We could get his voice from those."

Rio looked skeptical. "That would be great—if we can get somebody to turn them over in the next few hours."

"I'll figure it out."

"Forgive me for kicking the tires, but even the great Macmillan—"

"I can do it," Macmillan said. "A few hours, a few supplies..."

"We have to secure the TZ," Rio said. "That is still my first allegiance."

Macmillan was about to say, "It's my first allegiance, too," but he stopped himself. He'd vowed to save Laney *and* get the TZ, but given a choice, he'd choose Laney.

The realization floored him.

He'd choose Laney.

Rio turned to him, brown eyes weary with understanding. Macmillan would choose Laney, and Rio knew it.

His old friend put his attention back on the road with a sigh. "What do you need?"

Macmillan put together a shopping list. In addition to clean clothes they needed a charger, food, water, and other essentials. They parked in a ramp for a crowded department store. Rio slipped out to go shopping.

He looked back at Laney. *I'd choose you,* he thought.

While they waited, he made a call to a contact to get the requisition for recordings of Rolly's phone calls started.

"This is a weapon of mass destruction?" she asked after he hung up.

"Yes. And I'm going to take control of it away from him."

"But it's not for sure you can."

He watched her in the rearview mirror. "It's what I do."

She monitored his eyes with that intensity of hers. "I was the exchange, wasn't I?"

His gut twisted. He hated that she knew. But of course she'd gotten it; she was an artist and language was one of her mediums. "Yes," he said.

"Bait for a trap?"

"It wouldn't be a trap."

"What does that mean?"

"It means the plan wouldn't be built around getting you back. We'd take advantage of an opening, but we wouldn't expect one. It's not like in the movies. This exchange would be a straightforward transfer."

She stared at him in horror. The Association had done this sort of ruthless thing before and he'd always gone along. It seemed monstrous now.

"Don't make me go back."

He turned—the hell with the pain. His voice, when it came, was low and gravelly. "I won't." He looked her straight in the eyes and made the promise with everything he had. "I won't let you go back."

"Thank you." She trusted him. He'd earn that trust.

She wanted him to be Peter, but it wasn't Peter who could keep her alive. It wasn't Peter who could handle this mission.

Rio returned with an armful of bags. A very efficient shopper. "The blue bag is food and supplies. The white ones are new outfits. You two need to dress up for the business sector."

"How'd you know my size?" Laney asked.

"I guessed," Rio said. "There's a neck scarf, too."

Laney's hand went to her throat.

Macmillan could kill Rio for saying something. "It's not so bad," he said.

Yet.

"But best to be unremarkable," Rio said. "Go ahead and change back there. We won't look." He pulled moccasin boots from another bag, along with thick socks.

So Rio had noticed the way he was walking. He'd guessed about his toes.

"You didn't have to."

"I think I did," Rio said.

Rio would do what he could to help him, but there was a limit even to what Rio would do. Rio wanted to get that weapon out of enemy hands as badly as anyone.

CHAPTER TWENTY-FIVE

New York

Dax stood at the window of his penthouse looking out at the lights along the pathways of Central Park, sliding his fingers up and down along the silk lapel of his Armani one-button jacket. Up and down, up and down, sliding along the cool grain. The monotonous motion sometimes soothed, but not tonight. He closed his eyes and tried to breathe through the sensation of an icepick rammed between his eyes.

Zelda walked up and put a scotch in his hand. "The mama's back," she said.

He lowered his gaze to the gargoyle fresco at the corner beneath the window, where a pair of pigeons had made their nest. He'd watched pigeons incubating their eggs and feeding their chicks for three years now. Helpless little beings at the mercy of everything. When the condo board voted to clear the stonework of nests and birds in order to preserve its historical beauty, Dax had fought it. When he failed, he bought out his neighbors in disgust. Some neighbors refused. So Dax had ruined them, and then he'd bought them out. Because nobody but nobody stood up to Dax's wrath.

Fucking historical beauty.

He put his hand to his head.

"Christ, at least take a codeine."

"I'm fine," Dax said. And if he was going to send a woman into the arms of a monster like Jerry Lee "Rolly" Drucker, aka Jazzman, the least he could do was stay awake and bear the pain a little longer.

"We'll find a way to pull her out," Zelda said.

"Mmm," Dax said. They both knew how that would go.

Jerry Lee Drucker had first met the Shinsurins during deployments in South Korea while he was with the Rangers, and later as a military contractor. The files Zelda had pulled on him showed him to be a formidable strategist and a fluid thinker with contacts across the world. It would be hard to save Emmaline, during or after the exchange.

He felt Zelda's eyes on him. "Generals have sent entire armies off to die for less," she said. "This is the TZ, Dax." She wore a chic green maxi dress with gold sandals. They'd been at dinner with one of the U.N. High Commissioners, talking him down. The various powers were getting antsy about the TZ. They wanted to move big against Jazzman. They didn't understand that it was too late to move big—not unless they were prepared to see part of Bangkok taken out.

Zelda looked at her watch. Had she planned to meet somebody later? She always seemed so painfully alone. She didn't even have a family, unless you counted her adoptive family. Which Zelda definitely didn't.

"You don't have to stay," Dax said.

"I do," she said simply.

Dax nodded. Zelda kept her personal life private, and Dax made a point of not putting too much thought into it, but he knew Association business pulled her out of social occasions far too often.

If only his original plan had worked. When word of the auction had first come out, he'd tried to buy the weapon himself through a straw man working on behalf of undisclosed Americans, but Drucker had sensed something fishy about the offer.

Well, something *had* been fishy. The straw man would hand the TZ over to Dax to be destroyed and buried. Once Dax was sure he had all the plans and the locations of the ground lasers, he'd have Drucker killed.

Yes, Drucker had a good nose; you developed that, being in the field as long as he had been.

But his ex-wife would be his soft spot. As soon as Macmillan and the girl were at the safe house, Dax planned to work up the exchange, with or without her consent. Or Macmillan's.

He'd approach Jazzman with a new offer. Cash and Emmaline, or Laney, or whatever she wanted to be called. It was an offer Jazzman wouldn't refuse.

A ringtone sounded. Dax grabbed his mobile from his pocket. A voice on the other end. Riley, an Associate and one of his most reliable investigators.

Four words. "They're in the wind."

"You're sure you had the right place?" Dax asked Riley.

Zelda swung her gaze to him. Dax put Riley on speaker.

"They were here. I can tell from the lookout nest," he said. "Maybe they smelled trouble and left. Maybe one of the teams from the auction pulled them out of here."

Dax exchanged glances with Zelda. More likely, Macmillan had guessed about an exchange. Or somebody had tipped him off.

Riley said, "Maybe he's going for equipment for his plan. To take it over via the voice security."

"And I'm sure he can succeed, given enough time," Dax said, "but he robbed us of that time when he blew everything to hell rescuing the girl, so that's off the table."

"The guys feel very confident he can succeed," Riley said.

Dax sighed. The other Associates loved Macmillan. But Dax needed a sure thing now. The fact that Macmillan had blown the element of surprise by saving the girl showed he was no longer reliable.

What the hell had happened to Macmillan?

"Go back to the Sawadee Hotel and wait with the others," Dax told Riley. "We'll see what turns up." He closed the line and turned to Zelda. "We can't send the Associates after each other. I won't force them to make that choice."

"Agreed." Zelda drained her scotch. She wore one of her definitive looks.

Dax knew what she was thinking. The Associates weren't the only players they had on the field.

"We have to put Thorne on them," she said. "You know we do."

Nobody knew that Thorne was Dax's man. Not even the other Associates.

He shook his head. "Thorne would have to grab the girl and then screw things up and fumble her to our buyer. It would destroy his credibility with Hangman. Possibly even his cover."

"Then let Thorne's credibility with Hangman be destroyed. Let his cover be blown. Let everyone be destroyed. This is the big fight, Dax, and we agreed that anybody and everybody can be sacrificed to win it, even Macmillan. Even Thorne. If we can't take the weapon away from Jazzman, we need to be the ones to buy it."

Dax stared out at the park. They'd been trying to get somebody inside Hangman for years, and Thorne had been brilliant, working his way up within the notoriously cutthroat organization to become Hangman Four. Thorne with his black hair and wild Irish blood—the man was dangerous and brilliant enough to lead the group one day. The prospect of controlling Hangman got Dax hard in ten different ways.

He looked up to find Zelda staring at him.

"Yeah," she said, eyes narrowed. She'd have guessed what he was thinking. You couldn't get anything past Zelda. "The TZ comes first," she said. "Think about the Glorious Light having that weapon. The New Tong. The North Koreans. Any of them. We'll all be living in burntout buildings fighting over dog meat if the wrong people get the TZ. Who said that? Can you remind me who said that?"

He'd said it. It was true, too. He watched the pigeon mama. "If we send Thorne out after Macmillan, that's a fight to the death. Especially with the girl involved."

Zelda swirled the ice in her glass. "If we don't send Thorne for her, somebody else will take her. Macmillan can't protect her—not with everybody who's coming after her."

"He thinks he can," Dax said.

"The arrogance of the overachiever," Zelda said.

She was right, of course. Zelda was one of the best minds he'd ever encountered; he sometimes wished she'd agree to go back out in the field.

"What do you think happened down in that basement?" she asked him.

"Things got personal."

Dax got Thorne on the line and explained what he needed. Thorne listened impassively, asking only the important questions. There was very little Thorne wouldn't do. He gave Thorne directions to a vendor stall on Thana Soi, the last known place Macmillan had been with the girl. With Emmaline Drucker.

If there were leads to be gleaned in that stall, Thorne would find them. "I want everybody to come out alive, if possible," Dax eyed Zelda as he spoke. "But the mission is primary. It won't be easy—"

"I understand," Thorne said.

"I knew you would," Dax said softly. "Thank you."

Thorne cut the connection.

Zelda furrowed her forehead. "Thorne sounds unhappy."

"You know how he is—half monster and half whipping boy," Dax said. "Kindness spooks him."

So it was done. They watched the pigeon mama.

After a while, Dax said, "Did you know that pigeons are one of the few species that can recognize themselves in a mirror?"

"I did not know," she said.

"Most other animals don't recognize themselves. Pigeons do."

"Mmm."

Dax watched the pigeon mama, wondering what that would be like to look at himself in a mirror and not recognize himself. To see only the endless and blameless world.

CHAPTER TWENTY-SIX

Bangkok

Ten minutes later Macmillan was driving through one of the sparkling, chaotic business districts. He dropped Rio off when he hit the edge of it, where the bustle of commerce collapsed into a drab residential area. The line that separated the two areas was formed by a row of low-rent business traveler hotels that stretched for blocks.

He kept driving after that, parking some ways away, and he got out with Laney. She wore the cheap blue dress Rio had chosen, along with a little blue jacket, plus a wig, a sunhat, and sensible flats—with knee-highs.

He locked the car door with a smile. "You packed the knee highs." Of all the things to take, she'd grabbed the knee-highs.

"It's not what you think," she said.

"Not because I like to ravish you in them?"

She smiled.

He went around to where she stood. "Why, then?"

"Rolly would hate them. And, it's just something of mine. For my birthday." She straightened his tweed sports coat and smiled up at him in his ball cap and wig. "You look so damn different."

"You like me as a brunette? Should I go brunette like you?"

She snorted.

He grabbed the shopping bag with the rest of Rio's purchases and set off. They had to walk this last bit to whatever hotel Rio selected, possibly through a gauntlet of hunters.

This was a transitional part of town; there was lots of neon when you looked up, but down on the street level all that flash got mixed in with hand-lettered signs and grimy shop windows.

They entered a department store with mirrored walls, silver mannequins, and deafening electronica. Up the escalator they went to a display of silver mannequins in beachwear overlooking the street.

Things looked clear—nobody had followed them, it seemed.

Eventually Rio called with a hotel name and room number.

They headed out onto a different street. As the poor-man's end of the business district, it had the best hotels for hiding—and for escaping. Rio had a few favorites on the strip.

It was a little risky—they weren't the only ones who would identify this as a good place to hole up, but that would be true of all good places to hole up. No reason to choose a bad place.

He worried about Laney, though. It wouldn't be long until everything crashed down over her head—the danger they were in, her brother, the fact that she'd killed Harken, their slim escape, seeing Rolly again. That mini-outburst in the stall was just a blip.

He'd help her. He'd see her through it.

They joined the throng on the busy thoroughfare, passing a row of beggars and lotto ticket vendors. "Just behind this area is an old city neighborhood that's like a maze—an instant getaway."

Laney nodded. She carried off the black wig well enough, what with her dark eyebrows, but she looked nervous. Too conscious of being chased.

She'd give them away.

Macmillan slung an arm around her. "Focus on something in your mind, Laney. A TV show or something."

"Okay."

The hotels were on the second and third floors, above the shops. The little doors had lit signs above them, lettering in Thai and English, sometimes Chinese. Some hand-painted. Family hotels.

Her gaze darted all around. *Damn.* He'd spot her a mile away if he was hunting them, just from the fear rolling off her.

"Be anywhere but *here.* A hunter will notice if you're *too here.*"

"Like what?"

"Anything."

"I can't just disconnect like that." Her voice sounded tight.

"How about a TV show? Do you watch that soap opera with the famous singer?"

He could see her trying to conjure it up in her mind's eye, practically sweating with the effort of it. She couldn't disconnect. No surprise there—it was against her nature. Only one thing would get her mind off the street. Connection.

He had to give her something real. Something of himself.

He took a breath. Was he really going to do this? He lowered his voice. "Remember when you visited me down in that cell the first time? And you talked about having to say goodbye to all the familiar people in your life?"

She slid her gaze to him, sensing a ploy.

"I had to do that once," he continued.

"For real?"

"For real," he said. "It was ten years ago. I was riding on a train in Mexico with my parents, my sister, and my fiancée. Gwen. The four people I loved most in the world."

She shot him a glance, caught by the past tense. "Loved?"

"We were traveling through an area of unrest to visit a colleague of mine. It was my idea to take the train. I was arrogant; I thought it would be safe. We were playing a word game that we loved. The adjective game."

Her expression softened. "It *sounds* like a game you'd love. Right up your alley."

"It was up all our alleys. With my family moving around, we were closer than most families; each other's best friends. You wouldn't believe how many stupid games we had. And Gwen just fit right into our world.

We were this...*family*." He took a breath. What had he gotten himself into? This wasn't a story he ever told. But it was shifting her focus—that was the important thing. "I was just a scholar. Peter Macmillan Maxwell, PhD. We were...happy."

A group of three hunters ahead; it was their stance that tipped him off.

"I'd gone back a few train cars to where the functioning restrooms were," he continued. "While I was waiting in line there, the train hit a series of bombs. Everybody in our car was tossed to the back, like dice in a cup. A violent halt. But all the front cars were destroyed. The car my family rode in, totally destroyed."

"Oh, my God. Maxwell."

"All of us survivors, we were pouring out into the jungle. It was night, middle of nowhere. Just the burning luggage and seats for light."

One of the hunters eyed them as they passed out of the shade and through a patch of sun. He cringed; wigs sometimes shone wrong in natural light. Doggedly he kept on, describing the juxtaposition of twisted, burnt-blackened metal, charred corpses, and bright fabrics as he watched the hunters from under his lashes. He didn't know what contingency they were connected to, but he knew that they'd spot them if he couldn't keep Laney absorbed. Connected.

"I figured out which was ours and it was...one of the worst. Everything hot or burning. And just...all the bodies. Parts of bodies. It seemed unreal." It tore something inside him to bring it back up.

No. It was too much. He couldn't function like this. He'd be no good to her.

He said, "There was a study once noting the high frequency of words like unreal and surreal used in circumstances of tragedy. Surreal is used nearly across the board—"

"Maxwell. Fuck!" She grabbed onto his sleeve. "Tell me."

He swallowed and forced himself onward. "I identified my family by parts. Their clothing. Gwen...a bit of scalp with a barrette attached, still holding her hair in place. It was a long time ago."

"I'm so sorry," she said.

They'd passed by the hunters without incident. But he could feel others around. Better hunters. The ones you didn't spot so easily.

"There were live people to save in other cars. A group of us worked all night, shoulder to shoulder, pulling people out, trying to calm them in their bewilderment as they died. People who die like that are bewildered. God, I'd never felt so helpless. And we'd try to get people out only to realize it was a part of a person—you would see that too late. There's a kind of horror in a human body part that no longer looks human," he said. "There was this hand that I pulled out—"

"Maxwell," she whispered.

It felt oddly liberating to confide in her. "I held it for a very long time. Too long, actually, but I couldn't let it go. I don't know why. I don't know if you can understand—"

"Probably not," she said.

"But I want you to," he blurted, startling himself. "I think you can."

She turned her clear gaze up to him. "What was it like? Holding the hand?"

"It was like the world fell out from under me," he said.

She nodded.

"But not like that," he added. "It was as if, everything was gone. Of me, of the world. Gone forever. I think of it all the time, Laney. That hand. Severed like that."

"A hand attached to nothing," she said.

"Yes. Exactly." She seemed to understand. "And my world fell away," he added.

The phone sounded. He answered it.

Rio's voice. "I see you from the room. You're almost there. Happy Traveler. It's the lit sign, middle of the block above the drugstore. Room 308. Don't fucking look around. There's a white Honda heading south. They're searching. Don't know if they see you."

"Got it." he hung up.

"It sounds…" she shook her head. "So your world fell away."

"My world, and parts of myself. The good parts, mostly."

"People don't lose parts of themselves—"

"I'm telling you what happened," he said, perhaps too curtly. "It fell away."

She bit her lip.

The white Honda slowed. "It all fell away," he said simply. "I lost the dog's nose under the table, you know what I'm saying? The kitchen hanging with a spatter on it. The telephone voice, shoes in the rain..." *Everything that made him human.*

"I'm sorry."

"Thank you."

"And then you started doing this? This secret agent stuff?"

"Tracking people by language," he said, but his mind went to his old dictionary, one of his mother's prized possessions. Sitting in storage. Probably eaten by mice. His mother had sent him off to college with it, and he'd used it and treasured it, feeling connected to his family. They'd used to play games out of it. *Cookbook full of wishes,* he thought with a pang. Fucking song.

"This is us." He pointed at a blue door underneath a cracked plastic sign lit from the interior by a flickering bulb; *Happy Traveler* was written in Thai across it.

They entered and headed up the steps and into a small, stuffy lobby clad in bright vinyl panels framed by wood. Four ratty chairs were clustered around a glass table, and a gold mobile presided over a dying palm in the corner. The clerk was so absorbed in a book that she barely looked up. That worked. They turned down a slim hall and headed up a dank stairwell.

"I'm so sorry," she said when they got to the third floor. "I can't even imagine. The world falling away."

Except she could; he knew she understood; this woman alone would understand; the goodness of that so overcame him that all he could do was squeeze her hand. She was with him in a way nobody else had been for a very long time. He wanted to tell her more, suddenly, but he wasn't sure how to start.

It was as if he'd forgotten how to connect. He'd told her this thing, but real connection was like an open valve, and it opened you to pain. He didn't know if he could stand it. "We have to focus, now," he said.

"Got it."

They stopped in front of 308. "Thank you for telling me," she whispered as she straightened his jacket.

Rio opened up.

"Go on in." Macmillan nudged Laney forward and she walked in.

"Good day for room service," Rio said in a low voice. The Association all-clear.

Macmillan gave the standard reply: "Clears the mind." He followed her in and Rio shut the door.

Room 308 had pink walls, a small desk, a struggling air conditioner, and a double bed with a jungle print spread that matched the curtains.

"No leg irons." Laney flopped down on the bed. "That oughta earn a few stars from you."

He caught her gaze. "It'll do."

"You have it for two days," Rio said. He didn't imply the *but*. He didn't need to. They had hours, not days.

Macmillan followed him to the bathroom and was pleased to find a large window that opened easily and silently. "You oiled it."

"Months ago. Still glides."

The window overlooked a sea of roofs and twisty alleys dotted with colorful awnings that would help conceal an escape route.

"The fire escape is stable," Rio said.

"Good." Macmillan also appreciated the poor bathroom lighting and the mirror spotted with black where the silvering had oxidized. It meant Laney wouldn't be able to see her soon-to-be-ugly neck bruises. He wished he could race back to that hotel and rip Rolly apart with his bare hands.

"This room has a telltale," Rio said. "A creak that travels from down the hall." He went out and demonstrated it. Sure enough, you could hear a creak when he was three doors down.

The window looked out onto a mirrored building across the street; the blue neon sign of an electronics company down the block reflected off it in wavy geometries. The room would be lit blue at night.

"See the muscle out front?" Rio asked.

Macmillan moved to the window, staying near the side. He saw who Rio meant—it was the way they loitered down on the sidewalk—too on-the-nose. When real people loitered, they had an almost vegetative quality. Macmillan didn't like that he hadn't seen that man. He'd breezed past, absorbed in his tale of woe. That couldn't happen again.

Rio stood next to him. "A lot of reasons for a guy like that to be out there. Still." Food vendors were coming out to set up for lunch down below.

"Trouble?" Laney got up.

"Probably not," Rio said. "Just don't stand in front of the window." He pulled the curtains shut and looked Macmillan up and down. "You look terrible. Sit."

Macmillan sat as Laney peeked out through a slit in the curtains. Rio pulled medical supplies from a small box. "Take off the wig." He put a hand to Maxwell's forehead. "Fever's gone. For now." He brushed aside his hair. "Gash the size of Bolivia on your head. Look at this, your hair's become a pathogen toupee."

"I hear they were all the rage during fashion week," he said as Rio pressed his fingers onto his head, palpating the bump where Dok had bashed his head with brass knuckles. He could feel Laney watching him and not liking that he'd made that joke. She took his pain so seriously. It was a strange feeling.

"Take off your shirt," Rio grated.

Maxwell protested.

"No time. Do it." Rio produced a white bottle and a wad of cotton as Maxwell peeled off his shirt.

Laney gasped.

Macmillan looked down to see a nasty scrape glowing inside a line of red-pink bruises on his ribs. More bruises bloomed around his arm and shoulder where he'd fallen, some impossibly dark green and yellow. And there were other bruises not as bad, red patches the size of fists with marble-sized dots of red inside them.

"I'm perfectly fine."

"Aside from being all beat up with a gash on your head the size of Bolivia."

"It's nothing," he said.

"Nothing," she said. "And here I thought you liked a precise word."

Rio's cheeks hardened, as though he was suppressing a smile.

Macmillan winced as Rio palpated his ribs, heading toward the possibly broken one, finally hitting the spot where the slightest touch felt like a dart of fire.

"Here? Here?" Rio asked, continuing the torture.

"Everywhere. Just patch the scrape and we'll tape all around."

Rio gave him a look, because of course it wasn't just a scrape. He started slathering on the topical all the same. When that was done to his satisfaction, he taped a gauze pad over one of the nastiest of the gashes, then bound his chest; it would at least offer a little support.

"Now the feet," Rio said quietly. "We'll soak them first."

They went to the bathroom and ran warm water in the tub. Soaking would be the best way to get the socks off.

When they were finished cleaning and bandaging his feet, Macmillan eased on the socks and moccasins. He saw his friend to the door and clasped his shoulder. "It's no small thing, pulling us out of there like that," he said softly.

"Just make it right," Rio said.

CHAPTER TWENTY-SEVEN

Thorne knelt in front of the rusted gate to the stall, fingering the smashed lock. Macmillan had been in a hurry to get himself and the former Mrs. Rolly Jazzman out of sight. But you could never hide, not really.

He went into the space and found multiple sets of dusty footprints, and he could see where they'd sat behind the crates. It didn't mean much.

Yet.

He stood and took it all in. The dusty case. The pattern of broken cobwebs. The ripped Orangina poster. There was always a clue to be found, even with one fugitive. Two people multiplied the likelihood. Three even more. Other people were a liability, even when they were helping you. One of the reasons Thorne was glad to be a lone wolf.

Being a lone wolf was especially safer when you operated under deep cover, the way Thorne did. The other Associates had no idea he worked for Dax—that's how deep his cover went. Technically, he wasn't even an Associate. He didn't have a brainy specialty or wear glasses, and his only talent was knocking heads and creating chaos. Definitely not a team player.

Thorne knelt next to a cigarette butt outside the gate. Judging from the pattern in the dirt, somebody had stood in that spot for a while. The ashes suggested a cigarette held, but not smoked. He picked it up with a tweezers and determined that it had been dropped well after the rains of the night. No way would Macmillan or Mrs. Jazzman have stood in front of their hidey hole, smoking. No, whoever smoked that cigarette was probably a third player. He eyed the windows that looked out onto the sidewalk. Somebody would've seen.

One hour, five busted doors, and twelve frightened people later, Thorne had his description. It was Rio who'd been standing out there, waiting for the coast to clear before pulling them out.

Gloomy, ruthless, stylish Rio the assassin.

Even though Thorne wasn't a proper Associate, he knew all about them. They were like a baseball team he followed from afar; he collected their cards, memorized their stats, and followed their games. He even knew the code they used between them, thanks to Dax: One Associate would say, *Nice day for a walk* or *Nice morning for doughnuts,* something along those lines. And then the other would reply, *Clears the mind.* The exchange was a kind of secret handshake that meant *all is well.* Not saying one of the two parts was a heads up: SOS. Trouble.

Thorne sometimes wondered what it would be like to be in a tight group like that with their codes and back-slapping camaraderie, though he understood perfectly why Dax wanted to keep him on his own.

In the animal world, you had species that were universally despised—Fleas. Cockroaches. Rats. People put a lot of ingenuity into killing them or at least driving them off.

You had that in the human world, too. All his life people had been trying to figure out how to send him away or else kill him. He'd been putting up with it for so long, he was used to it. In short, he was a natural villain. He fit right in with the guys at the auction.

And Dax couldn't have found anybody more suited to infiltrate that group of crazy, fucked-up, dangerous cretins known collectively as Hangman. Hell, even the Hangman guys were wary of him. Thorne was Hangman four now, and he'd be Hangman three soon, and he planned to climb all the way to the top. He didn't know how; he never knew how he'd do a thing until he did it. His idol, Bruce Lee, always said to be open to every possibility.

He got Dax on the line. Dax was surprised to hear Rio had been there. Rio should have been on a hit across town during that time frame. Pinned down, Dax thought.

Dax got over his surprise soon enough and gave him a list of the Bangkok hotels Rio liked. Thorne assured him again he'd take the girl away from Macmillan and hand her off to Dax's own buyer. It wouldn't be easy, but Thorne would make it work; a reputation as a crazy bought you some leeway, that's for sure.

No way could the TZ get out—Thorne understood that better than anyone, thanks to his position inside Hangman. In fact, Hangman was possibly the worst group to win the auction. They loved chaos and senseless violence way too much.

He'd never gone up against one of the Associates, but he'd do what needed to be done, even if Macmillan stood in his way, which he would.

Macmillan: Cool and smooth, even in a firefight. Always ready with a joke. A shining golden boy, loved by all. Macmillan was everything Thorne could never be.

Well, he'd fight him all the same.

CHAPTER TWENTY-EIGHT

After Rio left, Macmillan used his phone to log into his personal cloud storage. Working on this tiny screen would be hell, but he could do it.

She sat on the bed, feet up, eating. "What's our plan, Devilwell?"

"I'm going to work out this problem." He started copying over his spectrogram software and unwrapped the earbuds Rio had purchased for him. He didn't need her hearing Rolly's voice over and over. Though most of his work would be on the screen.

"What do I do?"

"Just stay away from the windows."

She stretched out on the bed and opened a package of crackers. "Maybe this is a stupid question, but why not just arrest him or kill him or something?"

"Because he's an army of one with that weapon, and if he dies, somebody else will control the weapon and be an army of one, and the plans will probably be sent all over. We need the whole package. Just taking Rolly out doesn't cut it."

"And you're going to try to get control of the weapon? With that phone?"

He nodded. He'd sure the hell try.

"How?"

"I'm going to use Rolly's voice to break the security on the control system. It uses biometric security. It's a type of voiceprinting."

She narrowed her eyes. "And it's easy to break?"

"Normal voiceprinting is. It's a discredited technology, but this is kind of an advanced form, so it's a little tougher."

"And you can beat it."

He could hear the smile in her voice. *Don't look up,* he told himself. Getting lost in her again was the last thing he needed. "Yes."

"A linguist secret agent. Did you grow up thinking, I want to be so goddamn cool someday?"

He bit back a smile. "No," he said.

She grinned. "You sure about that? Because a linguist secret agent. It's so Indiana Jones." She stuffed another cracker into her mouth. "You don't want any?"

"No thanks." Even food could dull that crystal-clear space of intellect he needed to be in. They didn't have much time.

"I'll shut up. You just let me know if I can help." Her cheeks and forehead shone with sweat and he wanted badly to go to her, to fall into her, to tell her more about the horror of the hand. But that Peter stuff wouldn't serve her now.

"I need you to make a list of everywhere you think has a voice recording of Rolly. Anything. Phone messages, mp3 clips."

"Got it." He felt the hairs on his arms raise as she moved close to him, as if she brought her own electricity.

"What?"

"Paper and a pen."

He opened the little drawer and produced a notepad and paper.

"I love hotel pads." She ran her thumbnail over the edge of the pad making a soft *thwick*. "And then you use a recording of his voice to fool the computer?" she asked.

"Yes, after a lot of doctoring to make him say what I want him to say."

She returned to the bed.

Getting Rolly's password would be the easy part. Rio's phone had just enough CPU to throw at a brute force attack, though he'd have to run it concurrently with the spectrogram processing. So it would take a while.

The really hard part would be the challenge question— the program would ask a random question, like, *what is three plus four?* And he'd have to answer *seven* in Rolly's voice within a short amount of time.

He'd use his software to create a library of Rolly's speech, sliced into the smallest building blocks of language

First he'd separate individual phonemes, consonants, and vowels. Then he'd have to identify the transitions between sounds. The plosives—P and T and K and their counterparts—would be easiest because they were typically preceded by a few milliseconds of silence—that pause where the flow of air was blocked. He could put any phoneme he wanted before a plosive. The other sounds would be trickier. He'd have to picture how the lips and tongue moved. Tedious work, but necessary for "Rolly" to sound like a person and not a computer.

Once he had the library set up, he'd integrate it with his home-cooked voice recognition application to help automate things. He'd trained it well—it could understand him whether he was whispering or shouting. He'd say the challenge word in his own voice and it would assemble the sounds for him, synthesizing Rolly's voice on the other end.

She finished her list quickly, and it wasn't much. Phone threats she'd made digital copies of for the divorce case and "asshole things he said while I was recording songs," as she put it. "Mostly wanting me to be more country western. He always thought I should change my music. I've got hours of music with his voice in between songs."

"Everybody's a critic."

Laney snorted. "You got that right. So you can pull that stuff off my computer?"

As it turned out, he could. Laney went off to shower while Macmillan separated and prepared the new samples. The voicemail threats featuring Rolly claiming ownership over her were chilling. *You're mine—forever.*

Macmillan bristled at the words. And then there were the bits of Rolly bellyaching between songs. *Bellyaching.* Her term.

Rolly's passwords were starting to fall. Sports teams combined with 437. *Gotcha,* Macmillan thought.

The bellyaches were as short as the threats, unfortunately. *Can't you get a more country-western effect?* It was ridiculous, like asking an apple why it doesn't taste more like an orange.

But then, he, too, had been hard on her songs.

It felt good to parse Rolly's utterances into senseless bits. Still, he needed more recordings of Rolly speaking. There were certain sounds he'd kill to have, like the *zh* sound borrowed from French—the last *g* in garage. A voiced post-alveolar fricative, rare in English. Garage as a challenge word would sink him unless he could get that.

His email icon flashed. His contact had hit a roadblock getting recordings of Rolly's prison phone calls.

His heart sank. He would fail this mission without those recordings.

She came out of the bathroom wearing the blue dress and stockings she'd had on before, her wet hair the only clue she'd showered.

He wanted nothing more than to go to her and kiss her lips and her warm, clean neck, and confess things to her; it was as if he'd opened a floodgate, telling her about the hand. He wanted to connect with her and unspool with her. Just be with her. He was so tired.

Dangerous.

She needed him grim and focused. He examined the differences between two different *uh* sounds. People thought there were just seven or ten vowel sounds. *If only.*

She took up her perch on the bed. "What will you do once you have control of it?"

"It depends. The general idea is to shut down the weapon, shut down the auction, then worry about the schematics."

"No, but, what will you make it do? Will you shoot him with it?"

"Probably not," he said.

"But you could."

"That's a level of control I don't need. I only have to make it look like it doesn't work. That's enough to break up the auction." He looked up and was struck again by her, just sitting there on the bed with the *Bangkok Post* spread out on her lap, fanning herself with the hotel pad.

"But if you shot him with his own weapon, think how poetic it would be," she said. "Tell me you at least could, so I can enjoy imagining it."

He remembered that sort of revenge fantasy—he'd had it with Merodeador. "With the right commands in hand, yes," he said. "But look, we *are* using Rolly's weapons against him. Every word he said on those harassing calls, and every criticism he made of your songs, all of that's like gold to me."

"How long?"

"We're far from it."

"How far?"

"Far. And I'm afraid it will be boring for you."

"I got a project." She grabbed her pad and paper.

He kept on separating sounds, inspecting them and listening to them, one earbud in. He didn't like to cut off his hearing entirely. In truth, he was starting to feel a bit desperate. Things were taking too long. Eventually, he became aware of her humming, like a soft splash of heaven right onto his hell.

Working on a song, he realized. Her dusky, breathy voice was evident even in whisper singing.

She looked up, as if she'd felt his gaze. "I'm sorry, am I distracting you?"

He didn't know how to answer that. She was, yet he needed her to keep going. Her stockings were distracting him, too, but he wouldn't have her take them off for the world.

"Devilwell?" she whispered. "I was just working out a tune, but..."

"It's no distraction."

She hummed on, but more softly now. He picked up his pace. Being near her buoyed him.

But why wasn't Rolly's TZ password falling? He tried something new and the phone froze. He was running too much at once. He needed something more than a phone.

"What is it?"

"Does Rolly watch anything but pro sports? Does he have a favorite city or community team?"

"No. Maybe a titch of college football. Texas A&M."

"Does he play on a team?"

"Why?" she asked.

"He uses a password system for his accounts. Lakers437, Dolphins437, Jazz437."

"We had a garage door password like that. Packers437. I forgot. Wow."

"Rolly wouldn't abandon his system. He's been systematic with everything."

She looked off to the side. "Mmm."

"What?"

"A weapon like this, and he uses a password like he uses on the garage?" She shook her head. "No."

"People rarely go out of their systems. Especially Rolly's demographic."

She looked into the distance, as if channeling something. "It would be something ultimate. No numbers to sully it."

"The probability of that—"

"Listen, he'd want it pure," she said. "This weapon, it's his big play, right? He becomes rich, he gets me back. It's the big kahuna. The password would be like that. Big kahuna. But not *that*."

He was about to tell her why that wasn't logical, but then he paused. "You think you can guess his password?"

She still had that faraway look. "It would be a different class of password. Dramatic, mean, maybe even jokey." She was a poet who got to the heart of things, a type of hacker in her own way.

A poet was a hacker of the heart.

She stared off into the distance, lips pursed in a pale rose, brown hair showing red highlights as it dried, as though her natural color was crackling through. All that hidden voltage.

He couldn't imagine the world without her.

She smiled. Triumph.

"Good stuff?" he asked.

"Only the best, Devilwell." She straightened, made a humorous face, as if to signal how ridiculous Rolly was, how predictable. "My little friend. But spelled *leetle* or *lee-dle*."

"My *leedle* friend?"

"From the movie Scarface. Al Pacino comes onto some stairs with a machine gun and says, *Say hello to my leedle friend,* and then he shoots the place up. God, Rolly loved that fucking scene. I wouldn't be surprised if Rolly got the super weapon just for a chance to use that password."

He tried the different versions. "Bingo."

She smiled. "Now you're in?"

"I need him to say it, just to be safe. I heard a *my* somewhere." They went back through the recording together. There was both an *fr* and the word *end,* too.

"We get this and we're in?"

"Not quite. Before it lets me in, it will ask me a challenge question. It could be a request to repeat a word like *sunshine,* or a question—*what's the opposite of day?* That word has to be in Rolly's voice. I need a complete library of building blocks to work with, spoken in his voice. That's what I'm making over here."

"You can't, I don't know, just talk like Rolly?"

"The size and shape of my vocal tract is too different from his. The software will know; that's the whole point of biometrics. Try to think of anywhere else I could get samples of Rolly's voice."

"I can't."

"Keep trying."

She whispered, "Don't let me go back."

"I won't." He went back to work, cobbling different elements together and half listening to her humming. He thought about that night when she'd hummed *You Are My Sunshine* as he laid his cheek on her chest, and how strangely soothing the vibrations were. He'd hated the feeling, like it was too much.

It seemed like another world, him hating something like that.

Even with the curtains closed, he could tell dusk was falling; the blue lights from the nearby sign shone through the filmy fabric, bathing the room in a blue glow.

Another diphthong dead end. He wanted to smash the phone. The drone of the air condition seemed to be growing louder. Was it even cooling the room? He felt hot. Trapped in a dead end.

He needed to step away from the problem. In normal life he'd go for a walk. He couldn't do that.

She hummed softly, sitting there against the head-board, one leg out at a haphazard angle, the other bent, forehead furrowed, trying desperately to remember.

He went back to his project. He was missing nine sounds. He simply didn't have the parts he needed. Insufficient data.

The mobile vibrated. A text. Another delay on the prison calls. *Sit tight,* the text said.

Sit tight.

He couldn't sit tight. He was out of usable samples. He needed to get the TZ away from a madman.

It was then he realized that Laney had been silent for a while. He looked up to see her sitting forlornly on the side of the bed, tears streaming down her face.

He stood. "What's wrong?"

She lifted Amy's coffee mug. The anemic little plant was bent over, its stem broken nearly in half.

He closed the distance between them and stopped at her knees, unsure what to do.

"She's gone," Laney whispered, cradling the cup.

He touched her hair, a stroke of his finger, then his whole hand. "Maybe we can put her in a little water," he tried.

"This kind doesn't root." She tipped the stem up but it just fell again. She bent her head into her hand as silent sobs convulsed her back.

"Hey." He sat next to her, unsure what to do.

"She's just *dead*. I must've smashed her coming up here or something, and then I just forgot about her..."

"You're okay," he said softly.

"How can you say that? Look!" She held up the mug as if it was proof.

So this was her falling apart. It was always the little things that put people over.

"Here." He tried to take it from her fingers, but she clutched it, looking wild. How had he not seen this coming? Dax would've seen it miles away.

He knelt in front of her and put his hands on her knees. "It's just a plant, Laney. It means nothing."

"*It means nothing.* What a shocker that you'd say that." She stood, nearly pushing him over, and stormed to the window with the thing.

He watched her, wobbled. "Away from the window," he warned.

She let out an exasperated huff and went to stand in the corner, cradling the little coffee mug with the broken plant.

"You're okay. You're not going back," he said, secretly stung by her words. *It means nothing. What a shocker you'd say that.* It was true, things hadn't meant much since the train bombing.

"I tried to save her," she said.

"You did save her."

"Does she look saved to you?" She hurled it across the room, mug and everything. The ceramic thunked against the wall. Dirt sprayed. She wrapped her arms around herself, sobbing, sucking in desperate breaths, well on her way to hyperventilating.

He crossed the room, feeling panicky; he grabbed her shoulders. "Stop it."

She shook her head, lost in her misery. "There was never any use."

"Don't say that!" He cupped her cheeks and forced her face to him, but she wouldn't give him her eyes. "You are not that plant," he said. "It's not you. It's not us. Look at me!"

She shook her head. Well, she was hearing him. Enough to disagree, at least.

"You're right here, Laney. You're with me."

She stared off to the side, eyes puffy, nose red.

He smoothed his hands over her shoulders. "You're okay."

She pushed at him half-heartedly. "Fuck off."

"Stop it." He needed her to stop. He needed her to be with him in this. "That plant was defenseless and alone and doomed, and you stepped in to save it. Because you're powerful and resourceful. You're nobody's victim."

She looked over where Amy lay.

He wiped a tear off her cheek with his thumb. "You're not Amy."

She scrubbed her face and pasted on a fake smile. She was so beautiful, even fake smiling. "Happy now?"

"I'm not happy at all." He would be happy if she were out of danger. He would be happy if he could love her the way the old Peter could've. "Do you want a drink of water?" he tried.

"No, I don't want a drink of *water*." She grabbed his shirt and shoved at him. "I want you to fuck off."

"I won't fuck off." His lips landed on her forehead. "I won't ever fuck off, okay?" He kissed a tear off her cheek.

She stayed completely still. Like she didn't want him there. His entire being clenched in agony.

"Come on, Laney." He kissed a tear off her jawbone, tipped his forehead to hers. "You're okay."

"Stop saying that." She still had hold of his shirt. She wasn't pushing him away, but she wasn't exactly pulling him.

He pressed his forehead to hers, panting, his nose to her nose. Then he bent his knees, lowering himself to kiss her straight on, pressing his body to hers. She felt soft, pliant. But she didn't kiss him back.

He angled his head and kissed her maybe too hard—he felt desperate to have her with him. Like a madman he pulled her closer, putting his cheek to hers, losing himself in the heat of her skin. He kissed her ear, her jaw, her neck, rough kisses on the tenderest parts. He pulled her so close her arms were smashed between them, killing his rib. Not that he cared.

He became aware of her moving, shaking her head.

He pulled away. "Do you want me to stop?"

She closed her eyes. She seemed so helpless, suddenly. What the hell was he doing?

He drew his lips to her closed eye and kissed the swell of her eyeball, a kiss like a feather, as if to prove how under control he was. "Do you want me to stop?" he panted.

"I don't want you to stop." She opened her eyes, brave and brown and shot through with gold. "I want you to mean it," she said. "Please just mean it."

Mean it. A jolt of fear shot through him and he cupped her cheeks.

Mean it.

"It's not in me anymore," he confessed. "What you want. What you need."

Her gaze softened. "That's such bunk, Devilwell."

Deep down she had to know—he'd told her as much, how everything fell away, all the good parts of him. He hated that it was true.

He shoved his fingers deep into her hair, cradling her head, watching her eyes all the way until he claimed her mouth. Maybe there was nothing good left in him and no heart, either, but he would give her all of it. All of the wreckage, all of the words.

She mumbled something into the kiss as she wrapped her arms around him, grinding against him. "More," she whispered. "I want more of you."

He let out a gusty breath he didn't know he'd been holding. He grabbed her ass and lifted her clear up, slamming her onto the wall, letting her feel the way he was shivering inside, because he was falling for her. He pressed his steel-hard cock into the cleft between her legs, crushing his mouth over hers. "If I can't be inside you I'll die," he gasped.

She grabbed his hair and yanked his head away from hers. "That works."

He stared at her, emotions on overload.

She smiled, and he crushed his mouth over hers as if to devour that smile and all of her joy. Everything.

"Uh," she breathed, voice heavy with desire. He could get drunk just off the sound of her saying *Uh*.

"Maxwell," she whispered.

"Peter," he said. "My name is Peter."

"Peter," she said, with that pan-southern twang of hers. His heart nearly broke to hear it.

She tightened her legs around him. *"Peter, come 'ere."*

But he was already there. And he had to bury his face against her salty-sweet neck to hide the rawness of it all.

CHAPTER TWENTY-NINE

Peter.

That name was real. *Peter.*

He kissed her neck, ferociously almost, as he walked her to the bed.

He threw her down over the mess she'd made of the quilt. "I need you naked. Beneath me. Now." He didn't wait for her to comply; feverishly he pulled off her dress, and she wriggled and helped him, then he took off her underwear, so that she was naked except for the knee-highs.

Her heart pounded. *Peter.* She propped herself up on her elbows.

He wore boxers and he pushed them down, freeing his golden cock, primitive and thickheaded, as though some force of nature had sent extra cave-man essence to that part of his body. It was darker near the head and totally hot.

He pulled off his glasses. This wasn't the controlled Maxwell of their first encounter who took his glasses off slowly and wanted to talk about the word *fuck*. This was a new man. She found this new man frightening and exciting and real as hell.

She scooted away, desperate for him to come to her with that loose, fierce passion.

That glint of humor was gone. Peter was serious, eyes shadowed, mouth in a strong line, bright white tape binding his chest.

She slid a finger under one of the knee-high socks. "And these?" He had a thing about them. He loved them.

"No."

"You sure?"

"Say it again," he grated. "Say it."

Peter, he meant. His real name. "Peter."

Something new came into his eyes. He was shining and brilliant. He crawled over the bed to her, just him and his primitive cock. She thought she'd lose it right there—Peter, crawling to her like a beast.

She closed her eyes and tipped back her head, baring her neck, wanting to feel him coming over her, to feel him take her like a lion. She would give him everything now. He didn't understand how cracked open she was.

He crawled over her until his hands were on either side of her. She gloried in the way his movement stirred the humid air, causing ghostly wisps of cool to kiss her bare, sweat-drenched skin. Her nipples felt rock hard, straining to be touched. He stilled, a predator surveying the full panorama of his feast.

And then he lowered his head and kissed her with unforgiving strength that sent waves of pleasure clear down through her belly. She lay back and grabbed his steely, sweaty forearms as he plundered her mouth, lowering himself, moving against her.

She loved the roughness of his chest hairs against her breasts, the feel of his cock pressing at her belly, and the sweaty weight of him.

He planted kisses on the tender skin below her ear, nearly sending her into oblivion. Again he pressed his lips to that spot, as if to drink up her racing pulse. She tightened her grip on his forearms as he kissed an unrelenting downward line, sending rich rays of feeling into her overheated core.

When he reached her breast, he took her nipple between lips hard as teeth, sucking and tonguing, feasting on her as he slid his cock against her slick folds.

But really, she was the one feasting, and she would never be sated. She moved under him, panting, burning for more.

He pulled away, stood on the edge of the bed.

"Where are you going?" she asked.

He devoured her with his eyes, letting his fingers play lightly on her ankles.

Nowhere, she thought, in answer to her own question. He slid his hands up and down the length of her calves, and then he gripped her ankles—hard—and yanked her across the bedspread to him so that she was laid out before him. He gave her a dark look, just a little bit savage, and bent over her, planting hot, wet kisses on her sweaty thighs.

Like a man possessed, he shoved apart her thighs and put his mouth to her sex, prowling her sensitive folds with his tongue and teeth.

"Yes," she whispered, grabbing fistfuls of golden hair. He'd been so verbal before, fucking her half with words, but this was just raw.

When he plundered her with his fingers, she bucked under him, tightening her grip on his hair.

"Careful of Bolivia," he grated.

"Oh," she smoothed her hands over his hair. "Poor Bolivia."

He rose up, sliding his fingers over her mound, fingering her tender folds. "Bolivia is already feeling better."

She raised up her hips, wanting him inside her. Even just his fingers again. He slipped one in, then two, spreading her wetness around.

"Peter," she said.

"You are so hot when you're right on the verge like that." He fucked her with his fingers, possessing her. "What do you want? Tell me what you want."

"You. More," she said as he slowed. "Faster." She gasped as he pulled his hand away. "No..."

He reached over and fumbled with his clothes on the floor, pulling up something crinkly.

"Oh, good," she said.

It was a bit of a jokey thing to say—*oh, good*—like somebody had brought out ice cream treats, but there was nothing sweet or sugary here.

He knelt between her legs and put on the condom, eyes intense and feral. "You are so..." He slid his hands around her belly, up and down her thighs, hitting her stockings. "So..."

She took it as a compliment, when he didn't have a word.

"Comere, Peter."

He came back over her, still with that serious look.

This, she thought. *This.*

He pushed apart her thighs, letting his penis slide against her slippery folds. Then he pressed the fat tip of his cock into her, filling her slowly, as if to wring out every bit of feeling. It was almost too much and she moved under him, urging him on, but he clamped his hands onto her thighs, holding her in place, forcing her to wait, to have him slowly. "I don't want to hurt—"

"You won't."

He stayed slow and strong, pushing deeper, keeping control of her thighs, moving in and out, kindling the sparks hotter.

She felt desperate and wild and she grabbed his ass, giving him her fingernails. "C'mon, fuck me, Peter."

A whoosh of breath, and he thrust deeper, harder, hair swinging over her, brushing her cheeks.

"Yes," she said, kissing him. "Fuck me."

He thrust into her all the way then, taking her lips in a brutal kiss. He felt so massive in her—the feeling of him reached clear up to her eyes, and he fucked her hard now.

"I know I said it right that time." She dug her nails into his ass, arching her back, urging him on. "I want you to fuck me forever," she said.

He grabbed her calves and bent her legs up so that her heels smashed into her own ass, and he pushed into her more deeply.

She let out a strangled cry. "Like that."

"I'll fuck you in every way you want," he whispered, warm in her ear. "I'll devour you if you let me."

She panted, dizzy from the savage friction of it. "Do it, do it."

He fucked her raggedly, planting sloppy, frantic kisses on her neck, then her shoulder, and then he bit her there, like he needed to hold on to her with his mouth, like an animal or something. The pain was a kind of wild pleasure, spearing through her as he drove into her.

He was fully out of control.

So was she—spinning, falling, holding on. From out of nowhere her orgasm grabbed her like a fist, shaking all the sense out of her and spinning her around until she was just stars and breath and a man coming inside her.

He cried out. Something senseless.

She lay in his arms after, and tucked a bit of blond hair behind his ear. There was so much she wanted to say, but just then his phone sounded. He snatched it off the bedside table. "Yeah." His face fell as he listened to whatever the muffled voice was saying. "Yeah," he said softly, clicking off.

"What is it?"

He kissed her on the nose. "You're beautiful," he whispered.

"The prison recordings—"

"Just a setback."

"You can't get them."

"No, but it's okay. We'll get out of this," he whispered. "The answer's there somewhere, I just have to find it."

"I know you will, Peter."

He stilled, and all at once she saw it—that his name was a tender gift. Like a key to him. He kissed her and then he turned over and put on his glasses. He lay there naked on his stomach, ass pale as ivory, mind back to his weapon and his wordy science. "I have to pull my mind back together."

"And I distracted you—"

"I was at a dead end anyway. Now I know I have to hack a new path. I—" In a flash he flipped over, finger to his lips.

She searched his face—*what?*

His whisper was soft and hot on her ear: "The creak. Get dressed and get into the bathroom. Slip out the window. Down in the warrens, follow a pattern—one right, two lefts, one right, two lefts. I'll catch up."

One right, two lefts?

With shaking hands she pulled her dress over her head and shoulders.

He was out of the bed, moving fluidly across the room, pale skin bathed in the blue light from the sign outside. In a flash he was crouched near the door, holding the gun, muscular thighs straining, skin glistening with sweat. But that white band his friend had wrapped around his chest flashed even in the shadows. It made him an easy target.

A beep broke the silence. The phone! Giving them away. Who would leave their room without their mobile?

He handed her the knit cap and jabbed a finger at the bathroom.

She had to trust him; he seemed to get out of everything.

She grabbed her pack, slipped into the bathroom, and eased the door shut. The window raised up easily, soundlessly, but she so didn't want to leave him.

Peter's voice: "Hold up, Laney."

She got down and peeked out to see Peter zipping up his pants. He opened the door. A big, battle-worn looking man in black cargo pants and a black shirt walked in, arms raised, gun in one hand. He wore black gloves and he held his lips smashed together and aimed upwards, like he was assessing the situation and just didn't like it.

"Clears the mind," Maxwell—no, Peter—said to the man, somewhat nonsensically.

The man nodded and lowered his arms. "Right."

"Come on out, Laney." Peter shut the door.

Laney came out and Peter introduced her to the man— Fedor, pronounced *Fay-door*. Fedor set his gun on the desk and took Peter's chair. Everything about Fedor was big; even invisible things, like the way he took over the room. The way he saw everything through those pale blue eyes.

"What do we have?" Peter asked.

"The auction's off."

"Completely?"

"For now. Our friend, ol' Jazzman Rolly Drucker, he's decided to hold a bit of a scavenger hunt instead. The prize for finding you and his ex-wife is a tasty one—the finder's bids are automatically worth double." Fedor looked over at her then. "Congratulations. You're worth hundreds of millions of dollars to this guy."

Laney felt faint. "He's a maniac," she said. "He'll never stop."

"Be glad he wants you alive," Fedor said.

Peter sat on the desk. "So everybody who came for the auction—"

"Is out scouring the city for you both," Fedor finished. "Two hours more in this place, that's all you've got. Tops. You've managed to elude the players who were already in town, but right about now I'd imagine the Bangkok airport's a *who's who* of bounty hunters. And then there's Dax. Dax wants you, too. Never underestimate Dax."

"I won't let him have her."

"It's not just her," Fedor said. "Jazzman Drucker wants *you* alive, too. God knows why. A hundred G's for bringing you in alive. I would've priced you more at $59.99."

Peter smiled.

"That's not why I came, though." Fedor pulled a laptop from his sack. "You're not going to like this. What you're trying, it won't work. The hack won't work. I've been studying up."

"No," Peter said.

"Control can't be shifted in the usual way once the laser head is engaged. It's a failsafe. And Jazzman? There's no way he hasn't engaged that sucker."

Peter's whisper was sharp and hard. "Locked down."

Laney tried to catch his eye, but he seemed so remote. Thinking about that train, maybe. Or the hand. That hand had crawled clear into his core.

Fedor crossed his beefy legs. "He knows the Association's in town, and this is exactly the kind of shit we'd try. Sorry, it's how the thing is set up."

"There has to be another way," Peter bit out.

Fedor's expression was unreadable. "I'm going out on a limb here and guess you have a password and voice samples. Am I right?"

"Yes, but not near enough to beat a challenge word. I'm missing key sounds." Peter checked his phone and slid off the desk. "Brussels was trying to get the prison phone recordings, but it's a no-go. What do you have?"

Key taps and clicks filled the stuffy little room. A diagram went up on Fedor's laptop screen.

Fedor said, "We've never seen this weapon up close, but I've been going over the work of Eiger, one of the three researchers. The guy was heavy into unmanned ground vehicles. He worked on a four-legged, talon-type robot for the Chinese—the kind they used at the Ground Zero cleanup, only it comes with weapons systems. They're controlled remotely, but here's the thing—Eiger always built in a maintenance override."

She heard Peter suck in a breath. Did that mean he was happy? "How do you—"

"I know an old colleague of his," Fedor said. "Eiger would've disabled the override before they sold the weapon, but they didn't sell it, did they? It was stolen while they were completing work."

"So the back door is probably still open," Peter said.

"Wide open." Fedor smiled, big and lethal. "And I bet Mister Jazzman Rolly Drucker doesn't even know. It wouldn't be in the documentation. If you can beat the challenge words you can transfer control to your voice and do a self-destruct."

"I just need more samples," Peter said.

"And you have to be standing next to it," Fedor said. "You can't do a maintenance override remotely."

Peter leaned cool against the desk. "So it'll be *that* kind of party."

"Hold on! You can't go back there," Laney said.

Peter cast a glance at her. "Sounds to me like Rolly would be happy to see me."

"Peter!"

"He has to be on site to access the weapon," Fedor said.

"No." She turned to Peter. "He wants you there so he can kill you in the most painful way possible. He'll want to make you scream and cry and beg for your death. He'll want to literally flay off your skin or pull out your guts or something."

"No offense," Peter said, "but your ex really is a boor."

"That's not funny."

Fedor went on, undeterred. "Jazzman is holding court on the rooftop lounge. We have a bartender informing, but he's scared shitless—he'll rabbit anytime now. A lot of cold operators up there, a lot of hardware." Fedor was back on the laptop. "You know what a 360-290 sighting array is?"

"Ooh," Peter said. So he knew. And he liked it.

Fedor went on—it was all very technical, something about a laser on a boom arm. You could aim and shoot the weapon with a phone or laptop. Like a video game.

They crowded together in front of the screen, finishing each other's sentences, scribbling on the hotel pad. Fedor seemed to be teaching him how to control the weapon and make the thing shoot itself. At one point they both paused and stared into nothing. Stumped. Fedor reached under his pant leg and pulled out a small knife. Casually as could be, he tossed it across the room.

Thwuck.

It stuck into the wall and they resumed their conversation, like it was normal for a man to throw a *knife into the wall.*

Together they manipulated diagrams on the screen, with Fedor jabbing the keyboard with his thick fingers. He talked about Eiger creations in a rough rumble, like a connoisseur. During another pause, Fedor threw another knife. Maybe throwing knives helped him think.

Peter borrowed one of Fedor's un-thrown knives to peel a mango. Fedor grumbled about the ants. Everybody knew eating fruit in a room meant an instant trail of ants—up the wall, over to the table. Even saliva on the lip of water bottles sometimes attracted them. Peter kept on, casually talking weapons and words with his strongman, knife-throwing friend.

This was his world, she realized.

Peter could probably throw a knife, too, except it wasn't his style. Magnificent, dangerous Peter. These guys clearly worked for a government of some sort. The US government? Military? Fedor sounded American, though his name wasn't. Peter had that slight Euro accent, like he was from everywhere and nowhere. Peter was talking about the difficulties of things called *alveolars* and the desperate need for more recordings of Rolly, but his eyes were on her.

He cut off a chunk of mango and, trancelike, he rose and brought it to her. "There's always a way," he said, handing it down to her.

She plucked it from his fingers. "Thanks."

"Always," he said, letting the meaning change to something more important. A promise. *Always.* A communication on another level.

"Always," she whispered. This was the Peter she'd fallen for—the Peter who dug behind language, the handsome scholar who knew about secret dragons.

Fedor shifted in the chair, one arm over the back, legs sprawled. He wore that assessing expression of his, eyes keen. Fedor was as surprised by romantic Peter as she was by covert operative Peter. It was there she got it: Peter hadn't lost parts of himself in the train bombing. He'd gained parts of himself. He was all of these things. Lover. Fighter. Scholar. Hunter. Killer.

Fedor stood and closed the laptop. "I'm leaving this with you. I'm going to try something to get those prison calls. We have to complete your library."

With that he left.

"You can't go back to the hotel," she said to Peter.

"He won't kill me," Peter said. "Not if he thinks I know where you are."

"He'd make you want to die," she said.

He went to the window and peered through the gap in the curtains.

"See anything?" she asked.

"Hunters."

"Crap!" She went to where he stood and he showed her where to look. Her heart pounded in her chest. "What do we do?"

"Nothing. They don't know we're here. It's the hunters I don't see that worry me. We need to get on the move." He turned to her. "I need more samples of Rolly's voice. YouTube clips. Instructional recordings. I don't need much—just a few sounds. The *oo* of book. The *zh* sound from garage. The *j* of *judge*. The *ch* of *cheese*." He showed her the hotel pad. He'd made a list.

Just a few tiny sounds standing between them and everything.

"I want to help you. I wish I could."

"It's okay." He touched her hand, sliding his palm along hers. A line of ants was already heading in from the edge of the window, trailing up along the wall, across the ceiling, and down to the wastebasket where the mango peels were.

It was then they heard it—the telltale creak. Then again, softer.

He handed her a gun and the knit cap he'd worn earlier. "It's not Fedor," he whispered. "Two, three guys."

She grabbed her bag as he pushed her into the bathroom. He lifted the bathroom window. The sea of metal roofs behind the hotel looked almost pink in the mixed light of the moon and a red neon cola sign high in the distance.

"One right, two lefts, remember?"

"Yeah." She put on the dark cap and slung her bag over her shoulder. "Aren't you coming?"

"I'll catch up. Don't argue. Don't stop no matter what you hear. Go!" The intensity of his command sprang her into motion.

She scrambled out the window and lowered herself onto the rusty fire escape landing. Her pulse raced as the window shut above her, and she had this fear that she might never see him again. Like the window was cutting them off from each other forever.

A helicopter chopped above. Probably just news.

She climbed down three flights toward the dark little alley, which wasn't quite wide enough for a car, and hopped onto a pile of cans and newspapers, making an awful racket. Down one side some chickens pecked at feed under an anemic light that swarmed with moths.

She turned right and ran. Buzzing bulbs illuminated her way, strung up via webs of wire. She came to a fork and looked left. Bikes cluttered the way, and a woman squatted in front of a cook stove; flames danced on the corrugated metal behind her.

Curry. Dinnertime. She slowed to a walk as she headed past, smiling, looking for the next left. Just then, a gunshot rang out. A chorus of dogs started up.

She slowed.

Another shot. From the direction of the hotel. *Peter.*

Don't stop no matter what you hear.

Trusting him had worked out so far. She went on, past a blue wall with blue painted spikes on top, taking a left into an alley thick with encroaching jungle and lined with corrugated metal full of graffiti.

Footsteps sounded nearby; she darted behind a trash can and drew the big Sig Rio had given to her, holding the fat grip with shaking hands.

Just kids. She pulled the black cap down further over her head and slipped out, gun hidden in the folds of her blue skirt. She tried to not look alert, to not look out of her mind with fear as she walked.

Another right. The next left. The next.

But something was wrong—she felt it deep down. She backed into a dark doorway, thinking maybe she should wait. Even the dogs sounded more alarmed than usual. If anybody would sense things, it would be the dogs. Minutes went by, or at least that's the way it felt. It wasn't a good sign that Peter hadn't caught up; it seemed to her that he would get to her right away...or not at all. She forced herself to count to 100, but she couldn't concentrate. Her heart was drumming in her ears.

The dogs were growing frantic.

What if he needed her help? She could backtrack...just to check it out.

She retraced her footsteps, doing the pattern backwards, but things looked different. She slowed when she came to the blue painted wall.

It was on the wrong side. Was she going the wrong way? Was it a different wall?

When she heard shots ring out—close by—she didn't even think, she just ran in that direction. People were coming out their doors; she sidestepped them, zigging and zagging her way to where she thought the hotel was. She nearly ran into a woman who was backing away from a corner. She flattened against a wall as a moped whizzed by. She kept on. Another blue wall.

Were there multiple blue walls?

A crash nearby. She spun, confused. She ran in the other direction.

Footsteps behind her.

She looked back. Somebody chasing her.

She poured on the speed, turning this way and that, not daring to look behind. She was just thinking she was home free when a pair of strong hands gripped her from behind and yanked her backwards into a hard body. A male voice in her ear. "Gotcha."

She tried to shake free of his rock-solid arm, but he squeezed tight as a python, crushing the wind out of her. He fished in his bag with his other hand.

She panicked, struggled, but it only seemed to give him opportunities for tightening his hold.

She wouldn't go back to Rolly—never! And he didn't know she had the gun, right? With crazy force, she twisted and struggled, enough to shift her arm down to her side—the just-right position to shoot his knee.

Her heart pounded. Could she? She twisted again, feeling sick to imagine a bullet piercing into human flesh, shattering bone. But she wouldn't go back to Rolly. She squeezed her eyes shut and pulled the trigger.

Bang!

The force of the blast shook the both of them, thumping them backwards into a wall.

"Fuck!" He tightened his grip on her and pinched her wrist in a way that made her instantly drop the gun. "Fuck!" he said through gritted teeth.

She could feel his breath jerking his chest. "You got my foot." As he spun her around, she caught a flash of dark hair and wild-as-hell blue eyes set over high cheekbones and a short beard. One of the guys from the hotel—the one everybody said was crazy.

Thorne, somebody had called him.

He forced her cheek against the hard concrete wall and forced her arms behind her back, right around the cushion of her backpack. He began binding her wrists with something cutting. A zip tie. "Takes a lot more than that," Thorne grunted. "Go for the artery next time." He yanked her off the wall and pushed her in front of him along the alley.

She locked her legs and dug in her heels. "I'm not going back."

"Yes, you are." Thorne shoved; she stumbled. She had to get away from him and get back to Peter.

She dug in harder. He was limping. Shot in the foot. Surely she could fight him. Not like he'd shoot her; he needed her alive to get the money. Every step took her closer to Rolly and further from Peter. She dropped to the ground, right on her ass, allowing herself to become deadweight. "I'm not going back."

"You are going back. The question is if you go back with broken arms or not." He yanked her arms upwards. The pain was so intense, her eyes streamed with tears. "Break them," she hissed. "I'd rather die than go back."

"Dammit." He picked her up instead and hauled her over his shoulder, fireman style. She felt so helpless with her wrists bound behind her back, but she tried to knee him in the head all the same. She couldn't. He was crazy strong and fast. They rounded another corner. A darker, less traveled place.

"Please. You have no idea what he'll do to me."

"I have a pretty good idea," he said.

"And you don't care? What? You have no humanity?"

"Humanity's irrelevant," Thorne growled.

Figures emerged from the shadows.

A voice, thick with a Russian accent. "We'll take her, Thorne. Hand her over and there won't be trouble."

"Want her?" She felt the world spin as Thorne flung her straight at a trio of guys. She felt strong arms catch her as the world erupted in gunfire.

The next minute she was lying on top of a pile of bodies.

Blood was everywhere. She scrambled backwards, hitting another body. A scream ripped from her lungs.

"Come on." Thorne yanked her up.

She tried to pull away from him, horrified. He'd thrown her at his foes and then mowed them down after they caught her. She struggled to free her arms. He picked her up—and then put her down—or more, let her fall again as he fought two more men who'd appeared from nowhere.

He spun and kicked one right in the head. The man crumpled. He began to fight the other. Another appeared.

She saw her chance and took it, running like hell in the other direction, zigging and zagging.

She rounded a corner and nearly stumbled flat on her face. She had to get her arms loose! Around the next corner a woman was cooking over a tripod camp grill—the one she'd seen before! She was near the hotel. The woman eyed her suspiciously.

"*Dai prot Chuay chan duay na kha,*" Laney said—*please help me*. "*Na kha,*" she added, doubling the politeness words.

"*Ma thi ni,*" the woman said softy. *Come here. Let me see.*

Laney went to her, twisting to show the woman what she was tied with, beckoning her to hurry.

The woman unwrapped a cloth roll that contained a knife and sliced her wrists free. She offered to hide her, to alert the police.

"No, but thank you." Laney asked directions to the hotel instead.

On she went. Things were looking more familiar. She finally came to the larger alley that ran behind the hotels. She recognized their fire escape and ran toward it.

Then slowed.

Her blood froze as she spotted a lump in the shadows beneath.

Peter.

She ran to him. He sat against a wall down underneath the fire escape, holding his thigh, hands wet with blood.

She knelt. "Peter."

"Get out of here."

"You're shot!"

OFF THE EDGE | 341

"Flesh wound," he grated. "You should see the other guys."

She looked at him in horror. A gun lay in his lap. And he was so bloody.

"I'm just resting," Peter said. "You have to get out."

"No, we're getting you medical help. You're losing blood."

"But I'm also producing it. I'm running the operations simultaneously."

"Don't joke anymore. I need you to be serious."

"I'll get help once my friends arrive," he said after a beat.

"Your friends are coming?"

"Just a flesh wound," he repeated.

"Oh, Peter." She squatted in front of him. He looked so pale. Sweat on his brow.

"Got anything in your pack you can rip a bandage out of?" he asked.

She scrambled off her pack and dug out the silk scarf.

"That's good," he said. "Got anything gauzy?"

"This is all." She ripped it carefully. "I'm not leaving you."

"If you stay, you'll get me killed." He ripped a giant hole in his pants. All she could see was blood inside. He tied the scarf around his leg. "This is just a flesh wound," he whispered. "My guys and I get these all the time." He finished tying it. "Much better." He looked up. His blond hair was hanging loose instead of neatly stowed behind his ears, and the gray shards in his blue eyes seemed too bright, like gray shards of pain. At least he still had his glasses, but they had a bloody fingerprint. She took them off him and cleaned them.

"I'm not leaving you."

"I mean it, you'll make me a target. Everybody's after you, and if you don't take this chance to run, you're going back to Rolly." He glanced over her shoulder as he spoke. "I didn't go through all this hell for you to go back to Rolly now."

"I can't leave you."

"It's the only thing that won't get us both killed."

She touched his sweaty cheek, feeling so helpless.

He glanced again over her shoulder, eyes roving all around, and then back to her. "You're so beautiful."

She thought to say the same to him, but men didn't like to be called beautiful.

The laptop case lay next to him, and he instructed her to go in there and get a wad of cash. She complied. "Take it and start walking. There are guys with motorcycles down there. Pay one to drive you to the train station."

"I'm not leaving you!" Her eyes were hot with tears. She didn't care.

"Don't make it worse for me," he said.

"I can't just leave you."

"You think I can't find you? You're not a good hider. Laney." He smiled, but it was a smile that didn't reach his eyes. "You can't be here when my friends come. Unless you want to go back to Rolly." He looked again beyond her shoulder. "Is that what you want?"

"No," she whispered.

He glanced again over her shoulder.

"Do you see something?" she asked.

"Kiss me," he grated with crazy intensity.

She bent forward and brushed her lips to his, feeling wild with fear for him. She felt his hand close around her hair. He tightened his grip, then he yanked her head down, pressing her head to his belly.

Two blasts sounded above her, loud as thunder.

"Holy hellbuckets!" She looked up, catching sight of his steely arm, straight as a girder holding a fat black gun.

"Stay small." He shot again—*bang!*

Boom. Boom. Bullets from an unseen gun pocked into the metal wall.

He shot again. *Bang!*

Then nothing.

"Okay," he said.

She looked around, dazed, ears ringing.

He tipped his head up. On that roof.

She spotted a body. Two.

"Every hunter out there is now heading for this neighborhood. Your window of escape is closing fast."

"No."

"I know it seems heroic to stay here, but it's the worst thing you can do for me. If you stay here, you'll force me to protect you, and I'll die, and you'll be back with Rolly. Is that what you want? Me dead and you back with Rolly? Because I'm going to be honest with you: it's not my first option."

"Don't be like that."

"Then get the fuck out."

"But—"

"I mean it. Now."

She stood. His friends were coming. Her presence endangered him. She had to go. And yet...

"What do you need? Runway lights?" He pointed. "Go."

Her heart pounded. Was this it? "Okay. I'll wait for you."

"Go!"

Still dazed, she forced herself to turn and run, knees shaking so badly, she could hardly keep a straight line.

She didn't want to leave him, but she didn't want to endanger him!

She would go to Koh Samui. She would wait there for him. She would wait there for him forever.

CHAPTER THIRTY

He'd never see her again. Macmillan wasn't one to lie to himself, and that was the strongest probability. They were doomed for sure if they stayed together, but even apart things were dicey. Especially for him. She could still get out of this.

The bandage was getting soaked, dammit. And he needed to move; he was a sitting duck where he was, lit just enough by the ambient light from the hotel roof sign. He spotted a gap between buildings some yards to the right. Bad to use the leg, but it wouldn't be good to be seen. He straightened his glasses, slung the laptop case over his shoulder, and limped over. Quick as could be he nestled in, pushing aside the newspapers and piling up a few crates to put himself in darkness.

He closed his eyes, hoping fervently she was on her way out, hoping that she'd be safe. She could still save herself; it was a good plan he'd supplied her with.

She'd wanted him to stop joking, to be serious, but she didn't understand—that cool, jokey part of him was the only thing holding him up, the only way he'd gotten the strength to let go of her like he had. Letting go of her was the most logical course. Highest probability of success. Best he could do for her.

Hardest-ever move.

But she deserved to live.

He'd lied about his friends, of course. They weren't coming; at least not immediately. Their numbers had been blocked. Dax didn't want him calling. Probably figured out he had Fedor's phone.

His leg burned and throbbed. Between the silk and his hand, he was staunching the bleeding—somewhat—but the bullet was still in there like a little piece of hell, tweaking some nerve. Every movement hurt. At least it took his mind off his toes, he thought grimly. He just needed to rest and get back his energy. He'd go back to the spectrograms. It would be his fault if the TZ got out. Getting the prison phone calls seemed a distant dream, but Brussels could still come through. He had Fedor's laptop in his bag—he could complete his library and get to the weapon. It wasn't impossible.

Just very improbable.

He could bleed out, too. That was probable. Without stopping the TZ. All those deaths would be on him.

It was his own damn fault he'd been shot back in that hotel room. His mind had been on Laney when Thorne and his guys burst in. He'd shot the guys, but he'd let Thorne destroy his rhythm. Thorne was a master at destroying people's rhythm. It was a miracle Thorne had left him alive.

He still didn't understand it. Alive but badly injured.

He thought about that time in her room. Lying against her belly and feeling the vibrations as she sang. He'd been so resistant to the good feeling of her, as if she would break down his walls, push him off the edge. Now, suddenly, it was all he craved.

Now that she was gone.

A pair of hunters strolled past. Peter's heart lifted when he caught snatches of their conversation. So she hadn't been found.

How long had it been? Ten minutes? Thirty? She could be out of Bangkok.

His vision swam, and the wound bit like battery acid. He was feeling hot, or maybe cold. Definitely lightheaded. Maybe he'd been too cavalier about the blood loss.

Some kids walked by, laughing. Macmillan called out in Thai, asking to borrow their phone. They just kept on.

This was bad.

Once you started getting woozy, you got worse at putting pressure on a wound, and when you got worse at putting pressure on a wound, you got even woozier. A vicious cycle.

It was probable, really, that he would die now, alone. But he'd been dead and alone ever since that train wreck ten years ago, ever since he'd stood there holding that hand, disconnected from everything. These last days with Laney had been like sunshine. It was a kind of cruelty, really, that he'd die when he finally had something to lose. But he wouldn't trade those days for anything.

Footsteps nearing.

He willed the person away, though he could tell they were coming in his direction.

This was it.

A voice over him. "Such bunk."

His heart lurched as Laney's head appeared over the crates. "What are you doing?" he hissed.

She pulled the crate aside. "Scoot down, Devilwell."

"Get out of here!"

"Scoot down unless you want me to stand here like a fool."

He dragged himself deeper into the crevasse. She scooted in with her bag and pulled the crate back in front of them.

"Bunk designed to hornswoggle folks." She knelt, pressed a cool hand to his forehead.

"What are you doing?"

"I got supplies. Gauze and tape and some coagulant gel hoo-hah the fellow at the *rankaya* swears by."

"You have to go," he said.

"Yeah, well that's *way* off the table. Tell me what to do with this stuff."

"Laney—"

"I know. Save myself. Leave you to die. Nothing good in you anymore. You and your stupid severed hand."

"*Excuse* me?"

"We have to stop the bleeding, right?" she asked. "Did it go all the way through?"

Stupid severed hand?

"The bullet, Peter, the bullet. Lie back. What do you want me to do? Concentrate." She pushed him gently.

He gave in and lay back, elevating the leg. "Roll that gauze into a pad as wide as your hand." He had a good idea what the coagulant was—it was a good choice, and he gave her specific instructions about slathering it onto the silk and fixing the gauze over that. He'd seen a lot of blood in his day, but he didn't think she had. Still, she was amazing. Like an angel. No, a warrior.

When she finished with his leg, she arranged the crates to look more natural. It was better, but they were still too vulnerable, dammit. He had one bullet left in the piece Rio had left him with. Maybe two.

A rhythmic noise sounded nearby. A bouncing ball and shouts. The boys were back.

Thwack.

The ball hit the wall right near their hiding place. A few feet over and it would take down the crates.

Thwack.

"I'll ask 'em to—"

"Shhh," he whispered as the sound of new footsteps grew louder. Large footsteps, followed by a deep voice asking the boys if they'd seen Laney. The man spoke a few words of Thai— "*Phu ying* American," he said. American girl. "*Pom see nam-dtaan,*" he added. Brown hair. Another voice repeated the phrases. American hunters, maybe Canadian.

He picked up his gun. "I tried to borrow a phone from those boys before," he said. "When I was under the stairs. There could be a slight blood trail from there to here. Not much, but..."

Laney nodded. If the boys thought to mention what they saw, the hunters would take a look and see the trail. But the hunters weren't very polite.

Thwack. That one hit too close.

The hunters kept pressing. *"Phu ying* American? You sure?"

Macmillan held his breath. Some six feet above them, a spider had spun a web between buildings. It was a beautiful web that caught the haze of light just so.

"That ball'll take down these crates," she whispered.

He nodded.

More voices.

Thwack.

"Hell," she whispered, eyes shut.

Thwack.

He squeezed her hand.

Thwack.

Finally the footsteps started up again. The hunters moving on.

"I'm going to talk to those boys," she said.

"Laney, no."

"Sorry, Devilwell." She pulled out the wad of cash and poked her head up over the crates and then she was gone. He heard her conspire with the boys, speaking softly and sweetly in Thai, wrapping them into the fun and excitement of helping her stay hidden from the bad guys. She had money for each of them. And if they did the job well, they'd each get more.

She was back, arranging the crates. The bouncing had started up again, but they were bouncing the ball on the ground now, counting. "They're to count bounces. And if anybody comes, I ran to the road long ago." She checked his wound. "It's not soaking through," she whispered. "So far so good."

Just when she'd settled in, the bouncing stopped. Uneven footsteps approached, like somebody limping. Macmillan recognized Thorne's voice, questioning the boys.

The boys directed Thorne to the road.

Thorne wasn't easy to fool; he needed to be ready.

Macmillan sat up, cradling the gun, fire tearing through his thigh. Laney shook her head, meaning *no, lie back down.* Macmillan ignored her.

After an excruciatingly long exchange he only caught parts of, the uneven footsteps headed off. Thorne actually believed them? A minor miracle. Unless it was a trick.

And the limping. Had Thorne been injured?

The bouncing and counting started back up.

"We have to get out of here," she said.

"Too dangerous to stay and too dangerous to go, dammit." Even she had to see that. Hunters swarming. The TZ on the loose. Everything gone to hell. He'd failed the whole damn world and worst of all, he'd failed Laney. He wouldn't be able to protect her if they were discovered. She deserved so much better.

His heart beat fiercely, as though his chest was nothing but the thinnest membrane separating him from the world.

Strength drain. Bad sign.

And then he laughed. "*Stupid severed hand?*"

"That's right, your stupid severed hand," she whispered back, making herself small with him in the shadows. "I think you got hornswoggled by your own metaphor there."

"You don't know—"

"Oh, I know well enough," she interrupted. "Hands are part of what makes us human and all of that. You standing there holding one disconnected from a body, I see why you took it where you did. All the world fallen away," she whispered. "Doomed to be disconnected. It's bull is all."

"Only shows you don't get it."

"I get it. I think you had to be disconnected to survive—hard and jokey and cut off as that hand. Chopping apart language like you do. I think disconnection is what saved you, but it's not your destiny."

He grunted in dissent.

"I'm telling you," she said, "nothing goddamn fell away. That's not how it works. You lost your people in that attack, yeah, but you didn't lose any parts of yourself. I say you gained something."

"Laney—"

"Shut up." She squeezed his hand. "You tell me, what is this?" She squeezed again.

"Is that a rhetorical question?"

"I'll tell you what it is—it's a hand that's connected to a heart so big I can't believe it sometimes. This is a hand that helped save my hide several times over."

He felt breathless. And not from blood loss.

"And what else?" She squeezed. "What else is this hand connected to? Right now? Who are you connected to right now?"

He looked into her eyes. "You," he whispered.

"Yeah, you got that right," she whispered.

He wanted to laugh and cry both at the same time. He had the impulse to make a joke, just to control the situation. Because he was spinning out of control. Because he was falling off the edge.

"What is it?" she asked. "You can tell me."

He pushed through the impulse to squash the moment with understatement. It's just that the feeling was too sharp, too intense. He swallowed. "It hurts," he grated out.

She sucked in a breath, staring at him like he'd uttered something amazing. "Where does it hurt?"

He looked at her, thinking about the question. "My thigh." But that was a half-truth. "Everything hurts," he said. "Everything," he whispered. "Beauty hurts. Darkness hurts. Love. Death—"

"Like hell you're dying."

It felt good to tell her. Like something essential, chunking into place. "Laney—"

"What, Peter?"

He was silent for a bit, absorbing the soft ring of his name. "It all hurts." The boys outside kept bouncing their ball. *Bounce. Bounce.*

"I know."

"Sing to me," he said.

She went still. "You want me to sing a song?"

"Yes," he whispered. Maybe he wasn't thinking straight, but it's what he wanted.

Her eyes filled with tears. She started to sing *You Are My Sunshine* as she had before.

"No," he said. "Sing one of yours." He wouldn't blame her if she refused. He'd ridiculed her songs right to her face. But now he wanted to live inside one of them.

He nestled his head into her lap.

"Which one?"

"The kitchen," he whispered. "With the cookbook."

She started to sing, soft and whispery and melodic. The cookbook full of wishes. The stupid kitchen hangings.

The emotions flowing through him were too sharp, too clean, like they might rip him up inside, like they might rip up the world, but he let it happen.

He was going off the edge and he no longer fought it.

He closed his eyes as she sang on, letting the lost things inside the song echo with all the beauty and ruthlessness in the world.

And the strangest thing: it was all okay.

She was on the part about her mama now, *catches tokens of life like fireflies, to enjoy when she was right as rain, but that day never came.* That was one of the lines that had suggested to him that her mother was an alcoholic hoarder. He'd used that knowledge to manipulate Laney before, but now he felt into it, and into what it would've been like for Laney, the abandonment with a mother like that, and no father. He'd had so much, really, with his own family. Gwen. He missed them, but they'd given him such gifts. Gratitude washed over him. He'd never gone near that feeling—the loss was too much for him to bear, but they were still with him.

The beats of the bouncing ball sounded far away as he abandoned himself to her song.

It was then that the answer came to him, in the form of a line from her mother song: *Greedy with memories.*

"Laney."

She paused in her singing. "Yeah?"

"She kept things," he said. "Your mother."

"Our place was piles of things."

"Memories." He turned his gaze up to her. "How did she keep memories? Was it photos, or did she do video?"

"Some video, but not of Rolly."

"What about your wedding? Did she video tape your wedding?"

She furrowed her pretty dark brows. "Mama was drunk off her ass—she couldn't have worked a doorknob, let alone a camera. I'm sorry."

He sat up, ignoring the blaze in his thigh. "The mother who keeps every last magazine and broken TV doesn't miss her girl's wedding, dammit. Somebody taped that wedding, and she got a copy. *Especially* if she was drunk. Especially then."

"It would be something ancient. Like VCR," she said.

"And who would have a VCR player? I bet your mother does."

"But we can't get it over the computer. It wouldn't be digital."

"Tell me you have one of the burners Rio grabbed."

She pulled a phone from her pack.

"Call."

She scowled at the phone, as though unsure what to do with it. "It's been so long. I don't know what I'll say." She looked up at him. "I never told her where I was. I couldn't trust her."

"You'll make it right."

"Maybe she knows what happened to Charlie."

"Call her. Make this happen. We need more of his voice." He fished the list from his pocket and put it on the ground. "We need these sounds."

She dialed while he fired up the laptop. It would be a bitch to clean samples recorded off a VCR played over a phone, but if he could record Rolly forming just a few more sounds, his library would be complete, and he could beat the challenge words.

Outside the bouncing ceased. Voices. He darkened the screen. More hunters.

"Eight in the morning there. Mama won't like that," she whispered.

"Put it on speaker when I say the word," he whispered, listening to the voices. He would pull the recording right into the spectrogram software. The bouncing started up again—the hunters had moved on. He nodded at Laney.

The phone rang. A soft, woozy voice answered. "Whadya want?"

"It's Emmaline, mama," she said, tears in her eyes.

"Baby doll? You okay? Where are you?"

"I'm fine, mama. I've been running from Rolly. I couldn't call—"

Her mother began to ramble angrily about Rolly. Smooth as a pea chicken, she called him. She seemed drunk.

"You hear from Charlie?" Laney asked.

"Yeah, your brother's in the looney bin, did you know that?"

"A psych ward?"

Macmillan's heart nearly flew out of his chest as she caught his eye. The brother was alive. "He signed himself in last month," her mother said. "Nobody can get at him. If that boy's crazy I'm a monkey's uncle, I'll tell you—"

He saw when Laney got it—Charlie had gone in to get away from Rolly. "Mama, I need you to do something really important."

"You're not going to ask how I am?"

"Look, I've got a heap of trouble, and I need a recording of Rolly's voice. I'm thinking you can put your hands on one. I'm thinking you might have a recording of the wedding—is that possible?"

"That man's got nothin' to say I want to hear."

Eventually Laney got her mother motivated. "Now you're glad for your old decrepit mama saving mementos," her mother mumbled, rustling in the background.

"I'm glad for you to save mementos," she whispered. "And you're not old and decrepit, and I miss you, but I need this bad. The wedding dinner," Laney said. "You got a tape?"

"Well, that cousin of Gordy's filmed the ceremony and the toasts. Don't know why I'd keep anything that scumsucker Rolly ever said."

"And I bet you got a VCR player in there somewhere. Bet you can get at it fast." Laney walked an expert line, applying just a bit of urgency, but taking care not to upset the woman. Over the next ten minutes, Laney's mother hooked up two VCR players, both of which turned out to be broken. Finally she found one that worked.

He whispered to her, "If I circle my finger, have your mother rewind a bit and replay." He showed her how he wanted her to hold the phone.

They waited as her mother fast-forwarded through a tape. They got to the wedding vows, but the sound was terrible. He shook his head. *No good.*

But then they got to the reception tape. The holder of the video camera was closer to Rolly. He was asking Rolly what he most loved about Emmaline.

"I look at her and I think she's the most beautiful thing alive," Rolly said.

He and Laney exchanged triumphant glances. There it was—the *oo*.

Macmillan adjusted the levels. He was feeling faint, but not worse. He could probably stay conscious if he didn't exert himself. "There's no other woman like Emmaline," Rolly droned on. "The way she sings, and the way she enjoys the little things. Her word pictures, they grab you."

Rolly went on, delivering more phonemes. More sounds. He started ticking sounds off the list. A gold mine.

"Emmaline finds meaning and beauty in what other people pass by, but she's the beautiful one," Rolly continued.

Macmillan straightened. Rolly really had loved her, but he'd let that love make him small and cruel. He'd tried to lock her down. Macmillan put a hand on her arm and squeezed. He held it until she looked back.

He didn't want to be a small man in a locked-down world—he wanted to tell her that. When he looked at Laney, he felt inspired to be big and true and reckless, to rise up to meet her.

Suddenly her pink lips spread in a cat-like smile. Rolly had used the word *beige*. The *zh*. The last of the sounds on the list.

Bingo.

He started separating the sounds while she took back the phone to speak quietly to her mother.

Ten minutes later he had a viable library. He transferred it onto the phone.

"What now?" she asked when she was off.

"I test it. Plug your ears if you don't want to hear his voice." He whispered *peanut butter* into the phone. The phone synthesized Rolly's voice perfectly: *peanut butter.* Laney widened her eyes. He tried it with a few other words. Macadamia. Intentional.

"Peter—" She didn't want him to go.

"I have to. And I'm rallying at the moment." The truth. The pain raged on, but he wasn't so tired anymore.

"What if they take your phone?"

"They're only concerned with guns."

"Let somebody else do it."

"I trained this software for me, and I'm the only one who can get up there alive. Rolly wants to be up close and personal with me."

"So he can hurt you."

"Not if I take over his weapon first."

"You think he's going to let you waltz up to his precious weapon and play it a recording?"

"He won't realize until it's too late."

"You're not the only person who can get on that roof alive," she said. "Let me help you."

The thought of her up there chilled him. "Never."

"I'll distract Rolly while you make for the weapon with your phone."

"I need to know you're safe." She'd been frightened of going back—for good reason. He just needed to get near the TZ, play the *Leetle Friend* password, beat the challenge question, and transfer control to his voice like Fedor showed him.

Simple.

His muscles fired as she helped him stand, sending merciless darts of pain through his thigh. He gritted his teeth and pulled himself together.

"You ready? Can you stand?" She let him go and he managed to keep himself upright.

"Wish me luck," he said.

She didn't wish him luck. Instead, she pushed aside the crates and walked out.

Shit.

He caught up to her as she was paying the boys. "What are you doing?"

"I'm thinking about grabbing a tuk-tuk to the Hotel Des Roses," she said, "but what are the odds we'll get a free ride? I think they're good, don't you?"

"Laney, no."

"I'm done running from Rolly. We'll do this together, Devilwell. We're stronger together." She headed to the main road and he limped after her, cursing. Her arm shot up in the air. A tuk-tuk stopped.

"No thanks," he said to the driver.

"Yes, thanks." She got in. "Hotel Des Roses on Tamroung Road."

"You can't," he said, well aware that she could. Even if he wasn't banged up, he couldn't yank her out, not in the middle of all these people. He felt eyes on them. Probably too late already.

"You coming?"

He got in, holding tightly onto the metal bar. "Bus station," he said to the driver, a large man with a red baseball cap.

"Hotel Des Roses." She handed money up front. "Des Roses, got it?"

The driver looked nervous. Macmillan was the man, but Laney had the money.

As it turned out, it didn't matter. Because a red car pulled up and squealed to a stop in front of the tuk-tuk.

South American muscle.

CHAPTER THIRTY-ONE

Macmillan's pulse raced at they were pushed into the Hotel Des Roses lobby by their three captors, a trio of burly thugs from Venezuela led by a man in a baseball cap. The men had tied their wrists and relieved them both of weaponry and the satchel with the laptop, but Macmillan still had his phone in his pocket. And his wound wasn't bleeding for the moment. Just blazing with pain.

Laney held herself perfectly upright, intense amber eyes fixed straight ahead, dark hair in a long braid. He'd give anything for Laney not to be there; at the same time, he was blown away by her bravery. Facing Rolly.

"Laney!" One of the girls behind the front desk called out. "What's going on?"

"Sirikit. I'm okay." Laney spoke in rough, rapid Thai full of affection. "Be careful. Be ready to run."

Macmillan was surprised when the bellboy accosted them—he stepped right up to the biggest of the bunch. "You need to let her go—she works here."

"Sujet, it's okay."

He wouldn't budge; the thug pushed him away. Sujet would've come again if Laney hadn't talked him down in rapid Thai. She wanted him to warn the staff that trouble was brewing. She'd worked with these people for two years, Macmillan realized. They'd be her friends. Good friends.

"Enough Thai," one of their escorts barked. The elevator doors opened and an elegantly dressed Thai woman stepped out. Rajini Shinsurin.

The woman widened her eyes. "Laney!"

Macmillan could feel Laney stiffen beside him.

"How could you?" Laney asked. "How could you?"

Rajini Shinsurin looked on helplessly as he and Laney were pulled onto the elevator. "I had to."

"No, you didn't," Laney said. "And you're not the queen of capers." The doors were sliding shut. Laney stuck out her foot. "I thought you were my friend," One of the guards jerked her in— "but you're the queen of cowardice," she called out just before the doors shut. "Fuck it," she said, tears in her eyes.

"She didn't deserve you," he said. All the guns and blood and violence, and it was her dear friend's betrayal that made her cry. That was Laney—bravery and loyalty and fire in the heart. He wanted to tell her that and more. There was so much to say—too much to say and not enough time. Taking over this weapon could easily cost him his life.

She stared balefully at the twin columns of lights on the elevator panel. The light for floor one flashed off just as two flashed on, then two flashed off as three flashed on.

It was then that he noticed the corners of her mouth twitching, as if she'd thought of something funny.

She turned to him suddenly, eyes full of laughter. She furrowed her brow, trying to contain her smile. "Escorting guests at gunpoint. This sort of service will cost the Hotel Des Roses at least one star."

He laughed. God, he wanted to kiss her. The man holding him gave him a violent shake, but he didn't care. "I agree," he said. "And binding guests' wrists? That will cost the Hotel Des Roses yet another half star."

Laney snorted. "It completely lacks in decorum. If the elevator operators at the Hotel Des Roses wish for the guests not to press the buttons, they should simply make that preference known. Today's traveler does not expect to be brutally restrained."

Macmillan laughed as the floor seven light flashed off.

"*Cállate!* Shut up!"

He was in no mood to shut up, and their captors wouldn't do anything more to them now. The floor eight light flashed on. "The customer service techniques here are woefully out of date," he whispered.

Laney grinned. "Zero stars. And that's final."

He watched her. He couldn't believe the miracle of her, or how beautiful and brave she was.

But that wasn't the phrase, not precisely.

She felt good and endless, and he wanted to never stop discovering her.

But that wasn't exactly it. And then he realized. He said, "Nevertheless, I give the Bangkok Imperiale Hotel Des Roses a full five stars," he said to her. "And I'd give more if I could."

She looked at him in mock surprise, but he was done joking. Floor thirteen had flashed on.

"It's because of the woman who sings here at night," he continued. The man jerked him harder and he took a step sideways, which sent pain up and down his thigh, but nothing would stop him now. He gazed at Laney. "It's because she made me feel passion again, and happiness, and life—everything I lost. Because you connected me back to my own heart, Laney, and finding you..."

"Devilwell," she whispered.

"Just listen," he said, even though what he needed to say was too big to fit into language. "I was barely alive before you, and nothing meant anything, but then these last few days—no matter what happens, this has been worth it. Because I love you. And I don't know how much time we have—"

"Don't talk like that."

"I love you—I need you to know. Three days I've known you. I don't care. I love you anyway. You're amazing and beautiful, but it's not because of that, it's more—"

"Fuck." Tears streamed down Laney's face. "I love you, too, Devilwell. I love you like crazy." Wildly she looked at the panel. Floor sixteen blinked out. Floor seventeen blinked on. She looked back at him, seeming so alone. And he loved her so much. "*Comere*," she whispered in a tiny voice.

He surged forward, pressing his body to hers, nuzzling her cheek, finding her lips. One kiss like heaven. It was enough.

Rough hands pulled them apart as the doors slid open. "*Vamos.*"

He was shoved out onto the rooftop of the hotel. He stumbled and lost his balance, managing to fall on his non-wounded thigh. It would be a disaster if that wound started bleeding again.

He lay on his side, gathering his strength, taking in the terrain.

The rooftop lounge of the Bangkok Imperiale Hotel Des Roses occupied just a portion of the rooftop, a plush oasis in a sea of buildings. Flowing white canopies stretched over the rambling cocktail area, which was fitted out with white armchairs, sleek steel tables, and potted palms, all lit by torchlight. There were maybe a hundred dealers and armed guards arrayed in and around the seating area, and they were almost all facing east, toward the helipad where three military-style helicopters formed a triangle around the TZ-5. The weapon looked small and furious with dark, blunt wings and a fat little body rife with rivets and receptors. A laser array came up out of its head. The powering laser stood on the ground next to it, beam deactivated for the moment. The ground laser would be hooked up to the hotel generator. That's how the weapon would draw its energy.

The man in the baseball cap pulled him back up.

The excitement in the air was palpable. All these men salivating over a dangerous toy. Everybody was there— the Finns, the New Tong, even Thorne had made it. He stood next to his Hangman buddies with a cane, foot in a special boot. A sprain?

Macmillan's heart lurched as the men pushed Laney toward Rolly. Laney was starting to resist; she couldn't help it.

Rolly stood. "My lovely wife."

He couldn't see her face, but the resistance was all over her body, and Rolly was eating it up. He grabbed her shoulders and planted a hard, angry kiss on her lips that made Macmillan want to rage out of his bindings and lay waste to the earth and the sun.

Rolly pushed Laney down in a chair next to his and pointed at a spot ten feet in front of them. "Put Macmillan there where we can all look at him."

Macmillan was made to stand in front of the assembly. Quite the reversal after spending so much time watching these men and women from the shadows. He'd endure what he had to now; he just needed to get near that weapon.

"Our Associate. I have to say, you don't look so good, but I'm glad you're here, I really am," Rolly crowed.

"He's shot!" Laney raged. "Leave him alone. I'm here. I'm who you wanted."

Rolly waved a hand in his direction. "Somebody, untie him."

One of the Venezuelans cut his bindings. Macmillan knew what would come next.

He removed his glasses and slipped them into his pocket, waiting, grinning. Rolly strolled up to him with murder in his eyes and slammed a fist into Macmillan's jaw, sending him stumbling backwards and onto the ground. Macmillan sat there, gasping for breath. He'd gotten a couple of yards nearer to the TZ. Good, but not nearly enough.

As Rolly stalked toward him, Macmillan spotted the key hanging around the man's neck by a chain. He recognized the White Crow insignia—it was the key to a workout gym locker. A chain of upscale gyms.

Bingo.

That's where the weapon's blueprints and plans would be stashed. It was a little ballsy to have the key visible—others could guess it, too. Then again, Rolly had a crew of thugs and the most dangerous weapon in the world at his command.

For now, anyway.

Macmillan stood again, backing up, limping badly. He'd do anything to get to that weapon, including allowing himself to look like a coward.

Rolly strolled toward him. He'd expected Macmillan to fight, of course, not back up, and a suspicious gleam appeared in his eyes. Couldn't have that.

Macmillan spat at him.

That did it. Rolly flew at him, fists flying. Macmillan defended himself this time, getting in enough hits to stay upright and stay moving back, which he did, until Rolly got him in the balls. Macmillan crumpled to the ground, nauseated. Dirty fighter.

And he still wasn't near enough to the TZ, dammit.

"What's wrong?" Rolly glared down at him. "You're just a wizard in the booth. A lot of nothing." And with that he kicked Macmillan's thigh, creating an explosion of pain. Macmillan's hands flew to it.

Rolly had seen the wound. He'd meant to re-open it. And he had.

Damn.

Somewhere far off, he heard Laney screaming.

Rolly turned. He was addressing the group. "I know you've all seen the clips of my TZ leveling buildings, but I've fielded some questions on its ability to pinpoint a human target. And there seems to be some curiosity about what a laser actually does to human flesh. I could stand here and tell you that it heats a person up, instantly boiling the water in the cells and setting the clothes on fire. I could tell you that the skin bubbles and blackens within the first ten seconds. But why should you take my word for it?"

So there it was. He would be the demo. He eyed the weapon on the helipad. *"You're mine,"* Macmillan breathed, curling up as if from the pain. Discreetly, he transferred his phone from his pocket to his sleeve. He put on his glasses, then fumbled his hands back to the bleeding wound.

His time was limited now. He thought about breaking away and sprinting to the weapon out of the blue, but he wouldn't have enough time to play the password and answer the challenge question before they pulled him back. And then they'd know that's what he wanted.

A crash. He looked up to see Laney running in the other direction. She'd kicked over a table. Providing a distraction. It was bad timing, but he had to take it. He rushed for the TZ, phone out, but a guard was on him too fast. He got his phone back into his pocket before he was hauled back to the space in front of the crowd.

"Put him out there in front where we can all see him," Rolly said. "Further out. Rolly directed them to put him between the viewers and the weapon. For the demo.

More men were coming off the elevator. Word that the hunt was over had gotten out.

Laney was back in her seat, watching, horrified. Macmillan caught her eye and warmth rushed through his heart. They didn't need words now.

A whir sounded behind him; it was the weapon powering up. The laser beam shot up from the ground like a white line into the belly of the thing. Rolly was punching something into a notebook. Macmillan needed to think fast.

A voice: "Wait."

Thorne stood with the help of his cane, managing to look proud and tall, even injured. "I have unfinished business with this one," he hissed in Macmillan's direction, hobbling over. "I found them first and he's the one who shot me in the foot."

A lie. What the hell game was Thorne playing?

"He didn't shoot you!" Laney cried. "That was me."

Laney?

Thorne kept coming, gazing at him strangely. A deep scar bisected his cheekbone at an almost perfect forty-five degree angle. The scar had the crosshatched look of a scar gotten very young, stretched over time.

Whatever Thorne had in mind, it wouldn't be good. But at least it was more time.

"You have two minutes," Rolly said. "If you kill him or knock him unconscious, you're the demo."

Laney cried out and tried to get up, but she was shoved back down by a guard. "Move again and I'll shoot your boyfriend now," Rolly said.

"He's already shot," she said, crying.

Rolly said, "Clearly not enough."

Thorne stood in front of him, blue eyes blazing. He punched Macmillan in the belly. Macmillan doubled over, seeing stars.

Thorne came near, standing completely undefended. It didn't make sense—Thorne was an expert fighter. But an opening was an opening, and Macmillan took it, bringing the fight to the ground. Thorne cried out, as if he'd been hit, even though Macmillan hadn't hit him.

Macmillan felt confused, hazy. Losing blood. They rolled.

Thorne was on top of him now, gazing down with that wild look of his, like he wanted to kiss Macmillan, or more likely, bite his face. Then he whispered, "It's a nice day to die."

The Associates' all-clear code.

Macmillan stilled. Could Thorne be Association? He took the advantage to get on top of Thorne.

Thorne stared up, waiting. Was he waiting for Macmillan's reply?

"Clears the mind," Thorne whispered, offering the reply himself. "I know what you want. I'll get you to the weapon."

It would be just like Dax to have somebody in deep cover inside Hangman. To keep it from them.

Macmillan didn't have much of a plan. He went with his gut. "Do it," he whispered.

A blast of pain as Thorne flipped them over, doing a leg destruction that wouldn't have hurt if he hadn't been shot.

Thorne jumped up. Jubilant jeers rose up from the crowd. They all hated the Association.

Thorne pulled a gun from an ankle holster and raised it over his head, shooting up into the air. "I want to see the spy kiss the TZ before the laser kills him!" Again he shot into the air. "Crawl!" he yelled. "Crawl to the weapon and kiss it! Kiss and be killed!"

Macmillan almost wanted to laugh. Crawl to the weapon and kiss it. That would do.

The man really was crazy.

"Kiss and be killed!" Thorne shouted, shooting the rooftop this time, a little too close. A spray of stucco stung Macmillan's cheek as he began to crawl.

Jeers and laughter rose into the night sky behind him; the whole place had the feel of a mob on the edge. Some of them shot up into the sky.

Thank you, Thorne. Macmillan whispered. He would get close now. If only he could last. If only Laney could trust.

He collapsed when he reached the foot of the TZ.

"Kiss it! Kiss it!" the crowd chanted.

He activated the recording on his phone, hoping it worked over the din of voices. Out came Rolly's voice: *My leetle friend.* The whir changed. A computer voice. "Salt. And..."

Macmillan whispered. *"Pepper."* Rolly's voice emerged: "Pepper."

Click click.

"Transfer voice command," Macmillan said. He gave it a new password, following the steps Fedor had outlined.

Click click. The weapon was his. He got up and kissed it. Cheers rose up. Macmillan turned to the crowd, the weapon at his back. He limped away, just to make it look good, then collapsed a few feet from it.

"You can limp," Rolly called to him, notebook in hand, "but you can't hide." He stabbed at his keypad.

A hush fell over the rooftop. The crowd waited. And waited.

Nothing happened.

Rolly's expression darkened—Macmillan could see that even from a distance. Rolly punched something into his notebook. He looked up, then back down. He hit a button and spoke at his notebook.

Dealers started to grumble. One of the New Tong got in Rolly's face.

Macmillan caught Laney's eye. He needed to get her out of there. He loved her. And she loved him.

Suddenly Rolly was back focused on him. He had his gun out. "What did you do?" He began to stalk toward Macmillan, murder in his eyes.

Macmillan had taken the weapon out of Rolly's control, but he hadn't thought much beyond it. This was it— Rolly would kill him. The man had nothing more to lose.

Macmillan pulled out his phone and dove behind the front wheel casing of one of the helicopters. He tapped the link Fedor had bookmarked as a bullet whizzed by.

"Sighting array," he said, sliding his thumb across the screen until he had an image of Rolly on his phone, running at the weapon. The crosshairs appeared.

"Fire," Macmillan boomed.

Out of the corner of his eye he saw three red beams come from the crown of the weapon and join into a bright, white line that connected instantly to Rolly's chest. The force of the beam stopped his forward motion, and he emitted a horrible strangled cry. His gun skittered, his arms reddened, and his clothes burst into flames. He seemed almost to collapse and implode on the spot, skin popping, bubbling, and finally blackening as he crumpled to the ground.

Macmillan stood, holding his phone. The smell was horrific.

"Anyone else?" he asked.

The pandemonium in the audience was instantaneous and violent as dozens of dangerous arms dealers ran for the doors and elevators.

Good. Macmillan's vision was going hazy now. He could make out Laney, running for him, arms still bound behind her back. She fell to her knees. "Peter."

He held on to her and kissed her for all his life. "You're okay," he whispered, keeping an eye on the fights breaking out at the elevator banks. Most of the dealers were taking the stairs. But she was there. It's all he needed.

She twisted and deposited a small serrated knife on the ground. "Free me. Tell me who to call."

He sawed through the zip ties and freed her. She punched in the number he gave her, looking so free and strong, hair blowing in the night breeze. She was the last thing he saw before he blacked out.

Colorado

Laney was supposed to be collecting basil, but she couldn't resist stretching out in the sun. She could see Peter through the open kitchen window, making tea in the chipped old tea pot they'd found at the antiques barn. They sometimes joked about it, their little cabin in the foothills of the Rocky Mountains, all rustic and idyllic. The chipped teapot. Texting side-by-side in their favorite chairs. Their red mailbox with a creaky flag at the end of the winding lane. She threatened constantly to put their life in a cornpone song, and sometimes made up silly ones. They got a lot of joke mileage out of it. You got a lot of mileage out of things when you were crazy in love.

They'd spent that morning working at their kitchen table, her on her songs, and him on his big database project.

He wasn't out in the field anymore with his shadowy cabal, as she called it—those days were over. But the voice and image database and diction recognition software he was working on would make a huge difference for his friends back in the field. It was the linguistics project of a lifetime, he always said, and he loved working on it so much, he sometimes forgot to eat. He really was just a

378 | CAROLYN CRANE

word nerd when you came down to it. And so was she. She would work on her songs, and sometimes sing in the local coffeehouse.

Language was everything.

Yet not.

She missed Bangkok, and she missed the friends she'd made, though she didn't miss the Shinsurins. The hotel had gotten shut down after the auction, and Dok and Jao were hauled off to jail. Rolly had killed Niwat. Rajini was by herself, running one of the other hotels. She'd written Laney a letter a month back, begging her forgiveness. Laney needed to think about that. It was a lot to forgive, what Rajini had done.

The door creaked open. Hedley, their old rescue dog, came bounding out first. She felt his nose on her toe.

Peter was taking a bit more time; he still needed to use a cane—for at least three more months, the doctors told him.

He'd nearly died.

She shaded her eyes with her hand and smiled when he reached her. He was like a glorious god up there, golden haired and happy. "What'dya think you're doing?" she asked.

He adjusted his glasses. "I could ask you the same thing. I believe you had a mission out here."

"I was looking at the sky," she said.

"Oh, yeah?" He lowered himself to the ground and stretched out beside her. The sky was like a lazy bowl of delicious, delicious blue that was darker in the center. But he was so much more delicious. He turned onto his side.

"I have something for you." He handed her a bright paper package. A book. A big one.

"What is this?"

"A gift," he said.

She smiled up at him and sat. "For what?"

"Open it."

She ripped off the paper. There inside was an old dictionary. Beautiful raised letters, well worn, well loved. She knew what it was before he told her—the dictionary that had meant so much to him before the train bombing so many years ago.

"My mother's," he said. "I had a few things sent from storage. From before."

She touched it reverently. Her own mother had been asking her when he'd put a ring on her finger, but this was bigger. So much bigger, so much more personal, more meaningful.

"Thank you."

"I love you, you know," he said.

She turned on her side and propped her head up on her elbow. "I love you, too." She looked at the dictionary. This was why he'd latched onto the cookbook full of wishes song. This book was more than a dictionary. It was dreams. Goodness. The future. Family. Hope. Play.

"You think I'm going to sit around looking things up for you now?" she asked in a small voice, not wanting to ruin the moment with too much seriousness.

Peter was having none of it. "Always."

"Always," she whispered.

He kissed her lightly, warm lips over hers, letting the book slide into the clover. She pulled him nearer, messing up his hair, enjoying his warmth, his weight.

They both lay back after a spell, breathless, looking at the sky, which seemed almost to vibrate with blue.

She fumbled for his hand and found it.

~THE END~

ACKNOWLEDGEMENTS

This book has taken forever to write, and I couldn't have pulled it off without my smart, generous, talented author friends. Each of them read this in different forms and gave me feedback that made this book so much better: Joanna Chambers, Lauren Fox, Carolyn Jewel, Jeffe Kennedy, and Katie Reus (Joanna and Katie read it twice!) as well as my writing group: Elizabeth Jarrett Andrew, Marcia Peck, and Terri Whitman, and my brilliant and handsome husband, Mark! I'm also grateful to my Linguistic Consultant, Joseph Devney, who provided smart ideas, excellent advice, and kept me from making a few big blunders; any remaining linguistics mistakes are my own doing. Big thanks also to proofreader extraordinaire, Sharon Muha, and to all my Indie writing pals out there who have been so generous with advice and help. You know who you are. And to all you bloggers and reviewers out there: thank you for taking the time to spread your passion for books and stories.

BIBLIOGRAPHY

One of my favorite things about writing this book was doing the research, which was just so very interesting. Three books in particular gave me a lot of insight into how Macmillan might work and think:

Coulthard, Malcolm, and Johnson, Alison. An Introduction to Forensic Linguistics: Language in Evidence. New York: Routledge, 2007. Print.

Pennebaker, James W. The Secret Life of Pronouns: What Our Words Say About Us. New York: Bloomsbury Press, 2011. Digital.

Olsson, John. Word Crime: Solving Crime Through Forensic Linguistics. London: Continuum International Publishing Group, 2009. Print.

About Carolyn Crane

I write romantic suspense, urban fantasy, and other tales of adventure and passion. My books have been published by Random House and Samhain, and I also go the indie route, in addtion to writing erotic romance as Annika Martin. I live in Minnesota (complete with an accent that people sometimes laugh at) in an old 1920's condo with my awesome writer husband and two cats. I love to run and also to read, even though I'm probably the slowest reader ever.

I'm a superfan of chocolate and Mexican food, and if you invite me to your party, your cheese plate will be in more danger than one of my suspense heroines. Also, I use too many exclamation marks, I care deeply about animals, I work a day job as a freelance marketing writer, and I dream that someday I'll having the time to do all the crafts in the many craft newsletters I subscribe to. But I guess I'm having too much fun throwing my favorite characters into dangerous and sometimes steamy adventures.

CPSIA information can be obtained at www.ICGtesting.com
Printed in the USA
LVOW08s2240120116

470290LV00008BA/749/P